AUTHOR OF THE SERIES "A WOMAN OF ENTITLEMENT"

Tory's
FATHER

BY MARY ANN KERR

THINK WELL BOOKS

thinkwellbooks.com

Tory's Father
Copyright 2015 by Mary Ann Kerr. All rights reserved

Published in part by Thinkwell Books, Portland, Oregon
The views or opinions of the author are not necessarily those of Thinkwell Books. Learn more at *thinkwellbooks.com.*

Design & Cover Illustration by Andrew Morgan Kerr
Learn more at *andrewmorgankerr.com*

Published and printed in the United States of America
ISBN: 978-0-9891681-4-4
Fiction, Historical, Christian

Books by Mary Ann Kerr

A WOMAN OF ENTITLEMENT SERIES:

Book One

Liberty's Inheritance

Book Two

Liberty's Land

Book Three

Liberty's Heritage

Caitlin's Fire

Tory's Father

DEDICATION

I dedicate this book, in order of their births, to:
Asriel Kathryn, Elizabeth Grace, Elias Stephen, Mikiah Joy,
Grace Elizabeth, Lydia Ann, Zachary Peter, Anna Christine,
Bethany Joy, Ellison Morgan, Saraya Hope, and Avarie Lynn,
my precious, precious grandchildren.
God bless you each and every one!

ACKNOWLEDGMENTS

TORY'S FATHER has an interesting beginning. I had decided to do a story without Liberty as one of the characters. Beginning to write, I placed the timeline at 1875. *Liberty's Inheritance,* as you know if you're a fan, begins in December of 1882.

The story went along just fine until I got to the end of chapter fifteen. I have never experienced writer's block, but by the end of that chapter, I wondered, What am I going to do between now and the end of the story? I set it aside for a few days, and was stepping into the shower when I realized what I needed to do. I needed Liberty's help! I went back and changed just a couple of things, and put Liberty in chapter sixteen, and the writing was a piece of cake after that!

I think I have a strange way of writing. When I wrote *Caitlin's Fire* I named the book before I began to write. Fire became her horse. I don't plot out a story, I have no idea from day to day what I'm going to write. I write in the omniscient point of view, according to my editor. I guess it isn't done much these days, but was very common 'back in the day'. Maybe it's why my readers enjoy my books so much! I am having the time of my life writing these stories. It's given me a great appreciation for writer's of the past who had to go to the library to do their research. At the touch of a finger, I can look up anything I need for historical writing.

Another thing I do is take an experience and shape it to fit into my story. An example is when Henry throws a temper tantrum in the dining room. He throws himself on the floor and Manning upends a pitcher of orange juice on him. My daddy did that when I was young. Throwing a temper tantrum, I would stiffen up, fall straight backward and kick and scream. I did it one day when he was coming from the barn with a bucket full of milk, having just milked our cow, Bossie. He proceeded to upend that bucket on me and I thought I was drowning. It was old fashion waterboarding!

Out of the many people who've encouraged me to continue writing, I'd like to acknowledge a few.

Dori Harrell, my editor, at Breakout Editing has been an overwhelming cheerleader for me. She loves my books and when we talk shop, it's hard to stop. Thank you for not only being such a wonderfully, encouraging editor, but for becoming a friend as well.

Susan Richmond owner of Inklings Bookshop carries my books and has praised the beautiful covers my son Andrew has created. I thank you for supporting so many local authors and for putting our books on your shelves.

Sue Griffin, in California, picked up my books and began to read and couldn't stop. We were stationed together in Frankfurt, Germany. Her husband told her she couldn't start another book until after Christmas, because she couldn't put them down! Such good memories I have of times past. Thanks for being a fan.

Donna Black, Freddie Leonard, Shar St. Hilaire, and Nancy Barrett who are friends, but were bosom buddies of my sister, Jeane. I thank you for all your love, support and of course our fun brunch get-togethers.

Allan Thomlinson and his wife Karen are such a wonderful support. Darcy Armstrong, Ena Riddle, Jan Young, Jan Hensley, Mike Broom, June Danielson, Fran and Dual Eldridge, Mary Fuget, Debi Caryl, Melissa

Peart, and Earl and Arlene Engle are those fans who get the book as soon as it comes out; it's so encouraging to a writer.

Michele Andrews and Dan Huffman, I haven't met either of you, but you've become friends. Nancy Kerns, Phil McHaney, Pricilla Lamm, Jaime Lee, Loretta Mapes...so many friends and fans, I can't list you all, but I thank you for your interest in my writing. Thanks for the prayers and good times.

I thank David and Evelyn Kerr, my husband's brother and wife. You are special people in our lives. Thanks for being active in politics and for your involvement in pro-life organizations. You bless me.

To my f-a-v-o-r-i-t-e brother, Peter Brown and his wife, Regina, I again thank you for such wonderful times when we get together. You really know how to make a person feel special!

To my niece, Angie Ellis, what a sweetie! And my niece, Elida, I treasure our relationship...thanks for being the sweet women you are.

Of course, I thank my sons and their wives, David and Rosie, Peter and Rebecca, Stephen, and Andrew and Shari. You are such special people and thanks for giving me those wonderful grandchildren!

To Phil, a huge thank you for your patience and for reading my stories and encouraging me. I love you!

To all my readers, I give you a big thanks! You can help me by writing a review on Amazon to help the cause!

God's blessings on you all.

mak

List of Characters

George Baxter . . . . Boston detective
Adeline Baxter . . . . George Baxter's wife
Christopher Belden . . . . Chief of detectives, Boston
Andre Dufort . . . . .Boston detective
Bradley Burbank . . . . .Past board member Brighton Bank
Mrs. Hadley . . . . .Bradley Burbank's sister
Mabel May Vickers . . . . Manning's new bride
Madeline Vickers . . . . .Mabel's thirteen-year-old daughter
Charles Vickers . . . . .Mabel's eleven-year-old son
Henry Vickers . . . . Mabel's seven-year-old son
Manning Brighton . . . . Victoria's father, owner of Brighton Bank
Victoria Lynn Brighton . . . . .Manning's eleven-year-old daughter
Laura Brighton . . . . .Manning Brighton's deceased wife
Mrs. Franks (Frankie) . . . . .Brighton's housekeeper
Janey and Lorna . . . . .Brighton's all-around maids
Cookie Roberts . . . . .Brighton's cook
Olivia Annette Anderson . . . . Close friend of the Brightons
Ralph MacCrath . . . . Brighton's stableman
Morrie . . . . Brighton's gardener
Armand Bouvier . . . . Liberty Bouvier's husband
Jean-Paul Colbert . . . . .Liberty Bouvier's driver
Elijah Humphries . . . . .Manning Brighton's lawyer
Stewart Grenly . . . . .Man on the freighter
Captain Eldridge . . . . .Captain of a Cunard Liner
Stanley Gilbert . . . . .Shipmate at the captain's table
María Fernando Esperanza de la Vega . . . . Shipmate
María Alphonse Esperanza de la Vega . . . . .Shipmate
Herr Bernhard Haas and wife, Marlene . . . . Shipmates
Meneer and Mevrouw Pieter Van Aalst . . . . .Shipmates
Contessa Viola Stella di Amalfi . . . . Widow in Santa Marinella
Father Lorenzo Stenali . . . . .Abbot in Santa Marinella
Sister Amalia . . . . Elderly nun
Luigi Aroni . . . . .Doctor in Santa Marinella
Brugali . . . . .Fisherman in Santa Marinella
Katarina Dyrbov . . . . .Madeline Vickers' roommate
Claire Lambert . . . . .Madeline's boarding school chum

THE STORM

The storms of life are heavy
A weight upon our back…
Throughout the storm we flounder,
Never knowing what we lack.

We cast an anchor into the sea
Hoping for some relief,
Our anchor simply drags through sand,
Or perhaps we snag a reef.

For a time the problems seem to ebb
As we try to push them aside.
But the waves roll, our anchor slips,
and we're on a downward slide.

Our anchor needs a Solid Rock
Where we can stow away,
When sorrow and trouble beat us down
A place…safe from the fray.

The storms of life can try us
The winds of adversity blow.
If we know Jesus as Savior,
We know where we can go.

The chains of our anchor bind us
To the One who can calm the sea.
Our anchor holds fast to Jesus;
He's waiting for you and me.

MARY ANN KERR

PROLOGUE

Be merciful unto me, O LORD:
for I cry unto thee daily.

PSALM 86:3

"**AND WHAT DO YOU SUGGEST,** George? Am I simply to walk into Brighton's residence and say, 'Oh, by the way, sir, you may be marrying a murderess?' He'd demand evidence. I would too, if I were him. We've looked for…ahh, let me see…it was back in seventy-three, wasn't it? Here it is, already the fall of 1875. We've been looking into this for nigh unto two and a half years, and we can't find any substantial proof."

Christopher Belden, chief detective for the Boston Police Department, felt it was time to step down. He was tired. George Baxter, his right-hand man, was the brightest mind in the department. He felt George was ready to step into his position.

George Baxter stared bitterly at Belden.
"Bradley Burbank's sister, Mrs. Hadley, has been down here countless times demanding an investigation. She is quite certain her brother was murdered, even though the Boston city coroner ruled it an accident. I fully agree with her, but we've hit a dead end. There are no witnesses,

no one yelling foul play except Mrs. Hadley. She says her brother stopped seeing the Vickers woman about a month before his demise. That's what sparked the fuse. According to Mrs. Hadley, her brother told her the Vickers woman was mentally deranged. It was the reason he stopped seeing her. Mrs. Hadley said when Bradley Burbank broke off the relationship, it made Mrs. Vickers furious."

"Well," replied Christopher, "you know the saying. 'Hell hath no fury like a woman scorned.'"

George, his voice sounding harsh, said, "We *know* she killed her husband, and we're quite sure she killed Bradley Burbank, but how can we prove it, sir? And surely someone should tell Brighton to watch his back and what he drinks."

The Boston Detective Agency had hit a dead end trying to tie one Mabel May Vickers with the murder of her husband and that of her male friend, Bradley Burbank.

The day was bleak. Rain threatened all morning, and the sky finally decided to spill its contents. Torrents streamed down rooftops. Gutters rapidly overflowed, making little rivers down the sides of the cobblestone streets. Thunder crashed and lightening streaked the sky as bright, crooked fingers stretched themselves across the heavens.

The girl, curled up into a ball of misery, lay on a settee in her own sitting room, her head cushioned on a pillow as tears streamed unchecked down her cheeks.

It's a perfect day for crying, she thought. *Looks to me like God's crying too. Oh, I just know Papa's going to be sorry once he marries that woman. I just know he is. Frankie thinks so too. She doesn't like her either, but she doesn't say so. I can tell that woman hates me. I see it in her eyes. I'd like to run away, but where could I go? Oh, how I miss my Mama! What in the world am I going to do? That woman is mean. Why can't Papa see it? Maybe I could go live with Aunt Olivia. Wonder, would Papa even allow it? No, I don't suppose he would, but that woman looks at me as if I were a spider she'd like to squish. Oh, what am I going to do?*

Victoria Lynn Brighton was eleven years old. Wise beyond her years, she could see where the household was headed with a new Mrs. Brighton at the helm. Her papa had met the woman at a dinner party and felt sorry for her. He'd begun seeing her about three months before, but already they had decided to marry. The wedding was on the morrow.

Mrs. Mabel May Vickers was a widow with three children. There was a girl, thirteen years old, and two boys, one eleven and one seven. Victoria had been told to be nice to them, but no one had told them to be nice to her. The younger of the boys, Henry, had spilled an inkwell all over her favorite floral-print chair and her Turkish carpet.

Victoria's mother had turned the nursery into a sitting room for her since there'd been no more children after Tory. Her books and special things were there. Henry, seven years old, was spoiled, in Victoria's estimation. He hadn't even apologized. The Vickers girl, Madeline, acted supercilious and had broken the spine on the locket Victoria's mother had given her for her eleventh birthday. It had a tiny daguerreotype of her mother and father on one side, and her mother and herself on the other. Madeline had apologized, but it had been out of the corner of her mouth, and Tory didn't think she meant it. She'd asked her papa to get it fixed, but it was still lying on his chiffonier.

Madeline, at thirteen, had not been sent to boarding school. Victoria had asked her papa why, and he'd said Mrs. Vickers had insufficient funds, so Madeline went to day school. The boy Victoria's age, Charles, was the nicest. He was a bit quiet but observed everything that went on. When he spoke, which wasn't often, Victoria listened because he was smart.

Victoria's mother, Laura, had died nine months earlier. Victoria was supposed to be kept innocent of the cause, but she was best friends with their housekeeper, Mrs. Franks. Frankie, Tory lovingly called her. She'd filled Tory in on all the details. Her mother had gotten pregnant again, but this time when she lost the baby, an infection had set in and she'd died from it. Tory had been desolate and inconsolable. The only time she

17

felt halfway fine was when she rode her horse, Commotion. Then, she could forget.

Victoria, still curled up, thought bleakly about Mrs. Vickers. Her deep-set blue eyes had icicles in them. They looked coldly at her, and her smile looked more like a grimace, her lips pulled back from perfectly straight, small teeth.

Tory sat up, staring bitterly at the stained carpet, trying to think how she could escape being around Mrs. Vickers. Life would be different beginning tomorrow, with a new Mrs. Brighton in charge. Tory dreaded it.

CHAPTER I

A continual dropping in a very rainy day
and a contentious woman are alike.
Whosoever hideth her hideth the wind.

PROVERBS 27:15-16b

TORY FELT AS IF THIS DAY COULD be a funeral, the death of a family…hers. Mrs. Mabel Vickers was now her mother. She spoke aloud but softly. "I shall never call her mother. She's not my mother, and she never will be. Oh Father in heaven, I need Your love to flow through me to that woman. I don't feel at all like loving her, but Frankie says I must, and that I must pray for her too. So I am, but I don't want to. I don't like being around her. Her eyes give me the shiv—"

Madeline opened her bedroom door without knocking and walked in, interrupting her prayer.

"Who you talking to?" she asked rudely.

"Excuse me, but you may not come barging into my room without knocking first. It's only politeness," Tory said, eyeing the older girl who was so unfriendly.

"Well, *little girl*, it's not your room for very much longer." She flounced to a chair and plopped down. "My mama says it's the biggest room, and since I'm the eldest, I get to have it." Madeline was still dressed in the outfit she'd worn to the wedding. It was pink with darker pink bows all over it. Tory secretly thought it looked like a young girl's dress, not at all the kind of outfit a young lady should wear. She'd felt sorry for Madeline when she saw her dressed in it. She didn't feel sorry for Madeline now. She felt sorry for herself.

She responded to Madeline's comment with an even voice, but her insides quivered. "I'm sorry, but she's mistaken. When I was old enough to choose, *my* mother said I could have my pick of rooms in this house, and this is the one I chose. I have decorated it the way I want it. You'll simply have to pick another one. There's plenty from which to choose."

"This one shall be mine within the week, I should imagine, and you can't do anything about it." Madeline spoke condescendingly. "I came in to say that *my* mama says you're to come down for dinner now. We're gathering in the parlor first, and you're to dress appropriately." Madeline arose, pink bows jiggling all over the dress, and flounced out of the room, slamming the door shut behind her.

"Misery, it's all a misery." Victoria swallowed several times in an effort to control her tears and tried her best not to cry. She felt tears start in her eyes and took a big breath, holding it for a full minute. She didn't want her eyes to look swollen and give anyone the satisfaction that she was unhappy. *I'd like to take a ride down to the beach on Commotion, or something. I'd rather do anything else instead of going downstairs to see that woman in my mother's chair at the dining room table, staring at me with those frigid icicle-blue eyes.*

Tory stood and slipped into the brown dress she'd worn for the wedding. It was the closest she could get to black, which was what she'd wanted to wear. Unless a body was in deep mourning, black was simply not allowed. It was considered bad luck for a wedding.

Before her mother died, she'd promised her she wouldn't wear black for more than three months. Her mother had loved her to wear cheerful, colored dresses. The brown dress was taffeta and rustled when she moved. It was one of her favorites. Tiny maroon flowers trimmed with little leaves in green velvet covered the bodice front. The long sashes, sewn at the sides, crisscrossed in the front and came around to tie into a bow in the back. She smoothed the ties and heard a tap on her door. *At least it's not Madeline. She doesn't knock.*

Sighing, she said, "Come in."

"I comed in to help you, miss. Came up the back stairs, I did. The new missus, she says we ain't allowed to use the main stairs no more." Janey's brown eyes were rounded. She looked nervous, almost frightened.

"That's ridiculous! Why, that would just make a lot more work for all of you to have to go all the way back through the house to the kitchen to come upstairs."

Janey was an all-around maid on whom Laura Brighton, Tory's mother, had taken pity. The girl had shown up at the service entrance when she was barely twelve. She'd been with the Brightons now for three years, sleeping in one of the attic rooms that was part of the servants' quarters. She nimbly buttoned up the back of Tory's dress as she chattered nonstop.

"Oh, miss—Mrs. Franks, she don't like the new mistress a-tall. I heard her talkin' 'bout findin' a new position. She said she may as well start a lookin' now 'cause she's likely to be given notice from here, anyways. She said th' new Mrs. Brighton don't like her. I think th' new Mrs. Brighton don't like any of us, 'scuse me fer sayin' so."

Victoria turned around, her hazel eyes staring into Janey's.

"Are you sure Frankie said that?"

"Yes, miss, it's 'xactly what she said."

Tory chewed on her lip and thought as she pulled out the combs from her mussed hair. *Frankie mustn't leave me here. I love Frankie. If she goes, I go!*

Janey picked up the silver-backed hairbrush and tidied Tory's beautiful honey-blonde hair. She reparted it in the middle and swept up each side with combs to hold it back. Curls spilled down her back.

"Thank you, Janey. Not only for helping me dress, but for confirming what I already know. That woman is simply not to be borne. I don't know what I'm going to do. Maybe I could run away, at least as far as Aunt Ollie's." She smiled to let Janey know she spoke in jest. "Well, I reckon

I'd better get myself down to the parlor. The *new* Mrs. Brighton has demanded my presence."

Victoria ran lightly down the stairs instead of sliding down the banister. When she reached the bottom, she made sure her hair was in place and straightened her dress. She took a deep breath to still her racing heart and entered the parlor with her shoulders held back and her chin well up, the way her mother had taught her a lady entered a room.

"There you are, sweetheart." Manning Brighton beamed down at his daughter. "You're looking quite lovely, my girl." He pulled her beside him, planting a kiss atop her head. He slid an arm around her back and held her close to his side.

"Well, now," he said, "we're going to be one big happy family." Everyone else in the room looked at him, surprised he would think so. He continued to speak. "Mabel and I have been making some plans for our new family. Madeline, your mother has decided you should go to boarding school. What do you think about that?"

"Oh! I'd love to go! You simply have no idea! Why, that would be simply divine!" she gushed. "I've wanted to go to boarding school for over a year, when all my friends left to go. Going to day school is strictly for babies."

Manning looked at the girl, wondering if it was a petulant comment or just plain rudeness. Her two brothers and Tory were in day school. He glanced over at his new wife, who looked lovely in a blue gown that enhanced the blueness of her eyes. She beamed at her daughter, seeming not to have heard the comment.

Mabel said, "Oh, darling, I am so happy for you. You will attend a very prestigious boarding school in France. It's where girls from really good families attend. In another year, Charles and Victoria will be off to school too. Then only my sweet little Henry will be left home."

"I want to go too, Mama. I wanna go to school too." Henry whined, his voice at least four notes higher than normal.

"You'll have to wait, my precious darling. I want you close to me for a few more years."

"But, Mama—"

"Dinner is served," Frankie said as she entered the parlor. She interrupted the beginnings of the little boy's tirade.

The newly formed family entered the dining room, with Henry still talking about going to school in a whiney voice.

Three chandelier lamps hung evenly spaced over the long mahogany table. The walls were wainscot and above it, a lightly flowered wallpaper. Fireplaces were lit at both ends of the long room, and an eight-foot sideboard with a mirror above it graced the inside wall. The wall opposite had wainscot topped by windows with only the frame posts in between. There were no curtains—only valances in a creamy-colored, textured cloth with pale green embroidery stitched on them, the color echoing the green in the wall paper.

Manning and Tory had not eaten in the dining room since Laura died. They started to one time, but it brought too many nostalgic memories to mind, and neither of them could manage it. They'd ended up in the kitchen where, until this night, they had eaten all their meals. Manning glanced over at Tory with no smile on his lips, his blue eyes darkened by memories. Tory looked back at him, and he knew exactly how she felt.

Both remembered the last time they'd tried to eat here.

Mabel, on Manning's arm, took one look at the dinner plates set all at one end of the long table and said, "Excuse me." She slipped out of Manning's arm and headed for the doors that led straight into the kitchen. The rest of the family waited for her to return before being seated.

Manning wondered why she'd gone to the kitchen, but it wasn't long before he found out. Mabel returned with Lorna and Janey in tow. She pointed to the place settings, and without a murmur, the two girls reset the table, placing a plate at the far end of the table, two in the middle on both sides, and leaving the plate on the other end of the table alone.

Manning started to say something, but he looked at his new wife's set face and closed his lips.

The four children sat in the middle of the long table, two facing two, only a centerpiece blocked their view.

Tory thought, since her father didn't speak up, she would.

She placed her napkin across her lap and said, "Really, Mabel, don't you think this is a bit ridiculous? We're going to have to nearly yell at each other if we care to speak to either you or Papa."

"Children should be seen and not heard, Victoria Lynn. Be glad, young lady, that you're not relegated to the nursery to eat."

"I've never eaten in the nursery in my entire life." She nodded her head toward Henry and Madeline sitting across from her and asked, "Have you?"

"No, but we had a smaller house and didn't have a nursery." Madeline blushed a little at the admission.

Tory noticed her discomfiture and gently added, "We have no nursery now, either. Several years ago my mother converted it to a sitting room for me."

"Manning, darling, do you think, perhaps, Victoria should go to school along with Madeline? I think she's quite the young lady, and she too needs more than a day school can offer."

"I don't care to go to boarding school yet. At least not for another year, and maybe even two," Tory said. "I'm quite happy with my day school." She glanced down at Mabel. Tory knew for sure, in this matter, her father would side with her.

"You will, my dear. You will want to go." Mabel's eyes glittered and she turned her chilly blue glaze on Tory. Shards of glass seemed to gleam from them. Tory held her stare. She wanted to look away but didn't want Mabel to think she intimidated her.

Manning felt a palpable tension between his daughter and his new wife. No one was talking, and the silence was deafening.

Manning, not used to someone else making major decisions in his home, looked askance at his new bride. His glance at Tory turned into a stare as Tory looked stone faced back at Mabel. His stomach began to churn as he realized for the first time that his daughter did not like Mabel, not at all. He leaned back in his chair and looked down the length of the table at Mabel. *Laura and I always discussed things of import together before presenting anything to Tory.* He swallowed and wondered what he had married himself into.

He cleared his throat. "Mabel, perhaps you and I should discuss this later. I think the two of us should go on that honeymoon trip together. I know you said you didn't want one, but it would give us time together without the responsibilities of children."

"Oh, Manning, I simply couldn't leave *my* children. Perhaps it wouldn't bother you to leave Victoria. I could well understand that, but for me to leave my precious Henry…no and no, I won't even consider it."

Manning looked at Mabel, eyebrows raised in disbelief. *Does she realize she just discredited my daughter and my feelings for her?* He looked down the length of the table at the woman he'd just married. *She's been so pleasant, so charming. Are the gloves now coming off? Is the woman I'm hearing the true Mabel?* He looked down at his plate, his appetite gone. He stared down the long table again and sat thinking for a long moment before he stood up. He went to the kitchen. Lorna and Janey returned with him, totally silent, their eyes round as saucers.

"Put the plates back as they were. We are now a family, not a formal circus."

The girls simply gaped at him, too astonished to move.

"Now," he said, crossing his arms in front of his chest. "I would like to eat my dinner while it's still hot."

"But, Manning—"

"Move, Mabel. We shall be a family and have no splinter groups. Charles and Tory, you sit here on my left. Mabel, you're on my right, then Henry and Madeline." He sat down before Mabel could say anything else. It was a quiet group that moved back to the head of the table, Mabel's children looking scared.

"Tomorrow, Mabel, you and I shall go to Italy as planned. I forgot to cancel the bon voyage party set an hour before sailing anyway, and I still have our tickets. I thought to surprise you, but you were so adamant about not going I planned to return them. In the busyness of getting ready for our wedding, it completely slipped my mind. I have decided we need to get to know one another. I don't believe I know you, Mabel. Our departure time is half past noon, so we need to be there no later than eleven. If you are not ready, you will go as you are, but believe me, my dear, you are going."

Mabel, for the first time, turned her icicle-blue eyes on her new husband. He was thoroughly shocked by the hatred he saw within their depths.

The children were quiet, except Henry. "Mama, you can't go without me. Mama, you need to stay here and take care of me." He whined and began to cry, putting his fists into his eyes. "Mama, I won't let you go without me."

Charles spoke up for the first time, ever, in front of Manning.

"Button it up, Henry. This is a great plan, and Maddie and I are here to take care of you." He looked at the man beside him with eyes full of admiration. Never in his life had he seen anyone stand up to his mother. He was grateful to Manning, yet frightened too.

CHAPTER II

A prudent man foreseeth the evil,
and hideth himself; but the simple pass on,
and are punished.

PROVERBS 27:12

AFTER AN EXTREMELY STRAINED AND QUIET dinner, Mabel abruptly excused herself, saying she had some packing to do. She left, her heels clicking loudly on the oak floor.

After she left, Manning said, "I need to go out and will most likely return within the hour."

Madeline and Charles went to their respective rooms, but Henry went to his mother's room, whining out loud all the way up the stairs. Tory decided to go to the kitchen and relate to Frankie, Cookie Roberts, Lorna, and Janey all that had taken place during dinner.

The staff were already talking together in the kitchen. Each one had rooms in the Brighton house except the gardener and those who were only day help and lived in their own homes. Tory was disappointed

Ralph wasn't with the others. Ralph lived over the stable and took care of the horses and carriages. He sometimes came in to eat, but it was rare for him to do so. He preferred to cook for himself.

Tory related the dinner drama; Janey and Lorna added a few words of their own. The women in the kitchen were clearly happy to hear that Mr. Brighton had stood up to his new wife.

"That's good news, Miss Tory," Cookie Roberts said. "That woman has some highfalutin ideas." She put the finishing touches on a cake she'd made for the next day and handed the frosting bowl to Tory, who licked the spoon.

"Pretentious, that's the problem with the new Mrs. Brighton," Frankie said. "Putting on airs of being grandiose. The good Lord made us all the same, no matter if we're high or lowborn. We're to treat everyone with respect. We each have value in His sight, being His creation." Tory liked that Mrs. Franks was a lady, but not one to put on a facade of being something she wasn't. She was a common sense, no nonsense person. Tory knew her father was happy with his housekeeper. Frankie was the epitome of good manners and decorum. Slender, she was a woman with a head of prematurely white hair that gave her an added air of elegance. She exuded grace and charm, and guests usually gave comment to her ability to make them feel at home. The Brighton household always ran like clockwork under her attentive management.

Tory adored Frankie, and the feeling was mutual.

"She was madder'n a hornet, and Papa finally got to see those eyes that look daggers at you. I wonder where he went? She's up packing for their trip. I'll miss Papa, of course, but we're going to have some more time without *her* around. I'm glad for that." She licked more frosting, smearing chocolate near her mouth.

"Well, we shall see, but unless she gets hold of the Lord, I certainly don't see her changing in the few weeks they'll be gone. We all need to pray for her. She must have a sad heart to act the way she does."

Frankie was a Christian and had led Tory to Christ when she was only six years old. Her father didn't go to church, except for special occasions, but both he and Laura, Tory's mother, hadn't minded that Frankie took Tory to church. She'd taught Tory much about loving the Lord. Mentoring her, she had taught the young girl to read her Bible and pray.

Cookie set cups of tea on the table. Tory sat with the frosting bowl in front of her, not yet finished with its contents.

Cookie finally sat down. She picked up her tea cup and asked, "So, who's going to take care of you children? Did your papa tell you that?"

"No, no he didn't. I guess he thinks everyone can take care of themselves, except Henry. My goodness, what a whiner he is. Mother would have sent me to my room if I ever whined like that. Remember when I started whining? Papa said if I acted and talked like a baby, then I'd be treated like a baby, and he wouldn't let me ride my horse or anything. It didn't take me long to lose the whine." Tory chuckled with remembrance, and the rest of them laughed.

Mabel strode into the kitchen, talking in a low, furious voice.

"Victoria, you go right this minute to your room. Have you never been instructed to not to mix with the hired help? What kind of household is this anyway?" She glared at Tory, her eyes like shards of glass. "I said go, and I mean now!"

Tory looked up at the woman, took another sip of tea, wiped her mouth, and said, "Yes, ma'am, I heard you, and I will go right now." She turned to the others and said, while she dropped a little curtsy, "Thank you for a lovely time. I'll see you all tomorrow." She started to walk with measured steps to the kitchen door, her shoulders back and her chin well up. It apparently angered Mabel as nothing else had done. She took a step toward Tory with her hand up as if to slap her. She stood and looked Mabel full in the eyes, hazel meeting icy blue.

Mabel gave Tory a resounding slap full in the face. Tory, stunned, turned her other cheek and pointed to it, the tears beginning to slip down her cheeks. Mabel looked at the girl, clearly angered almost beyond endurance.

She screamed at Victoria. "Get out of here now!" Then totally ignoring her, she turned to face a wall of incredulous hostility. "Didn't any of you hear me ring for help?"

Tory left the kitchen, head up and shoulders squared until the door closed behind her, while Mabel began to harangue the staff.

Once the door closed, she ran on silent feet to the bottom of the stairs. Victoria charged up, taking them two at a time. Her face stung and was red hot as tears coursed down her cheeks. She heard the front door open and close and glanced down through the railing that ran the width of the front entry below. Her papa was home.

Manning heard her running steps and looked up in time to see Tory sprinting for her room.

He climbed the stairs slowly—reluctant to talk to Mabel. *What a muddle*, he thought. *Here it is my wedding night, and I find I've made a colossal mistake. Well, it's too late now. I'll just have to make the best of it. Where was it I heard love is an emotion, marriage is a commitment? Ah…I remember, it was my old friend David, several years ago. Am I committed?*

He tapped on Mabel's door, but there was no reply. He entered, thinking, perhaps, she was in her dressing room and didn't hear him. After peeking in, he saw she wasn't there. He started to walk out but, glancing down, saw something shiny in her trash basket. It was Tory's locket. He picked it up and noted the chain had been broken in several places and the locket front smashed. The tiny pictures were still in place, and he breathed a little sigh of relief. He could replace the locket, have it custom made if he needed to, but the pictures were irreplaceable. He felt heartsick for not having shown more discernment. He'd thought to have playmates for Tory and to once again have a home full of life and laughter. *Both Tory and I were too quiet, still mourning Laura, I suppose. I wanted a home that was cheerful again, with a charming woman as my partner.*

He walked slowly out of Mabel's room to see his sedate housekeeper, Frankie, running down the hall, a cloth in her hand. He strode swiftly after her. Without knocking, she entered his daughter's room, and he followed behind her. As he started into the doorway, he saw, out of the corner of his eye, Mabel coming up the main stairs.

"Tory! What happened?" He watched as Frankie applied the cool cloth to a cheek that was an angry red.

"N-nothing, Papa, nothing." Tears ran down her cheeks, but she wouldn't look at him.

"Tory, look at me," he said. He strode to the bed and scooped his daughter onto his lap despite the fact she was eleven years old. He took her quivering chin in his hand and gently lifted her head, but she closed her eyes against him, tears pouring unchecked down her cheeks.

"Darling, what happened?"

"N-nothing, Papa," she said, and she burrowed her face deep into his chest, her shoulders shaking with sobs.

"Mabel," mouthed Frankie, who laid her hand on her own face over Tory's bent head.

His eyes widened and he nodded, but his gut churned. He kissed his little girl and gave her a gentle squeeze.

"I love you, sweetheart. I love you so very much. Better than anyone in this whole world. I don't know what's going on, but it will be straightened out, right now."

He left, gently closing the door behind him. He entered Mabel's room without knocking this time. She was in a state of undress, but his look at her was disinterested and cold.

"Did you, by any chance, slap my daughter?" Each word was clipped out and enunciated clearly, the voice of a very angry man.

"Yes, yes I did. I will not tolerate any disrespectfulness toward myself. I asked her to go to her room, and she—I don't have to answer to you, nor explain myself. Suffice it to say, I will not be made a fool in front of the staff by an eleven-year-old girl."

"Madam, don't ever—do you hear me clearly? Don't you ever lay a hand on my daughter again." He turned abruptly on his heel and strode from the room, sick at heart, his stomach a roiling mass of nerves.

"Why didn't you tell your papa what happened, dearie?"

"Oh, Frankie, she's his new wife. He has to live with her. If I told him what happened, it will simply cause a problem between them, and I don't want that."

Frankie was surprised by the maturity Victoria exhibited.

"Well, she needs to be held accountable for her actions," Frankie said firmly, her lips pressed together.

"I'm not telling Papa what she did. They're going away tomorrow, and I am hoping she lives day in and day out with a good man and sees what being good is like. I don't think she knows. Her eyes give me the shivers."

Frankie took the cloth from Tory's cheek and bent over to kiss her. "I know what you mean about the shivers! I love you, little girl. I love you so much! I know you've had a rough time of it this past year, but remember, sweetie, all that comes your way is filtered by the hand of the Almighty God. Let me pray for you." She sat on the bed and wrapped her arms around Tory. "Dear Lord, we thank Thee for Thy infinite love—love much deeper than we could ever imagine. I pray, Heavenly Father, that Thou wouldst grant Tory wisdom and strength. May she know Thy hand is upon her. Comfort her mourning heart, and I pray we will show the love of Christ to all. Father, if it were up to our feelings, we would hate the new Mrs. Brighton, but Father, we don't go by our feelings. We do our best to obey and follow Thy Word. Help us to have a forgiving heart and love as Thou wouldst love. Thou hast taught us to love our enemies. Many times, we seem to overlook the commands we don't like, but Father, we cannot do that command…to love our enemies…without Thy help. Therefore, we pray for Thy help. Fill us, Father, with Thy wisdom. We pray this. Oh, and Father, we also lift up Mr. Brighton. Lord, grant him faith in Thee and wisdom to know how to deal with the new Mrs. Brighton. We pray these things in Thy peerless name, the name that is above every other name. Amen.

"Here, ducky, let me help you with your dress." Frankie began unbuttoning the back of the brown taffeta dress as Tory pulled the combs out of her hair.

"Frankie, be sure to pray a lot for Papa. He's beginning to realize the huge mistake he's made. I think I was wrong not to let him know how I felt about Mabel. Sometimes it's better to say how we feel, isn't it?" She held the cool cloth against her hot cheek but pulled it away as she turned to look at Frankie.

"Yes, I suppose sometimes we think the problem will go away, dearie, and we don't deal with it or make our wishes known, or we think we're being considerate when, if truth be told, we need to speak up. We seem to think others can read our minds, but they can't. We all need to communicate and not bottle things up inside. It's not healthy to have your stomach in knots because you don't share how you feel about things." She slipped the nightgown over the girl's head, smoothing it down. "I will certainly pray for your papa. Are you all right now, or do you need me to stay awhile longer?"

"I'm fine, truly. I'll be all right. Frankie, you're not going to find a new place of employment, are you? Janey said you were going to look for another job. I couldn't bear it if you did." She reached up and hugged Frankie. "Thank you for helping me."

Frankie kissed Tory's cheek and after hugging her, patted her on the shoulder. "No, I know I need to stay here unless, of course, the new Mrs. Brighton dismisses me. Good night, sweetie girl." She left Tory's room and gently closed the door behind her.

Victoria brushed her hair out. One hundred strokes the way her mama had taught her. When she was finished, she braided the bright curls, brushed her teeth, and filled her glass with fresh water from the jug. Opening her armoire, she picked out a dress to wear the next morning and laid out her undies and long stockings. She crawled into bed and picked up her Bible from the nightstand. She slipped out of bed again and carefully turned up the wick on her lamp. Settling against her pillows, she began to read the fifth chapter of the book of Matthew. She loved to read the teachings of Jesus. She read the Beatitudes and remembered what Frankie had said about them. *They are the attitudes we are supposed to have and follow. Tomorrow is Sunday, and I'll be going to church with Frankie.* She lay quietly and prayed for everyone she knew. She prayed especially for her father, who must be quite miserable on his wedding night. She prayed that he too would come to know Jesus as Savior.

Frankie lit a taper and made her way downstairs. She went to the kitchen, which was tidied up for the night. Her shoulders felt achy from the tension of the last few hours. She thought back to Mabel coming into the kitchen right after the wedding. She had stood there in all her finery and told the staff things would be different from now on. Her eyes had glittered as she announced her position as mistress of the Brighton household.

Frankie made herself a cup of chamomile tea, and while it steeped, cut herself a small piece of cake. She tapped out the tea ball into the waste bin and made sure to clean up after herself, as Cookie didn't like to enter a kitchen with a mess in it.

She went to Laura Brighton's sitting room and made herself comfortable, putting her feet up on the ottoman. She leaned back with a sigh and thought about poor Mr. Brighton. She should have said something to him, especially when she knew how Tory had felt about the woman.

Ah, well, she thought. *What's done is done. There's no going back. Now, I can only pray.*

CHAPTER III

*A merry heart maketh a
cheerful countenance*

PROVERBS 15:13a

MANNING BRIGHTON LAY AWAKE long into the night, wondering
how he could help Mabel, or survive her. He could think of nothing.
When she'd turned her eyes on his, full of hatred, he had been shocked
beyond belief. *Did she marry me for my money? Why else?* That there was
money was quite evident in his dress and mode of living. Manning
Brighton was a wealthy man. He didn't need to work, and he could afford
a house much more ostentatious than he had. He'd inherited not only
from his father but from a bachelor uncle as well. He chose to work
because it gave him a sense of well-being—a sense of accomplishment,
and he felt his bank benefitted society.

Manning thought back to the first time he'd met Mabel. It'd been at
a dinner party hosted by Bradley Burbank, a past board member of the
bank. Mabel had been an entertaining dinner partner well-versed on a

variety of subjects. His mind flitted to the tragedy of Bradley. He'd been found drowned in his bath. Bradley had been a bachelor. The coroner had ruled it an accident and no foul play had been suspected. It was believed he'd slipped in his bath, hit his head, and drowned. Bradley had been seeing Mabel. *I wonder if Bradley knew Mabel as she revealed herself to me this evening. Perhaps he had and wanted to foist her on me. I'll wager that's why he seated her next to me—an eligible widower.*

That was quite a conversation I had with Frankie. How could Mabel so lose control that she slapped Tory in the face? She's not the woman I thought I married. Am I that naive and shallow? Did I only look at her outward appearance and not see her true character? How could I not have seen what she is really like? Do I simply see what I want to see and not the truth?

I'm grateful Olivia is going to come watch the children. That's one thing I won't have to worry about. The three of them will be in good hands while I'm away. We'll take Madeline with us. We're going to France first, anyway.

Manning, under Mabel's direction, had sent money to a reputable girl's school in Reims, France, the month before. Mabel said it wouldn't matter if her daughter, Maddie, wanted to go to the school or not…she needed to go.

Manning had gone out earlier in the evening and bought Madeline's ticket. She'd be sailing with them on the morrow. Packing shouldn't be a problem. She wouldn't need much in the way of clothing because she'd be wearing school uniforms most of the time. After purchasing the ticket, he'd stopped by Olivia's to see if she would be willing to watch the children. He'd told her that Henry was going to be a handful, but she'd laughed and said she was up to the challenge.

Olivia Annette Anderson had been Laura's dearest and best friend. She was considered an old maid at thirty-one. She simply had never been attracted to any men she deemed marriageable material. Much sought after for dinner parties and soirées, she kept a busy social schedule, which she said she would be willing to forego for the next six weeks or so. Manning was thankful for her willingness to come.

Wonder why Victoria wouldn't tell me Mabel slapped her? I guess I thought we shared everything. I think I've been so caught up in my own affairs, I never asked Tory what she thought of Mabel. What a fool I've been. He tossed and turned, finding sleep elusive.

Victoria awoke early the next morning. She lay quietly for a few moments in hopes of going back to sleep, but thoughts of Mabel prevented her mind from dozing off. She stretched and sat up. It was still nearly dark, the days getting shorter and shorter. *Think I'll go for a ride down on the beach.* The realization that it was pouring down rain hit her. She pulled back the curtains. *Oh bother! Guess I'll just go mix with the hired help.* She smiled at her thoughts. She wrapped a light-green satin robe around herself and slid her feet into fur-lined house shoes. Quietly she opened the door, slid down the bannister, and headed for the kitchen.

"Good morning, Cookie. What's for breakfast?"

Cookie Roberts jumped. "Land sakes, child, you like ta scare me ta death! I'm certain you just took ten years off my life!" She stirred the batter for pancakes.

"Sorry, I just thought I'd come mix with the hired help," she said with a cheeky grin.

"You'd best be careful 'round the new missus. How's your face this morning? That was quite a smack. Scared me and no mistake. It was a shock, uh hum, a real shock. Not like a lady, that one. Couldn't believe she'd do that."

"Oh, I'm fine." She touched her cheek gingerly. It was still tender. "Think I should take up boxing lessons?" Tory laughed at her own jest. "Papa said they were leaving for Italy today. Do you know what time?"

"No, I'm just the cook. I'm not in the master's personal confidence." Cookie smiled, her big tooth-gapped smile, missing one of her front teeth. She said her husband took a fist to her mouth and knocked the tooth right out of her head. She went on to say she broke his nose with a fry pan before she walked out on him. No one knew the real truth, and Cookie never talked about her past. Someone in her former life had taught her how to cook delicacies fit to please a king. She was clean, organized, and coveted by other households. Tory knew she had loved Laura Brighton with a passion, and she loved Manning and Victoria. This was her home. They were her family.

Mabel awoke slowly. Memories of last night flooded her consciousness. She knew she had behaved badly. *Oh well, it's not the first time, and it certainly won't be the last.*

Mabel knew she had a problem. Sometimes she felt well and healthy, and other times it was almost as if someone else took over her body. She was afraid of being locked up in some institution because she was crazy. *I'm not crazy. I'm not. I wonder what's the matter with me? One thing is certain. I'm not sorry for anything I've ever done.*

She swung her long, slender legs over the side of the bed and sat a few moments as other memories came flooding into her brain. Sometimes, it was as if she could see outside of herself. She had a quick flashback of Horace drinking a glass of juice she handed him and then seeing him in a casket. She put her hand up to her head. *I hope I'm not going to get one of my headaches.*

She felt a growing excitement about going to Italy. Never having had money to take any trips, she could travel now, and in style. She rang a bellpull for someone to come help her dress. Overnight, she had become a lady of means. *I need to look into hiring my own personal maid. The few they have here simply won't do. I need a French maid, or perhaps a Spanish one.*

Manning arose and dressed himself. He had never liked the idea of another man dressing him. Even as a boy, he'd insisted on dressing himself. He quietly opened Tory's door and peeked in to see how she fared this morning, surprised to see she was already up and about. He would miss her.

He was nearly ready to go on a trip he didn't look forward to. Frankie had packed most of his luggage. He had only a few items left to include. After breakfast, he'd collect his razor, strop, and soaps. As he went down the stairs, Manning made a mental list in case he'd forgotten something.

He entered the dining room, glad to see the sideboard was already filled with hearty breakfast food. Pouring himself a large glass of orange juice, he glanced up as Tory entered with a tray of scrambled eggs.

"Good morning, Papa. I've already eaten and need to get ready for church."

"Good morning to you, Miss Victoria Lynn Brighton." He smiled. "And I don't believe you're going to church this morning, sweetheart. Frankie needs to help Madeline pack." He hugged Tory and she kissed his cheek.

He said, "I love you so much. I'm going to miss you, my little sweetie pie. How's your cheek?" He turned her chin sideways and perused her face carefully, noticing a slight bluish swelling, but said nothing as he gently kissed it.

"It's fine, Papa, but where's Madeline going?" Tory's eyes were round. "You're not taking her to Italy and leaving the rest of us here, are you?"

"No, of course not. No one else knows it yet." He dropped his voice and held his forefinger to his lips as if relating a secret. "But we'll take her to France and drop her off at school before we head to Italy. I don't think many of her things are unpacked yet, so it shouldn't take long to get her packed up. We, Mabel and I, were to sail to Paris for a few days before heading to Italy anyway. Taking Madeline works out best for everyone." He dished up a sizable plate, having eaten little the evening before.

"Oh well, she said she wanted to go. She'll probably be very happy to go now. And then I'll be able to keep my bedroom."

"What are you talking about?"

Not answering his question, she asked, "I nearly forgot. Papa, while you're gone, do you think Ralph could get a couple more horses so Charles and Henry can ride?"

"That, young lady, is an excellent idea. I'll certainly mention it to him. He's got an exceptionally superior eye for a good horse. I don't believe any of Mabel's children ride, and Ralph can teach Charles and Henry. You are brilliant, Tory." He patted her shoulder.

"Before I sit down, I'll talk to him." Taking the cover off the muffins, he covered his own breakfast with it.

He strode into the kitchen as Mabel entered the dining room from the hall. Tory stood, gave her a curtsy of respect, and said, "Good morning, Mabel."

"Good morning. Do you always dish up your own breakfast?"

"No, ma'am, only on Sundays. Weekdays we are served, or if one wishes, they can have breakfast alone in their room. I only do that if I'm sick." She sat back down and started eating after saying a quick prayer of thanksgiving.

Manning came back into the dining room and eyed his new wife with obvious misgiving, wondering what kind of mood she was in this morning.

Mabel glanced away and said, "I want to apologize for my behavior last night. I was totally out of line." She looked first at Manning and then at Tory, her eyes clear and sweet. "I must say, I'm very sorry."

Tory looked astonished, but Manning felt a good deal of skepticism. He thought of the locket he'd placed in a pair of folded socks in his chiffonier. *I don't want Tory to come upon it accidentally nor have Mabel see I have it.*

The hansom cab driver jumped down from his perch and opened the carriage door to help the svelte woman alight. Her hair gleamed a shining raven black under her elegant hat. She smiled up at the tall man who held an umbrella for her and said, "Thank you, kind sir."

"You, madam, are most welcome." He looked at her face, which was unremarkable except for the peaches-and-cream complexion, but humor and a zest for life sparkled out of her tawny-colored eyes.

She turned and scooped the large, wicker-covered basket toward her. As she picked it up, the driver said, "Madam, let me get that for you."

"Oh, it's all right. It's only Snuggles, and he doesn't weigh all that much." She pulled the basket into her arms, satchels hanging from each elbow.

He took the hamper from her and heard a low growl from within the basket.

"What kind of dog is it?"

"He's a Schnauzer—doesn't shed, and that's important to me." She laughed up at him. "As you can see, he's my protector." She laughed again.

Rain poured off the huge umbrella, but to the cab driver, it seemed as if a ray of sunshine peeked out from under it. They walked up the cobbles together, and the woman used the knocker as he hurried out to get the rest of her luggage. It took three trips for her two small trunks and several hat boxes. The door had swung wide open, and a girl stood hugging the lady for all she was worth. "Oh, Aunt Ollie! Papa didn't tell me. Oh, we're going to have such fun!" She turned shining eyes on her papa as he entered the front foyer.

Olivia straightened to her full height as she felt Manning's eyes upon her. She looked up to see his new wife right behind him. Glancing swiftly at Mabel's face, she saw opaque blue eyes that held no curiosity.

"Hello, everyone." Olivia straightened her shoulders. "I've come to be nanny for the next few weeks." She smiled pleasantly, but Mabel didn't smile back.

Manning didn't say much last night, but since it was his wedding night and he left the house, hmmm. Olivia could read between the lines and knew something was definitely wrong, but she surely didn't care to get into the middle of anything.

"Are you going to stand there gaping at me, or am I allowed to come in out of the rain?" She laughed, a sweet contagious sound. Tory laughed, and Manning smiled.

"Come in—please do come in," Mabel said, but her eyes said something else.

Manning drew Mabel forward. "Mabel, this is a friend of the family, Olivia Anderson. Olivia, my new wife, Mabel."

41

Frankie came down the main stairs, breathless. "Oh, Miss Olivia, welcome, welcome. I'll get Ralph to carry up your things."

"Don't bother, Frankie. I can get the trunks," Manning said.

"Oh, Aunt Olivia, you've brought Snuggles. Can I hold him?"

The sweet-faced woman smiled down at Tory with eyes full of love. "A bit later, Toralina Lou. He's probably all a jumble right now, but after he's settled into my room, you are more than welcome to play with him. Now, which room am I in? The lilac room or the lilac room?" She laughed. "I'm always in the lilac room, aren't I?"

"No, not this time," Frankie said. "Miss Madeline is in the lilac room. You're in the end suite this time."

"Oooh, the one reserved for special guests. My, I'll have to behave myself, won't I?" She laughed again and picked up the basket she'd set down. "Let's be off to it, then." She glanced at Mabel, who stared at Manning with daggers in her eyes. *Oh dear, isn't that just like a man. He didn't tell her I was to come watch the children. Well, it's not my problem.* She followed Frankie up the stairs, Tory carrying her satchels and Manning bringing up the rear with one of the trunks.

CHAPTER IV

Shall not God search this out?
for he knoweth the secrets of the heart.

PSALM 44:21

MABEL WAS LEFT STANDING ALONE in the front entrance. She walked with swift steps to the library, picked up an inkwell, and walked back to the remaining trunk. She started to unhook the lid but heard a sound behind her. It was Ralph, who'd come in by way of the kitchen. Cookie must have notified him that help was needed. Mabel straightened, hiding the inkwell in the folds of her dress.

"Good morning, ma'am. Come to help, I am. Where would you like me to stow this?"

"Mistress Anderson is staying in the suite of rooms at the end of the hall. I'm sure you'll find Mr. Brighton there." Her tone deliberately undermined Manning's integrity. She noticed Ralph's glance to see if that was the case, but he promptly looked away. She kept her face stony and implacable, not caring the atmosphere was extremely uncomfortable.

Mabel started back to the library to replace the inkwell. *What was I going to do with that?* She went back to the dining room to finish breakfast.

In the meantime, Manning chatted with Olivia a bit.

Sill in the room in which Olivia would be staying, he spoke to Tory, who was on the floor trying to peek into the basket. "Tory, I want you to go wake up Madeline. She needs to get ready. I'm sure there are some of

43

her belongings that need to be shifted. She won't be wanting to take everything with her."

Tory said, "Yes, sir." She stood rather reluctantly, which cued Manning onto the fact that his daughter was not on the best of terms with Madeline.

Tory looked up at her father. Seeing his questioning look, she dropped her eyes and headed slowly down the hall.

She tapped on the door but got no response. Knocking harder, Victoria pushed open the door.

Madeline sat up. "What do *you* want? I don't remember saying *you* could come in here. This is *my* room for a few more days."

With a pleading look on her face, Tory replied, "Madeline, can we start over, please? I know I'm two years younger than you and that you know a lot of things that I don't, but I don't want us to be enemies…I'd like us to be friends. I'm very sorry we got off to a bad start."

Madeline stared at Victoria, clearly astonished at the younger girl's offering of an olive branch. Tory had no doubt Mabel duped Madeline into believing Tory was a selfish, spoiled brat.

"In truth, that would be all right by me. I'm sorry too. I don't like being at loggerheads with someone else. Living in the same house, why, it could become very tiresome. And, if we're to be friends, you may call me Maddie."

"Well, that's good news for me." She walked over and sat on Maddie's bed, looking into her serious blue eyes with a twinkle in her own. "Bet I can make you get out of that bed in less than three seconds, once I tell you something."

"Tell me what?"

"If I tell you what, then it won't matter, but I really do bet I can make you get out of that bed in less than three seconds."

"You're on. Bet you can't."

"All right, are you ready?" Tory stood and backed up to get out of the way.

"Yes. In truth, I'm glued to this bed and there's no way you're getting me out of it." She grinned at Tory.

"All right...today..." Tory said and looked at the chime clock on the mantel, "in...let's see, less than three hours, you're going to be on a ship headed for France and boarding school."

Madeline screamed, jumped out of the bed, and ran toward her clothespress. "You win, Tory!" Maddie laughed. "You win! Oh, I'm so excited. I've dreamed and dreamed of going off to school."

"Won't you miss home? Won't you get homesick?"

"I can tell you one hundred percent, no and no, but I'm not going to explain."

"All right, but I'm sorry now that you're going away. I think we could have been good friends."

"Well, we can still be that. I'll write and give you my address, and then you can write me. That way we'll learn a lot about each other. After all, you're my little sister now."

"I'd like that, Maddie. I'd like that a lot. Is there any way I can help you?"

The two girls chattered happily together as Tory helped the older girl pack.

Mabel had finished breakfast when Olivia and Manning joined her at the table.

"Are you all packed?" Manning asked Mabel, his tone stilted.

"Yes, yes I am."

"Mabel, I went out last night after dinner to get another ticket and stopped by to ask Olivia if she'd watch the children while we're away."

"Who's the other ticket for...my Henry?"

"No, I thought we should take Madeline to school and get her settled in while we're in Europe."

"That's a brilliant idea, Manning. I'm sure she'll be delighted." Mabel poured herself another cup of coffee as Manning dished himself up a new plate of eggs and bacon.

Olivia took a couple rashers of bacon and poured herself some steaming hot coffee.

"Mabel, is there anything I should know about Charles or Henry that will make them more comfortable with me?"

"No, not really. They have stayed with friends before and are able to do fine on their own."

Nodding her head, Olivia said, "All right...no special foods they like to eat or games to play?"

"I've already told you, no!" Mabel's voice rose a bit. She was not happy this woman would be watching her boys. *She's quite charming. What if Henry starts loving her more than me? I don't care about Charles. He's close to hating me already, but I'd be mightily put out if Henry switched his affection and loyalty to this woman instead of me.*

The two boys entered the dining room, and Charles went to the sideboard to dish up his breakfast.

Henry ran to his mother. "Mama, Mama, you're not going to leave me, are you? Mama, you can't leave me here with strangers. You can't!"

"Oh, darling, it won't be for long. We're going to take Maddie to school and before you know it, we'll be back."

"I don't want you to go!" Henry screamed at her. He turned to yell in Manning's face. "I don't want you to take her. Do you hear me? You leave her here with me!" He threw himself down on the floor and began to kick and scream in a fit of temper. "You can't go! You can't go, Mama!"

Olivia looked on with a shocked expression, likely wondering how his mother could tolerate such horrible behavior.

Manning stood, grabbed the pitcher of orange juice, and poured the rest of its contents on the boy's face. Henry stopped screaming immediately. He sat up, clearly in shock at the vile treatment.

Manning had the boy's attention.

"That, young man, is not allowed. No temper tantrums nor screaming in this house, do you understand?" Manning was not angry. He wanted to laugh but tried to look stern. Charles chuckled and belted out a full-bellied laugh. Manning watched as Charles' eyes caught his mother's horrified look, and the boy laughed even harder. Henry looked at Charles laughing, which wasn't a common sight. Manning had never heard him laugh before.

Henry's lips turned up and he started laughing too, his tongue beginning to lick the orange juice from around his mouth. Olivia and Manning joined in, relieving the tension that had permeated the room.

Olivia knelt to help the boy after a glance at his upset mother, who continued to sit, her lips turned down in disapproval and a scowl marring her forehead.

"Henry"—Olivia choked on her laughter—"let's go to the kitchen. I'm sure we can get you fixed up." She led the dripping boy out of the room.

Charles said, "Let me help with the floor." He too went to the kitchen, but he couldn't stop laughing.

Tory and Madeline came into the dining room. It was nearly nine, and Madeline said she was hungry.

"Be careful where you walk," Manning said, humor still lurking in his eyes. "We've had an accident in here."

He could see Mabel was angry, but she hadn't voiced it.

"A deliberate act is *not* an accident." Mabel couldn't seem to move. She felt sick and excited at the same time. She looked at Madeline, whose cheeks were reddened with excitement. She knew hers probably looked the same. She felt upset about Henry, but deep within her she didn't care about him at all. She only cared that within the hour, she would be on a trip to Europe with no cares, no responsibilities, and no eerie feeling that someone followed her. She had that feeling every time she went out. Even the day before at the wedding, she felt as if someone were watching her.

"What happened?" Tory asked.

"Nothing of any import," her father said. He smiled widely at Madeline. "So, young lady, how are you this morning?" He could tell her smile was genuine.

"Oh, I'm enraptured! It's divine! I'm beside myself with excitement! I've been pinching my arm to make sure I'm not dreaming. Tory told me, and I almost didn't believe her."

"Are you packed?" Manning asked. "We'll need to be gone from here within the hour."

"Yes, Tory helped me, and I'm ready to go right down to my satchel. I will never, ever be able to thank you enough for this gift. I thought I'd never be able to go off to school and wondered if I'd ever have the education I want. You see, I'd like to teach French and deportment. Perhaps I could even run my own establishment someday. Without an education, my hopes were…well, they were hopeless. Thank you again, Mr. Brighton."

"You are most welcome, and I think you should call me Manning or Pops or something else rather than being so formal. You are now my stepdaughter, and you are an exceptional young lady to have set such goals at your age. I am proud of you." He was amazed at the transformation in this girl from yesterday, when she'd seemed so moody and quiet. This morning she was vivacious and friendly.

"Well, again I thank you. I decided a long time ago that I wanted to be a teacher."

Mabel looked at her daughter with cold eyes and stated, "I think it's a pipe dream. I don't expect you to amount to a whole lot, Madeline, taking after your father the way you do."

Manning's jaw dropped, and Tory looked at the woman with something near to horror in her hazel eyes.

"What a cruel thing to say to your daughter!" exclaimed Manning. "I have no doubt she will attain to whatever she aspires to do." He was staggered at Mabel's seemingly detached behavior and careless words.

Tory had heard enough out of that woman.

She turned her back on Mabel and took Madeline by the arm. Smiling into her eyes, she said, "I think you are most likely quite brilliant. I have no idea what I want to be when I grow up. It's time to dish up some breakfast, Madeline, but first let me introduce you to one of my most favorite people in the whole world."

Olivia had returned to the dining room. The girl turned to give Olivia a hug. "Aunt Olivia Anderson, this is my new sister, Madeline Louise Brighton. Maddie, this is Olivia Anderson."

"I am pleased to make your acquaintance, madam." Madeline dipped a little curtsy. To Tory she said, "But my last name is still Vickers, not Brighton."

"Well, Miss Madeline Vickers, I'm quite pleased to make your acquaintance. What a young lady you are!" Tory liked the way Olivia always seemed to put people at their ease.

She watched as Madeline looked closely into Olivia's clear, shadow-free eyes.

"If you'd like, you may call me Miss Olivia. You are certainly in for a treat, sailing to France." Olivia smiled her best smile.

"Come, Madeline, you need to eat," said Mabel a little irritably. "We'll be leaving shortly." She threw down her napkin and excused herself, saying she had a few more things to pack. Tory thought the atmosphere in the room warmed up significantly after she left.

Charles came back with a mop, and Janey and Lorna followed him. He began to mop up the mess of orange juice off the floor, and Janey went over it with a clean, wet cloth to make sure it wasn't sticky. Lorna scrubbed it again, making sure all was clean.

"Papa, did you talk to Ralph yet?"

"No, it completely slipped my mind. I'll do it right now. Thanks for reminding me." He took a last bite, swallowed down the rest of his coffee, and wiped his face with his napkin. Getting up, he excused himself. He left, going through the kitchen to the back door.

The Brighton stable was huge. Manning owned one stallion and one gelding, both beautiful horses. Tory was the proud owner of a sweet mare, a palomino named Commotion. Besides the three riding horses, Manning owned Glad and Glee, who pulled the carriages, and lastly, a pony born to Commotion in the early spring. It was a sweet little filly, now seven months old. Tory had been allowed to watch it be born and thought it such a miracle. She'd named her new little horse Sensation.

There was a huge field behind the house, a fenced-in paddock, and a wooded area with tons of trails for riders. Ralph also stabled his horse in the Brightons' stable. His was a gelding called Castanea Denata, named for an American chestnut tree that was dying out due to a bark disease. Casta—for short—had a glossy, chestnut-colored coat.

"Ralph...say Ralph, are you in here?" Manning entered the small side door to the stable. Ralph was in the tack room and hadn't heard

Manning. He hummed happily to himself and interspersed his humming with prayer.

He turned when he heard a footstep. "Mr. Brighton, you gave me a fright an' no mistake."

"Good morning, Ralph. Sorry I startled you. I called out, but you didn't hear me. We'll begin to load the wagon in about twenty minutes. I can help you with those trunks."

"Aye, sir, Glad and Glee are all ready to go, and I'll be gettin' Morrie ta' help me wi' the trunks."

"Oh, is he here already? I asked him to cut down that old twisted willow on the corner of the paddock. It drips leaves and branches all the time. Be sure he remembers, won't you? The main reason I came out was to ask you to purchase a couple horses. One for Henry and one for Charles. I respect your eye for good horseflesh and give you full rein, so to speak. Neither of the boys ride, and if you could spare the time, I'd like you to teach them. If you don't have the time, I'd like you to find someone to give them lessons, but not at the same time. I don't want Charles shackled with Henry's tantrums. I want the boy to enjoy himself without the extra worry of his little brother."

"Very well, sir. I'd be tickled pink ta do that. Ye ken how I be a lookin' at the horses. I takes me time, I do. Mayhap, I'll take the older boy wi' me."

"Clever idea, thank you so much, Ralph. Keep an eye on my little girl while I'm away, won't you?"

"Aye, sir, that goes wi'out sayin', sir."

"Thanks, I'm grateful to have a dependable man such as yourself." Manning clapped Ralph on the shoulder and started out the stable. Turning back he added, "We'll be gone nigh unto eight weeks, I should imagine." Ralph nodded.

Once the trunks were all loaded onto the wagon, Manning drove the carriage with Mabel, Madeline, Olivia, and Victoria to the docks.

A stilted conversation ensued inside the coach. Mabel continually cut Madeline and Victoria off midsentence, so the two girls stopped talking. Olivia tried to talk to Mabel, but she rudely ignored her and looked out the window, twisting her new wedding ring around and around on her finger. A strained silence prevailed.

Ralph followed behind Manning and drove the wagon with the two boys sitting beside him. Henry bounced on the seat, wild with excitement. He couldn't stop talking, and even Charles, who was normally so quiet, added a comment here and there.

The two boys carried satchels and some lighter items onboard, and the heavier things were loaded by a porter. It didn't take long for the trunks to be trundled down to their stateroom. The main compartment had two connecting rooms. Everyone, except Ralph, who stayed with the carriage and wagon, went onboard to the Brightons' cabin, oohing and ahhing over the beautiful accoutrements. Manning had ordered caviar, crackers, Brie, and Stilton along with champagne to celebrate their departure. The children drank ginger ale, which was a treat. Several other couples, who were friends of Manning's from the bank, joined them to wish the newlyweds a bon voyage. There was much laughter and excitement as people chatted together.

CHAPTER V

The bloodthirsty hate the upright:
but the just seek his soul.

PROVERBS 29:10

GEORGE BAXTER, THE YOUNG detective from the Boston Police Department, was at the going-away party. His wife, Adeline, was on his arm. She'd been a close friend of Laura Brighton, but George didn't know Manning all that well. While everyone was busily chatting, the detective approached Manning.

"Could I have a word with you, sir, just for a few minutes?" He spoke quietly.

"Of course, Detective Baxter. I'm surprised to see you here." Manning eyed the detective curiously. He hadn't invited George and his wife to the bon voyage party. It piqued his interest.

"Yes, I'm surprised to see me here too. It's not official business, you understand, but I've always admired you, sir. My Adeline, as you know, was such good friends with your Laura. I asked her to accompany me today because I don't want my presence here suspect, but I thought it only right to warn you." He dropped his voice even more. "Brighton, we've never been able to prove it, but your new wife is suspected of poisoning her late husband and also having something to do with your late friend, Bradley Burbank's, death. Please watch your back, Brighton. Please...be very careful."

Manning Brighton's eyes widened in stupefaction, and it took every ounce of willpower not to turn around and stare at Mabel.

George was surprised that Brighton didn't turn to look at her.

It would be a natural reaction given the information he'd imparted. It gave George a measure of assurance that Mr. Brighton was a man in control of himself, easing his mind a bit. Manning Brighton was no fool.

"Thank you, Baxter. Thanks for the warning. I will take it very seriously. I certainly witnessed some extremely bizarre behavior last evening. I wish you'd have told me of this earlier."

"Without proof or knowing about last evening, would you have believed it?" George Baxter asked. He stared at Brighton, who simply stared back. "Enjoy the sights, sir, but please, do watch your back." He strolled over to Adeline, who was in conversation with Olivia. He bowed politely, listening to small talk.

Finally the ship's earsplitting blast sounded out, and it was time for all visitors to exit the ship. Manning shook George's hand and thanked him again. He hugged Charles, whose blue eyes shined up into his with respect. He gave Henry a hug and ruffled his hair. Turning to Victoria, he picked her up and whispered into her ear.

"I love you, darling. We'll be gone about seven or eight weeks, I should imagine. You take care. Ohhh, I love you so much." He squeezed her and put her back down.

He turned to Olivia and took her hand in both of his. "I can't begin to thank you enough for taking the children, especially on such short notice."

Her cheeks reddened slightly, "Oh, Manning, don't you know I'm delighted to do it? I plan to have great fun with them while you're away."

She turned and pulled Mabel, who'd hung back, into her arms. "God bless you, Mabel, and I hope you have a wonderful journey. Italy will be beautiful this time of year."

Mabel stood stiffly, smiled brittlely, and replied, "Thank you."

Her eyes stared at George Baxter's back. He was leaving the stateroom with his wife. She wondered who he was. She knew she'd seen him somewhere before.

When the blast of the whistle sounded, George had taken Adeline's arm and they left the stateroom.

Descending the gangway, George was deep in thought. He and Adeline walked slowly, arm in arm, toward their hansom cab while he murmured a prayer.

"I hope I did the right thing. Lord, please keep Manning Brighton safe. I pray he takes the words I spoke to him with seriousness. Lord, please help us find proof that Horace Vickers and Bradley Burbank were, indeed, murdered."

Adeline murmured, "Amen."

The noise of the children, as Charles hugged his sister Maddie and Henry cried for his mother, drowned out everything except the sound of the second warning whistle. With much noise, laughter, and scurrying of feet, the nontravelers descended the ship posthaste. Henry's hand was held firmly by Olivia, who had to tug and pull him with the help of Charles on the other side.

The wind was blowing hard, and the skies overhead darkened with heavy clouds. The gangway was quickly drawn up into the ship. With another long moaning blast of the horn, the vessel began to cut the water slowly as it made its way out of port and into the bay, its flag flapping wildly in the breeze. Olivia and the children stood waving until the people at the rail were no longer discernible.

Henry stood with tears raining down his cheeks, his hands tightened into fists, but at least he was quiet. The little group stood on the pier until the ship became a dim outline.

Olivia said, "Let's join hands. I want to pray for their trip." Still holding Henry's and taking Tory's hand in her own, she looked on with a smile as Tory and Charles held hands, but Henry put his free hand behind his back.

"Henry, we are praying for your mother to come back safely and that they have a good trip. This isn't about you, and I want you to join the circle."

Begrudgingly, Henry took Charles' outstretched hand, but his lower lip stuck out in a pout.

Olivia said, "Thank you, Henry. Now, let's bow our heads. Lord Jesus, how thankful we are to have a wonderful Savior like Thee. Thou knowest our needs even before we voice them. We pray a special blessing upon Manning, Mabel, and Maddie. We pray for a trip of Thy choosing. May Madeline enjoy her schooling and make many new friends. May Thy blessing be upon her and help her to grow. We pray for Manning and Mabel. Father, I pray that they enjoy each other's company and enjoy the history and beauty of Europe. May Thy will be done. And now, Father, I pray for Charles, Victoria, and Henry. May we have a wonderful time of our own. I pray we enjoy each other's company and savor the time we share with one another. May our actions and speech be pleasing to Thee. We Thank Thee, Lord Jesus. Amen."

"Amen," said Tory. "Thank you, Aunt Ollie. Now I feel better about them going. How far is it to Europe anyway?" Tory was close to Olivia, who had been her mother's best friend.

"Normally, it's close to a week for an ocean liner to get to France. If they run into a storm, it can take longer. If they have fair winds, it can take a shorter amount of time. Let's get back to the carriage. I see Ralph heading toward the wagon, and look, the sky is getting darker. Looks like more rain."

Tory turned to Charles and Henry. Her eyes shone brightly as she looked over their heads at Ralph climbing up the wagon. "That reminds me—you'll never ever, ever guess what my Papa asked Ralph to do."

"What? What did he ask Ralph to do? Tell us, Tory. Come on, tell us!" Henry was full of curiosity, but it was Charles' clear, blue eyes she held with her own.

"Papa told Ralph to buy two new horses so you both can learn how to ride."

"He did?" Charles' eyes shone back at her, clearly excited at the prospect.

"Yes, and you are to have separate lessons. Ralph wants to teach you himself, so you will learn correctly and at a pace he feels is good. Isn't that exciting? We'll be able to ride together and have fun jaunts down on the beach. It won't take you long, Charles. You'll probably catch up with me in no time."

Henry chimed in. "Me too. I'm going to learn fast too."

The four of them headed for the carriage as great droplets of rain began to fall.

"Well, I guess I'm in for it," laughed Olivia. "I'm supposed to drive back."

"Can I ride outside with you?" Charles asked. "I don't mind getting wet."

"Of course." Olivia began to walk briskly, still holding Henry's hand. They were almost running. Her silk dress would most likely be ruined. *Oh well, it can't be helped.*

Christopher Belden, head of the Boston detectives, knew his prized detective would most likely warn Brighton. In truth, it was necessary, yet without proof, that's exactly what it was, simply a warning. If Brighton took it to heart, it might just save his life.

Without any proof, he thought, *it's impossible to arrest that woman.*

The problem was having no witnesses. No one saw anything. Not one person had come forward. Not one person at the department believed Burbank fell in his bathing tub. The depression on the top of his head was not consistent with the tub's edge, but it's what the coroner had ruled…death by accident. Christopher Belden hoped Manning Brighton had eyes in the back of his head.

The captain of the cruise line went out of his way to greet Manning Brighton. His home base was Boston, and he had his account and line of credit with Brighton's bank. The two men had met several times for lunch. Both seemed to share the same politics, and a mutual respect had grown between them. Manning met up with him in the ship's lounge, and the captain invited him to sit at his table that evening.

"We've been invited to sit at the captain's table. It's quite an honor. Dinner is at six o'clock," he said, smiling at Madeline. He studied Mabel to see what kind of mood she was in. He would go up to the top deck and decline the invitation if Mabel didn't want to attend.

"I suppose we'd better get dressed, Maddie, darling. Manning is correct. It is an honor, and the captain's table is usually a dress-up affair. Pretty soon you'll be old enough to wear long dresses and have your hair up, but for now, wear your best dress."

There were two bedrooms in their stateroom, one with a huge bed and the other with two twin-sized beds. Mabel had stated that she and Madeline were taking the room with the twin beds. Since talking with Detective Baxter, Manning was glad for her decision.

Mabel dressed herself in a beautiful midnight-blue gown that enhanced the blue of her eyes. Maddie fastened the clasp of a necklace around her mother's neck. Last month, Manning had given Mabel a beautiful sapphire and diamond necklace with matching earrings and a wide bracelet of sapphires, studded with diamonds. He'd said it matched the brilliance of her eyes.

Madeline's best dress was the pink one, the young-girl dress she'd worn to the wedding.

She hated it. The bows all over it were pitiful. If she could get rid of the bows, it wouldn't be quite so bad. Her mother had picked it out over her protests. She decided she'd wear her green dress that was second best but more appropriate for her age. At thirteen, one thing she knew for sure was that she had an excellent eye for haute couture and none of her clothes came close to fitting into that splendid category.

Dinner was an elegant affair, the food perfection itself. The mix of passengers gave way to scintillating conversation and much laughter. Manning secretly observed his wife, seeing the woman he'd been attracted to over the past few months. He remembered a Charles Dickens' quote he'd memorized. *We forge the chains we wear in life. Well, I've forged mine, marrying a woman I thought to be something she is not. Wonder if George Baxter is right? Could my wife truly be a murderess?*

Olivia Anderson thought she'd never enjoyed herself more, not since she was a little girl. Henry was a bit of a challenge, but it didn't take him long to realize that whining and shows of temper got him nothing.

Charles had never, in his entire life, been so happy. Now that his mother was away, he felt a measure of relief and enjoyed himself more than he could ever remember. Mabel's mercurial temperament constantly had him on edge and frightened by what she might do next.

Today, Charles was to go with Ralph and pick out a horse for himself. He hadn't been around Ralph much, but the groom seemed like a very nice man. He went out to the stables to find him.

Ralph thought Charles an amiable enough young fellow.

He saw the boy enter the dimness of the stable and said, "Good morning, Master Charles. Hope this day finds you in high spirits. You look like a young man ready to go horse shopping, Charley, me boy. First, I have a very personal question to ask you."

Charles stiffened, standing still as a post. Ralph saw the change and wondered what was the matter with him.

"My question is, do you want this to be a strictly manly outing, or can we be invitin' Mistress Victoria ta go with us?"

Charles didn't realize he'd been holding his breath.

It whooshed out, and he grinned up at Ralph. "Aw, she's quite nice for a girl and doesn't seem to be a nuisance at all. I vote let's take her with us. She'll want to see what you decide to pick. I'm so excited. This," he said and waved his hand expansively around the barn, "is so wonderful. I'm having the best time of my life."

"Well, scoot on in and tell Miss Tory to get herself out here, directly, but don't be a lettin' Henry know, or we'll be saddled with him fer th' whole afternoon."

"Believe you me, I won't!" Charles raced across the stable yard and entered the house by way of the kitchen.

"What're you up to, young man?" Cookie asked when he banged the door shut.

"Ralph and I are going to look at some horses. I'm to ask Tory if she wants to come, but we don't want Henry to hear about it." He grinned as Cookie pressed a couple oatcakes into his hand. Hers were quite special, as she put frosting on them. "Thanks, Cookie." He pushed through to the dining room and took the stairs at a run.

Cookie stared after him.

"What a difference there is in that boy and in just one week too." Cookie was always talking out loud to herself. "He's settlin' in and I'm glad. He acted so quiet and...and old. Too quiet for a young man such as he," she muttered to herself.

Charles made a beeline for Tory's sitting room. He opened the door a crack and looked in to see if Tory was still in there with Miss Olivia and Henry...she was.

He peeked his head in and made a sign to Miss Olivia and said, "Tory, could you come help me a minute? I've forgotten how and need you to show me how to adjust the stirrup again."

"Certainly, I'd be glad to help."

"Me too, I wanna watch too." Henry began to whine, but when he saw the look on Olivia's face, he brought his voice down to a normal pitch. He turned to look at Charles, obviously sensing something was up and wanting to be a part of it.

Olivia said, "Oh pooh. Well, all right, go ahead and go with them if you like, Henry. I was hoping you'd come with me to feed the ducks. Oh well, maybe next time." She winked at Tory and shooed her out with her hand. Charles appreciated that she'd hooked Henry with her enticing offer. Henry's head swiveled around to stare big-eyed at Olivia.

"Oh, I don't haf ta go with them. I'd much rather go feed the ducks with you."

Once in the hall, Charles said, "Ralph wants to know if you want to go with us to look at horses. If you do, he said to get yourself to the stable right away."

"I'd love to come. Let me change my shoes, and I'll be right there." She ran down the hall to her room. Charles decided to wait for her on the top of the stairs. He sat down with his chin in his hands, elbows on knees. *God, I don't know how to pray properly. I don't know You, but Tory says You know me. Please, please keep Manning Brighton safe. I'm really scared for him. I feel so badly. I should have told him about mother.* Guilt weighed heavily on the boy's thin shoulders.

CHAPTER VI

A virtuous woman is a crown to her
husband: but she that maketh ashamed
is as rottenness in his bones.

PROVERBS 12:4

MANNING THOUGHT SETTLING Madeline into boarding school was much easier than he'd anticipated. The headmistress was politeness personified and everyone else most helpful. Manning and Mabel spent several days sightseeing in Reims to make sure Maddie would be happy at the school, but they needn't have worried.

She knew a bit of French and had enrolled in intensive French classes. With her willingness to learn, it wouldn't be long before she'd be not only proficient, but fluent. Mabel constantly fussed over her but secretly, Madeline couldn't wait until her mother was gone. She had to spend her after-class hours in Mabel and Manning's company and go sight-seeing when she'd rather be making friends.

For three days, while Madeline attended classes, Manning and Mabel toured the city. They'd gone to the famous cathedral, Notre Dame, and were awed by its splendor and beauty. They'd toured the champagne cellars, for which Reims was so famous, the Palace de Tau, the basilica, and so many beautiful sights. The food was *ne pas être égalé*, not to be equaled. Sitting in small cafés over coffee had been pleasurable. Mabel excitedly made small talk. She seemed to enjoy the doors money opened for her. If Manning hadn't seen her previous behavior, he would have had trouble believing it existed. *George Baxter was right*, he thought. *I don't think I would have believed him. I would have believed Tory, but I never thought to ask her what she thought of me marrying Mabel. What am I going to do? George thinks she murdered her husband and Burbank. I'm beginning to think that perhaps it's a physical disorder that causes her to go off on these tangents and horrible behavior. Perhaps we should travel up to Switzerland after Italy. There are some well-known clinics that deal with mental disorders. She seems happy enough right now, but how long will it last?*

Finally with tears on Mabel's part and a bit of relief on Madeline's, the couple left Reims to make their way back to the coast by train.

Charles carried a heavy, dark secret and whenever it cropped up, he slammed a door shut in his mind. He put the secret, which only he knew, in a box in a dark corner labeled Do Not Enter. He'd awakened abruptly, his body covered with sweat as his mind slowly came out of the throes of a horrible nightmare. *Only it's not a just a dream, is it? It happened. I saw it happen.* He rolled onto his tummy and pulled his pillow over his head. He wished somehow, someway, he could erase the memory that persistently invaded his mind. He groaned inwardly. Charles carried a burden far too heavy. He lay still and wondered if he should tell someone, but if he did, what would happen? He lay there, his mind in a fever pitch of anxiety. It was a long time before he was able to relax and go back to sleep.

Tory awoke not long after dawn. She was a good sleeper and an early riser. She had a wonderful time looking at the horses with Charles and Ralph the day before. They were going to return today and see if they felt the same way about the animals. If they did, they'd be the proud owners of two more mares.

The horses had been found at different studs. Ralph said they were fine specimens of horse flesh. One was an Andalusian, a beautiful white horse, which Ralph said was known for its sweet temperament. The other was a Canadian. Tory hadn't heard about this kind of horse before, although she'd studied breeds because she was so interested in them. Ralph said the Canadian was one of the sturdiest breeds and could do almost anything, from pulling carriages to lugging a plow—which they wouldn't need—to being a jumper. The mare they'd looked at was a beautiful black one with a broad chest and shiny coat. Tory thought the two horses together would make a striking combination...one totally white and the other totally black except for one white foot.

Victoria threw back the covers and hurriedly dressed into a split skirt. She was still allowed to ride astride and dreaded the day she'd have to ride sidesaddle. She was particularly happy to be up and about so early on this morning because she wanted to ride before breakfast. She ran lightly down the stairs and out to the stable. She hadn't ridden much in the last week and a half, not wanting to make Charles feel bad that he couldn't ride. He was a quick learner. Ralph said he was a natural and would be riding as if he were born to it in no time at all.

She entered the stable quietly, but Commotion heard her and whickered. Tory gave her a lump of sugar. She looked into the tack room but didn't see Ralph. Carrying her saddle and blanket out of the tack room, which was no mean feat as it was so heavy, she saddled up Commotion, tightening the girth a second time. When Tory climbed on Commotion by herself, she would back her horse out of the stall, turn Commotion around, and back her into the stall. She stepped onto a slat of the stall so she was tall enough to step into the stirrup. It was still early, and as she walked Commotion out to the stable yard, she saw, out of the corner of her eye, Ralph coming to feed the horses.

"Off to the beach, air ye?" Ralph grinned. "Have you eaten yer breakfast yit, me girl?"

"No, I want to ride before the rest of the household is up."

"Away wi' you, then, little one." He slapped Commotion lightly on her rump and Tory was off at a gallop.

The groom understood Tory wanted a good ride before Charles was up. He never ceased to be amazed at the sweet nature of one Victoria Lynn Brighton.

The horses were a great addition to the Brightons' stable. Charles chose the black Canadian and named her Ebony. Henry took several days to name his. He could be seen, chin in his hands and elbows on his knees, sitting on an upturned bucket staring at the beautiful white horse. He couldn't believe it was really his. Finally, he came up with two names but had trouble deciding between them.

"I'm going to name her Snowball or else Crystal," he announced. He asked Olivia what she would name it, but she told him it was his horse and she didn't want to influence him. He asked her to pick between the two names he'd chosen but she refused to tell him anything.

Henry had nearly stopped whining and seemed a much nicer boy. He loved Snuggles, Olivia's dog, and could be found in Tory's sitting room playing with the little dog that enjoyed a good game of tug of war. This day, they had one of Manning's old socks from the wash. It had a knot on both ends, and Snuggles could hold his own against Henry.

Olivia sat in Tory's favorite wingback, her legs curled underneath her. Two days after her arrival, she had taken Tory into the heart of the city. They'd picked out a new floral print and had the chair, which Henry had ruined with ink, reupholstered. They'd also bought a beautiful wooden rocking chair and had pillows made to match. The refurbished chair had arrived yesterday as good as new. She still needed to replace the stained carpet.

Olivia sat and thought about Manning and especially his new wife, Mabel. The day after her arrival, Olivia discovered two of her favorite dresses had been slashed with scissors. Unpacking one of the trunks, she'd been horrified. She didn't tell anyone about it. There was nothing to be gained except anxiety. She prayed for Manning's safety on this trip more than once a day since they'd been gone. She tried not to worry about him as her motto was, worrying was fruitless.

Today, Frankie, who routinely checked out clothing, had gone in to check on Manning's socks to make sure there were enough and that they had no holes in them. It seemed he'd gone through several pair recently. An aghast Frankie had brought Tory's smashed locket to Miss Olivia.

Olivia looked at it, saddened. She remembered when she'd gone shopping with Laura, a little less than a year ago, for Tory's eleventh birthday. She'd helped Laura choose the locket, which now lay broken and battered in Frankie's hand. Put it back, she'd told Frankie. Manning had to know about it, or it wouldn't have been hidden in his socks. Olivia wondered if Mabel was deranged.

Maddie took great pleasure in boarding school. She'd made several close friends and blossomed under the careful guidance of her teachers and the program of classes she was taking. Her popularity soared, and to sit next to her in the dining hall was a coveted prize among the girls. There weren't many students who were from America attending the school. Maddie had a great sense of humor, and her droll comments were repeated among her classmates as if she were a celebrated wit. French, with diligent study, began to roll off her tongue; she loved the language. Mathematics was Madeline's most difficult subject, and she spent nearly two hours every afternoon trying to make sense of some of the problems. Her roommate, Katarina Dyrbov, hailed from Russia and was brilliant in mathematics. She helped Madeline with numeric problems, explaining the numbers in such a way that Maddie began to look forward to solving them. In exchange, Madeline taught the Russian girl English. They communicated either in French or by sign language. Maddie liked Katarina extremely well, and Katarina seemed more than pleased to room with her.

Horseback riding was an actual class, and riding sidesaddle was considered a must at the boarding school. Maddie learned how to ride with aplomb.

She'd written one letter to Victoria and had received one back from her and one from Charles. Life was more enjoyable than the girl could ever remember. She began to hope she'd never have to go home, not ever again. One of the girls had already invited her for the Christmas holidays in England. She hadn't accepted yet but thought she might. For the past two years, Maddie had been having stomachaches, and they seemed to have vanished. She was quite certain her mother's capricious temperament was to blame for them. Home had never been a happy place.

Mabel was enjoying Italy immensely. She was quite tired and felt she should slow down. Sometimes, too much activity or tiredness brought on headaches or the voices. The voices told her what to do, and she knew the voices were much wiser than she. She'd been listening to the voices since she was fifteen. Thinking back, she realized it was the same year she started playing with tarot cards and the Ouija board. She had been told they were satanic games, but she didn't think so. They were harmless; she was sure.

Manning had been especially considerate on this trip, and Mabel had enjoyed his company. They had separate rooms in the hotels as he'd insisted she needed her rest. Mabel was glad, as it put the onus on him. She didn't have to feel guilty for never having performed her wifely duties. Manning didn't seem to care.

Mabel thought Manning a bit strange. He would not take a drink of anything unless he himself opened the bottle, or their waiter opened it in front of him. She had never been around a person so conscientious about the source of his drink.

They landed in Genoa, a northern city in Italy, and were slowly making their way south. There was so much to see and such a huge amount of history that Manning said they would limit their sight-seeing to major places of interest. If they tried to visit every little town, they would saturate their brains, and the end of the trip would become monotonous and repetitive. He'd mapped out their itinerary, starting with

Genoa and traveling south. They'd seen much in Genoa and were now headed to Florence.

Manning was tired and on edge.

He felt as if he couldn't let Mabel out of his sight nor ever let his guard down. Protecting himself was harder than he'd thought it would be. He locked his bedroom door every night if they had a suite. He kept his windows locked, not sure if Mabel would try to come in one of them. Food and drink was much easier to control. If Mabel had killed Bradley, she had no fear of entering someone else's room without permission. He knew she'd been in his suite of rooms the first day they were married, since she'd taken Victoria's locket. *Poor Bradley. He had been looking for a wife. Poor me. I now have one.*

He came out of his room and tapped on her door. They had different compartments on the train to Florence. He rapped louder, wondering if she could hear him above the clatter of train wheels.

"Mabel, Mabel, it's me, Manning." She didn't answer her door. He jiggled the handle. "Mabel, are you in there?"

"No-I-am-not." In a strident tone, her words were pronounced in a staccato-like burst.

He turned to see the glitter in her eyes and felt his insides squeeze in a huge feeling of dread. *Here it is again*, he thought. *I've got to try to get her help. She must be quite insane.*

"Are you ready for dinner?" he asked gently.

"Do I look as if I'm ready for dinner? Can't you see the way I'm dressed? I am not dressed to go to dinner, fool!" She looked him up and down, her eyes like crystal slivers. Suddenly, she raised her arms and her fingers reached for him like claws. He grabbed her wrists and yelled her name.

"Mabel! Mabel!"

Her eyes blinked and she went limp. He let go of her wrists to catch her. Too late, he realized his mistake. She stiffened straight up and raked his cheek with her nails. Turning, she ran to a restroom, slammed the door, and locked it behind her. She crumpled to the filthy floor, curling up into a fetal position.

Manning sat nearby and dabbed at his cheek with a handkerchief. With bowed shoulders, he felt totally dejected. He decided right then they would cut Italy short and head for Switzerland and a hospital that would know how to deal with the problem.

CHAPTER VII

Hear, O LORD, when I cry with my voice

PSALM 27:7a

OLIVIA WAS EXCITED. SHE'D BOUGHT tickets for Tchaikovsky's

First Piano Concerto, which was to premiere on Monday evening, the twenty-fifth of October. She wondered if Henry was too young to enjoy it. She hoped he wouldn't become troublesome during the performance. Olivia, looking at the book calendar, suddenly realized it was only two days away. *Goodness, without keeping all my social commitments the way I'm used to, the days are simply flying by. I've lost all track of time. I need to tell the children. I'm sure they will be delighted.* It was a Saturday, and Manning and Mabel had been gone nearly three weeks. *Lord, I don't know why I feel such a heavy burden to pray for Manning, but I do. I lift him up to Thy precious care. I know he's not a believer, but I feel in my heart that one day he will come to Thee. Please protect him. Wrap Thy wondrous arms of protection around him. Thank You, Lord Jesus.*

Olivia planned to go for a ride with the children. Ralph was to go along with them. The plan was that all of them were to have a picnic lunch on the beach. Cookie had prepared a basket, and the smell of fried chicken made Olivia's mouth water, along with the chocolate cake she'd seen being frosted earlier. "Tory...oh Victoria," Olivia called down the stairs. "I need help, Toralina Lou. Could you please come up here?" Olivia had left her personal maid home. She'd thought to give her a bit of a holiday, but she found dressing herself a chore. *I think, for the concert, I will send for Lucy and let her get me ready. I can't manage a corset. In truth, it's been wonderful to forego it since I've been here.* Olivia normally dressed more formally. Caring for the children, she'd mainly brought casual day dresses. She'd dropped off her two favorites at her dressmaker, asking her to make replicas and to take the material from the two damaged ones to make dresses for Tory.

Being a discreet dress shop, Mademoiselle Monique's Haute Couture was, Olivia thought, the best place in all of Boston to have clothes made. Mademoiselle was quite young, but her unerring ability to dress women in styles that best suited their figures was unequaled in the entire city. She said nothing as she looked at the dresses that had been cut with scissors. If a customer volunteered information, it never passed her lips to anyone else. She knew how to run a business and keep customers. Mlle. Monique was not cheap, but she was quite discreet and worth every penny.

Tory came running up the stairs, stopping abruptly when she saw Olivia.

"What a gorgeous habit!" she said. "I like the color."

"Thank you. It's not new, but it's one of my favorites."

Olivia's habit was a forest-green affair with a matching toque. The two entered her room and began to chat.

Victoria loved Olivia. Because she'd been Tory's mother's best friend, some of Olivia's mannerisms reminded Tory of her mother and brought a warmth to her young heart.

Seeing the jacket part of the habit lying on a chair, Tory exclaimed over the soft velvet trim, a suntan yellow that also outlined the matching toque. She began to fasten the buttons that ran up the back of Olivia's habit.

"Do you miss Lucy?" Tory was quite familiar with all Olivia's staff, as she and her mother had often spent the day at Aunt Ollie's. Tory wondered that she had ever thought Olivia plain. *She's beautiful,* Tory thought. *Her eyes sparkle and she's full of...of...spice. That's what it is. She's full of spice.*

"I haven't missed Lucy until now. Oh, Toralina Lou! Do I have a surprise for you!" Olivia often called her that, and Tory loved the nick name.

"What? What is it, Aunt Ollie?"

"We..." she said, placing her forefinger to her lips, "you, Charles, Henry, and I, are going to a concert on Monday night—Tchaikovsky's *First Piano Concerto*. Oh, I'm so excited!"

"Oh, Aunt Olivia! Oh, how wonderful. I know Charles will love it too. How shall we keep Henry still for that long?"

"I have a feeling he'll enjoy it. I purchased a set of colored pencils, and I'm taking them and some paper in my satchel just in case. I think there will be enough light for him to draw if he gets restless."

"Have you told Charles about this? He's going to love going to the concert. I know he will."

"No, I haven't told him, but I shall shortly." Olivia smiled at Tory. She reached out and drew the girl close to hug her. "How I do love you, Toralina Lou-Lou!" They went down the wide staircase holding hands.

Ralph had the horses saddled and ready.

Charles was quite proud of his new knowledge of horses and their accouterments. He'd saddled his own horse, Ebony, and was glad she wasn't like Tory's horse. Ebony didn't blow up her stomach when she was saddled up the way Commotion did, making a second tightening necessary. Charles had also saddled Ivory. He thought it humorous that his little brother had definitely decided the name would be either Crystal or Snowball but came up with the idea of Ivory, saying it was so beautiful and white. The name was a good counterpart to Ebony and it fit Henry's horse.

Ralph, an excellent equestrian, had spent quite a lot of time teaching the boys good horsemanship.

He looked appreciatively at Olivia as she walked into the stable yard. He thought her quite the looker with her lustrous black hair with red highlights. Her hair gleamed even if it wasn't sunny. He cupped his hands and interlocked his fingers to give her a boost onto her horse. She rode a stately gelding he'd fetched the day before from her own stable. Miss Olivia had named her horse Sandoval but called him Sandy. He was a spirited horse but seemed to have a good disposition. Ralph could see how the nickname was fitting. *He'll blend right in when we get to the beach.*

"Victoria, you'd best be a checkin' your girth agin afore you get on that Commotion. I tightened it twiced, but twiced mightn't be enough this day. Henry, ole chap, let me gi' you a boost up." Ralph cupped his hands again and lifted the boy so fast that he almost went flying over the top of his saddle.

"Whoa, Ralph! You almost threw me over onto the other side of Ivory!" Henry was clearly excited to be going for a ride and for a luncheon on the beach.

Tory slapped her horse's side and pulled hard on the strap, getting it one hole tighter.

"You're a stinker, Commotion. Do you want to go dragging me, saddle an' all, down to the beach?" Tory asked her horse as she waited for a boost up from Ralph.

Olivia asked, "Well, Mr. Ralph MacCrath, do you have our vittles with you?" She smiled and it melted Ralph's heart.

"Yes, ma'am, that I do. Cookie gave us a veritable feast. All right, children, away wi' you, now. Let's be away." He kicked the stallion he rode. Midnight was coal black and a beautiful horse. Usually, Manning kept him well-exercised and Ralph didn't ride him much, but if Mr. Brighton was away, Ralph kept him in good shape until the master returned. The groom planned to have a fast, hard ride on the beach and looked forward to it.

It was a short distance to the strand, and Tory led the way for Charles and Henry, keeping to a more sedate pace as Olivia and Ralph pounded their way down the sand along the water's edge.

It was a beautiful Indian summer day. The sky, a clear blue, faded to a haze where it met the ocean. Clouds, fluffy and white, scudded their way across the blue expanse, and gulls swooped and soared, screaming their delight. Terns, flocks of them, dipped their heads or sat riding the waves in bunches. The tangy smell of salt coupled with a fresh breeze vibrated the air with energy.

The children rode the opposite way from Ralph and Olivia. Charles kicked Ebony into a canter and the other two followed.

Henry yelled, full of exuberance. "I love to canter! It's is a lot more fun and much smoother than a trot."

Tory yelled back, the breeze snatching her words. "You're right. It's a whole lot smoother."

Charles simply grinned.

Tory had caught up with him and grinned back. The thought came to her that he didn't look well. She wondered at the dark smudges under his eyes. Although he smiled brightly, his eyes looked shadowed. She decided to ask Olivia about it.

They cantered until they came to an outcropping of rock, where they turned the horses back. They chattered as they walked their steeds to the place where they had decided to have lunch.

The opposite end of the long stretch of beach had a cliff that formed a cove, where Ralph and Olivia turned their rides around.

Olivia laughed. "My, you left me in the dust. I suppose I should say... sand. That is some horse Manning has. Wonder if he'd let me ride him?"

"Fer a stallion, he's quite the affable horse. My guess is, he'd take ta ye just fine. I've watched ye, and ye have strong wrists—I think ye could handle 'em all right." They talked while walking their horses down the beach, splashing a bit where the water climbed its way up the sand.

"Miss Olivia, I be a bit concerned aboot Charles. I don't be a knowin' for sure, but I think sumptin's wrong. He's beginnin' ta look a bit peaked. Ha' ye noticed it, ma'am?"

"N-no, in truth, I haven't. I will though—I'll make it a point to take a good look at the boy. Maybe he's ill." Her tawny eyes looked concerned.

Ralph felt he'd left the matter in capable hands. Miss Olivia would take care to see if there was a problem, and a burden lifted from his shoulders.

Manning lay in his train compartment, one arm crooked behind his head, staring at the ceiling. It was too warm with a window that didn't open. Sweat covered his bare chest, which glistened. He felt in need of a bath.

The click of the rails hadn't been noticeable earlier. Last night it had seemed soothing. Tonight it was an irritant. He'd stopped tossing and turning and lay still, deciding he needed to figure out some kind of a plan.

I now know why unhappy men take to drink. If I didn't need to keep my wits about me, I'd most likely drown my sorrows. Mabel scares the wits out of me. The scene she made this evening in the lounge was the most embarrassing moment of my entire life. I certainly don't want her around my Victoria. The fact that she crushed Tory's locket gives evidence to a violent nature. The fact that her first night in my home, she slapped my little girl tells me her temper displays are not solely directed at men. I feel so helpless. Why, oh why, did I ever take a second look at that woman? Wonder if I could have her committed to an institution where she'd get some help? At least I've set the stage for a trip to Switzerland. I know I lied, but she now thinks I need to see a Swiss banker. I think what we'll do is continue south to Rome, but that will be the end of it. I'll get tickets on a ship back up to Genoa and take a train from there inland to Bern or someplace closer if I can find something. Perhaps I should cable George Baxter and have him confirm to the doctors that Mabel is dangerous. Wonder, since our marriage hasn't been consummated, can I get an annulment? I'll have Elijah look into that.

Henry sat totally enthralled with the music. He'd never heard violins before. *To play like that, to hold people spellbound, is what I want. I want to play the violin. Mama would never get me one, but I bet Aunt Ollie would.* The music soared and his little heart soared with it. He was enraptured, touched in his inner being like he'd never been before. He had no idea, sitting there in the darkened theater, that he would feel this passion for music the rest of his life.

After the concert, they took a hansom cab to the Oyster House on Union. Olivia enjoyed being with the children—she'd never enjoyed herself so much. They chattered with one another about the performance.

Henry said, "I have never ever, never ever, ever in my whole life liked anything the way I did that concert. Aunt Ollie, thank you very much for taking us."

Tory and Charles looked in amazement at Henry, who acted and spoke as if he were a contemporary, someone eleven, not seven.

Olivia said, "I believe we all enjoyed it. It almost makes one tired inside from all the emotion we experienced. It was, without a doubt, one of the best concerts I have ever heard." Olivia was delighted that she could provide such an evening for these precious children. It wasn't simply entertainment; it was an education in the arts, and Henry had been a model of good behavior.

A man came up to their table with a woman on his arm and spoke. "Good evening, Olivia. Eve and I noticed you at the concert. We've missed you at soirées, and Eve said you haven't been to any tea parties either. You haven't been ill, have you?"

"No, not at all, thank you for asking. I don't suppose you've met Manning Brighton's daughter or sons. This is Victoria, Charles, and Henry. I've had the opportunity of staying with them for a few weeks and have been having the time of my life." She turned to the children. "Victoria, Charles, Henry, this is Mr. and Mrs. Chester Wyngham, friends of your father." She nodded at Victoria. "And friends of mine." She smiled, a little proudly, as the children all stood up. The two boys sketched a bow and Tory gave a little curtsey, each saying a how-do-you-do to the couple, who were obviously charmed by their sweet manners. Once they left, Henry turned his gaze back to Olivia, his eyes serious.

"Aunt Ollie, I know it's asking a lot, but I want above all things, a violin. I want to learn how to play like that." He waved his hand as if including the whole orchestra that had accompanied the pianoforte. "I want to…" Henry's eyes shone but his voice trailed off.

Olivia stared in surprise at Henry. She could feel this was important. It wasn't a whim or a passing fancy. It was a desire that would push everything else out of the way.

"We'll go tomorrow and see what we can do toward purchasing you a violin. I will also begin asking my acquaintances if they are aware of a violin master who gives lessons. Henry, I congratulate you. I believe you've found what you want to do with the rest of your life. You are fortunate, young man. Some people never find out."

CHAPTER VIII

And ye shall know the truth,
and the truth shall make you free.

JOHN 8:32

MANNING AND MABEL'S SOUTHERNMOST stop was Rome.

When they arrived at their hotel, Mabel said she needed to lie down and rest until dinner. Manning stifled his relief as he accompanied her to their suite of rooms.

Once she was settled into her bedroom, Manning waited a few minutes to see if she would come back out. He left the room and ran lightly down the stairs. He asked reception where he might cable to the United States, and they told him it would be where he had arrived on the train. He sighed inwardly with relief that he would be able to get a message off to George Baxter without Mabel being any the wiser.

Manning hailed a cabriolet for the short ride to *Roma Termini*. He overpaid the cabby, asking him to wait. With long strides, he arrived at the ticket booth and sent off a cable in a speedy manner. The telegraph operator asked if he expected a reply, and Manning told him no.

He ran back to the cabriolet and was back in their hotel is less than a half hour total. Their accommodations were quite exclusive. Located near the Spanish Steps and the Via Veneto, Mabel would be able to shop to her heart's content. He breathed a sigh of relief as he reentered the hotel. He went into the restaurant and ordered coffee at the bar.

George Baxter was surprised when the errand boy showed up at his office. He pulled a couple coins out of his pocket for him and closed the door with his foot while he ripped open the missive.

It must have cost Brighton a pretty penny to send such a detailed cable, he thought. He reread it a bit slower the second time and took it down the hall to Christopher Belden's office. His chief beckoned him inside, and the two men sat chatting about their plan of action. George sat sideways to Belden's desk, his arm resting on its top, drumming his fingers steadily on its surface as they conversed.

"So, if she attacked him, it still doesn't prove anything, but I believe she's our murderess. I feel it in my gut, Chief. I believe she murdered those two men. Whether she was aware of it or not has no bearing on the fact that she's dangerous." George sat pondering what course of action they should take. It sounded as if Manning hoped to have her institutionalized. He kept drumming his fingers, but it was quiet drumming as his boss thought about a plan.

"All right, Baxter, I want you to go to Italy. Find the Brightons and make sure that woman is not only institutionalized but interned in Switzerland. She's dangerous, not only to Brighton but to others as well. Given the fact of the smashed locket, slapping Brighton's daughter the first night of their marriage, and then attacking Brighton, she could harm anyone. I'd like you to leave as soon as possible. Brighton sounds like he'll cut the Rome visit short and head back up to Genoa, via ship.

You head to Genoa and hopefully pick up his trail from there. I hope Adeline won't mind you leaving on such short notice. Get yourself down to the Cunard Lines and buy yourself a ticket." He handed George a letter of credit he kept on hand for emergencies.

The day after the concert, Olivia took Henry violin hunting as promised. They visited several music establishments but none had what they were looking for. Henry, elated in the beginning, began to feel dejected. He wasn't big enough for a full-sized violin, and that was what the shops seemed to carry. Finally, they came to a shop that stocked full, three-quarter, and half-sized violins. Olivia told the proprietor, Mr. August, that she wanted something fit for someone who would, one day, be quite good. She didn't smile when she said it. She told Henry she could feel, in her heart, that he would one day be a virtuoso.

The man eyed the small boy. Henry stared right back, keeping his jaw set and determined. He wanted a violin.

"I have one violin that might just be the ticket," the man said. "An elderly lady brought it in. She said it'd been in her basement since she was a little girl. She thought, perhaps, her grandfather had played it. It has a stamp bearing Giovanni Paolo Maggini, but there are questions as to whether this particular violin was made after the famous violin maker's death. The problem is there is no provenance accompanying the instrument."

Because of that, the price was within the range Olivia proposed to pay. It was a three-quarter size and would fit Henry quite well for a long time.

Mr. August said, "I know a concert violinist who is in need of funds and would be an excellent master teacher for your son."

When Olivia didn't enlighten the proprietor and even smiled at his assumption, Henry looked up at her questioningly, but he didn't correct the man either. He felt as if last night, he'd suddenly grown up. There was an overriding compulsion to take the violin the storekeeper held and start playing. He knew in his heart the violin would be the love of his life.

Olivia took down the tutor's name and address. She said she'd visit him this very day. The case of the violin was battered, but there was rosin and a rehaired bow included in the price. Olivia said she was thankful, and was sure it was a good violin, and that someday, Henry would make it sing. He believed her.

Manning hoped his temper would remain unflappable, as his body, along with his brain, was exhausted. He wished he could turn the whole problem of Mabel over to someone else and let him take care of it. With no return address to give to Detective Baxter, he'd wired that he would send another cable when he arrived at a hospital that would accept Mabel.

They'd been in Rome for four days and were leaving on the morrow. Manning had purchased tickets for Genoa on a steamer, hoping to be done with all his problems within the week. He'd taken Mabel to the Colosseum and Roman Forum, but they just looked at it from outside rather than tire her with a tour. They visited St. Peter's Basilica, Trevi Fountain, and of course, the Spanish Steps near their hotel.

Manning wished he were accompanied by someone he trusted. He wanted a wife like Laura, one he could enjoy and cherish. Their last stop was the Villa Borghese gardens. In the late afternoon, they were back to their hotel and packed for the steamer. Manning dreaded dinner. Mabel had made a scene the evening before, and he'd been embarrassed beyond measure by the stares in their direction. He was hopeful there would not be a repeat performance. That his wife was insane or possessed of an evil, he had no doubt.

The next morning dawned fair and bright. A freshening breeze kissed their faces, and the skies were clear and blue. The night had been cool, but now it looked glorious outside. They took a train to the coast, and it was nearly noon when they arrived. Manning found a small eatery for them to have a bite of lunch before going to the docks.

They boarded the steamer and descended the stairs to their berth. The room, though fairly small, still had two bedrooms. After stowing their belongings, they returned to the top deck to enjoy the general excitement that always accompanied a boat leaving shore. There seemed to be some delay, and Manning could feel his gut tighten. All he wanted was to be underway and headed toward some normalcy in his life. An announcement was made that there was a problem with the boiler. Finally, they were under way. Manning breathed a sigh of relief as he eyed Mabel who looked tired and strained. It was a look with which he happened to be quite familiar…it preceded an episode. Manning was filled with dread.

George Baxter had been fortunate. He'd gone to the Cunard Lines directly after speaking with Christopher Belden. There had been a cancellation on a ship headed out the next day for northern Italy, and he'd been able to purchase the ticket for the cancelled berth. Costing a bit more than the allowance from the department allowed, George felt blessed that he'd found one leaving so quickly. He could easily make up the difference. Adeline had been a Cunningham before her marriage to him. The Cunninghams were Boston Brahmin…the highest class of society in the city. He'd fallen for her like a ton of bricks before he'd known she was an only child of rich parentage. It didn't bother him at all that she used her money to make their life much more comfortable than he could afford. He worked hard but could never have afforded the house, lifestyle, or entertainments they enjoyed because of her inheritance. He was thankful and did not feel diminished by her private income. They had no children but took much delight in each other, which eased the pain of childlessness.

Adeline was a devoted Christian. They'd met at a special revival service, a tent meeting. She, along with some friends, had attended the large gathering, and George had been lucky enough to sit next to her. Within four months of meeting, they'd become engaged. Adeline's parents had been a bit wary of him at first. He wasn't in their social circle of friends, and they were on the lookout for fortune hunters. However, it wasn't long before he won them over. George was nothing if not diplomatic and charming. Adeline marrying for love pleased her parents. They didn't care about social connections or more money, for that matter. They had both. George had come to love Adeline's parents as his own.

Olivia sat in on the first few lessons while the young tutor instructed Henry so she could help him to remember everything when he practiced on his own. Everyone was a little in awe of the fervency with which Henry took to the violin. The young boy was thrilled beyond measure. He had his violin and poured over the book the young man had given him, memorizing *E A D G* as the strings with which he could make music. He learned the parts of the bow and to never tighten the screw too much, and how to apply the rosin to his bow, always going one way and starting at the ferrule. The battered case also contained a pitch pipe, and his young instructor showed him how to tune the *A* string and to listen carefully while tuning the others from that string. There was a pianoforte in the house if he needed to check his notes. It wasn't long before Henry made a lot more than squawking sounds on the precious instrument.

Olivia decided it was time to have a private talk with Charles. Ralph was right. Something was definitely wrong with the boy. She wanted to find out if he felt ill or if something else might be the cause of the purple shadows under his eyes. It looked to her as if he wasn't sleeping well. She'd observed him every day since the outing on the beach.

Charles, always aware of his surroundings, had noted Olivia's keen eyes on him. It had made him uncomfortable.

He was nervous as he entered the sitting room. Most days, Olivia could be found in Tory's sitting room, which he felt had a much more comfortable atmosphere than this room.

Laura Brighton had loved her sitting room, and Olivia had spent many a happy hour in it with her best friend.

"Good morning, Charles. Please, sit down." Olivia indicated a chair opposite where she could face the boy. Morning sunlight filtered into the room, which was the reason she had chosen the sitting room and this time of morning. She wanted to look clearly into the blue eyes of Charles

Vickers and see every nuance and every expression in his eyes as she talked to him. She'd ordered scones and tea for their little tête-à-tête, knowing it would put the boy more at his ease.

"First, I want to show you the telegram that arrived. Please, help yourself. You do like milk in your tea?" She poured the two cups and added a bit of milk to hers but no sugar.

He selected a large lump and stirred it into his cup and said, "Yes, please, a bit of milk would be perfect. Who sent the telegram?" He looked at her curiously.

"Your mother." She handed him the missive that had arrived earlier that morning.

He took it and read:

HAVING A WONDERFUL TIME STOP MADELINE LOVES SCHOOL STOP NOW VISITING ROME STOP BE HOME SOON STOP CAN'T WAIT TO TELL YOU ALL ABOUT IT STOP MOTHER STOP

"Sounds as if she's enjoying herself. Henry will be happy to read it." He handed the paper back to Olivia; his hand shook slightly. Charles took a deep breath and tried to act normal, but his heart was pounding so loud he felt he couldn't hear. He wanted to pour out his trouble. He wanted to let someone else take care of the secret he'd guarded so carefully.

"Charles, I've come to care for you very much. You do know that, don't you?" Olivia looked at the boy with tawny-colored eyes full of warmth and concern, which communicated itself to the eleven-year-old.

"Yes, I know. I feel the same way about you. You're wonderful and… and you're not only nice, you are always the same. There's no guessing game as to how you are feeling."

"What do you mean by that, Charles? What do you mean, no guessing game?"

"With my mother, I never know how she's going to react to anything that's said. I have learned to be quiet and observe. It's kept me out of trouble more than once," he responded seriously.

"Why *is* that?" Olivia asked him.

"Aunt Ollie...I...I think my mother is very sick." He glanced at the door to make sure it was closed all the way. He dropped his voice, and tears began to course down his cheeks. He set his cup down with a rattle because his hands were shaking so badly. "Sh...she killed my father, Aunt Ollie. I saw her do it. She put something in his juice and served it to him, and he started choking and grabbing at his neck and his eyes were bulging...and...and...he died." Charles could barely speak, his voice clogged with tears. "I stood in the doorway of the kitchen, and mother's back was to me. I turned and ran. I was barefoot and ran back upstairs as fast as I could and got back into bed. I was s-so scared she'd come get me too. It was early morning, before Papa went to work."

Charles sobbed uncontrollably, and Olivia was horrified. She'd had no idea the problem with him was so catastrophic. She knelt before him, pulling him into her arms. She rocked him and rocked him, trying to soothe him. She smoothed back his hair and murmured love words to him.

Charles sobbed. "I...I think she killed that other man too, Mr. Burbank. I'm quite sure she did. Oh, Aunt Ollie, she's very wicked, and I'm scared of her. I'm so scared of her. I didn't want to tell anyone. I feel guilty because I didn't help my father, but I couldn't help anyway. It was too late, and I was afraid she'd find out I knew and kill me too."

Olivia let Charles cry for a bit. It was good for him to let go of the pent-up emotions he'd carried for so long.

Oh Lord, help me to comfort this boy and help him. Would You please wrap Your wondrous love around him? Please let him feel the love You so richly pour out. And please protect Manning. Oh Lord, please protect him from that wicked, murdering woman.

Charles cried and cried but continued to talk. "I am so afraid for Mr. Brighton," Charles' teeth were chattering. "He stands up to Mother and doesn't let her get away with her behavior, and I know...I just know she'll go after him too. I should have said something to him before they left. It's just...they left so suddenly...it all seemed to happen so quickly, and I didn't get any time with him alone. I was afraid Mother would see me. I know I'm fearful. I should have said something. I haven't been sleeping very well because I'm scared for

Mr. Brighton. Oh, Aunt Ollie, what if something happens to him because I was too scared to warn him.

CHAPTER IX

*[He] commanded that they which could swim should
cast themselves first into the sea, and get to land:
And the rest, some on boards, and some on
broken pieces of the ship. And so it came to pass,
that they escaped all safe to land.*

ACTS 27:43b-44

OLIVIA'S HEART ACHED FOR THE INNOCENCE lost to this boy
and the horror he had witnessed. She prayed for wisdom before she spoke
to him.

"Charles, first and foremost, if anything should happen to Mr.
Brighton, it won't be because you didn't warn him. He already knows there
is something drastically wrong with your mother." She thought of the
crushed and broken locket in Manning's sock drawer. "I can't tell you for
sure how I know that, but I know it from the bottom of my heart." She
squeezed the boy's shoulder.

Olivia rose, straightened her skirts, and sat again, facing him. So he
could look her squarely in the eyes and know that what she said to him was
the truth. Her mind flitted back to the man she'd met at the bon voyage
party in the Brightons' stateroom, before they'd sailed. Manning

had introduced George Baxter to her. She was quite well-acquainted with his wife, Adeline, and had seen George at dinner parties, meeting him only briefly. She knew him to be a Boston detective. Her mind came back to the present, and she prayed she could help this boy.

"Charles, we can't control what other people do. It might have been a good thing for you to warn Mr. Brighton, but on the other hand, what if your mother *had* walked in while you were doing it? My question to you is, are you willing to tell a detective what you told me? I think you're correct in saying your mother is ill. She fluctuates between good behavior and wicked. She needs help and can get good care. Mr. Brighton has pots of money and can get her the best care imaginable."

Charles took a huge breath. It was as if a heavy yoke had been lying across his shoulders and suddenly had been lifted off. Olivia could see what she said made sense to him. He agreed it would be wonderful if his mother could get help.

"Yes, I will tell anyone you think it important for me to tell, especially if Mother can get help."

Adeline had wanted to accompany George to Italy, so he'd gone back to Cunard Lines to purchase her ticket. It didn't cost as much as his, as he already had a stateroom; it was simply an extra passenger ticket. George and Addie packed with the help of servants and headed for the ship.

The morning was bright with sunshine, another beautiful Indian summer day. Fluffy white clouds scudded overhead in the breeze. Whitecaps slapped at the sides of the great ocean liner while terns rode the waves, bobbing up and down. Seagulls cried overhead or strutted on the pier, hoping for crusts of bread. The pungent smell of salt and sea carried itself on the freshening wind.

The two departing for Italy waved good-bye to Christopher Belden, who had accompanied them to the liner.

Chief Belden waved up at George and his wife. He grinned, glad Adeline could go with George and keep him company. They laughed down at him, and Adeline held her toque with one hand lest it blow away. The ship, after a few deafening blasts, pulled out of the harbor, making its way out to sea. Chief Inspector Belden stood there until the couple was out of sight. He climbed into the hansom cab waiting for him and thought about the mound of paperwork he needed to wade through today.

When he arrived back at headquarters, he was surprised to have a woman and boy awaiting his return. A clerk had them sit outside his office, telling them the chief would be back shortly. Chris invited them into his office and wondered what was on their minds.

"Good afternoon, I'm Chief Inspector Christopher Belden. How may I help you?" He smiled pleasantly and tried to put them at their ease.

He saw the woman note the Bible lying on his desk and heave a huge sigh, it seemed, of relief.

"Inspector Belden, my name is Olivia Anderson, and this is Charles Vickers. We came to speak with Detective Baxter, but the clerk said he was away."

Surprise etched itself into his eyes when he heard the name Vickers. She proffered her hand and he shook it. He offered his hand to Charles, and the boy grasped it as if it were a lifeline. The inspector took a long look at the boy's clear, honest blue eyes and wanted to hug the nervousness out of him.

"Please, won't you sit down?" He waved them to a couple chairs facing his desk and sat facing them, the light from the window behind him on their faces.

Olivia spoke. "I have charge of Manning Brighton's children until he returns from his honeymoon. We have come to ask for your help and direction." She nodded at Charles. "This young man has been carrying a very heavy burden and would like to share it with you in the hopes his mother can get some help." The chief never took his eyes off the two. She laid her hand on the boy's shoulder and gave it a gentle squeeze. "Charles, I'd like you to tell the inspector everything you told me."

Raising blue eyes misted with tears that threatened to spill over, Charles began to talk. He took a shuddering breath. He not only related what had happened the morning his mother had murdered his father, but he told of other incidents of behavior so bizarre that had the boy not been so obviously open and honest, it would be hard to credit someone with such acts of violence.

"My mother needs help, sir. She's done things, horrible things, but perhaps she doesn't know what she's doing. I'm so afraid for Mr. Brighton, sir."

"I can definitely tell you this, young man, and hope it relieves your mind. Mr. Brighton was forewarned, even before he set sail. He is watching your mother...carefully watching her. More than that I cannot tell you at this time. Suffice it to say, he's planning to get her help and has communicated with our office to that effect."

Charles looked with eyes full of incredulity at the chief Inspector. He took out his handkerchief and blew his nose. The chief wished the boy had known to do this a long time ago rather than suffer the way he had, keeping it all bottled up inside.

The woman let out her breath slowly and said she had not realized how afraid for Manning she had been since Charles had told her his story.

Chief Inspector Belden said, "Miss Anderson, Master Charles, you have done a great deed by coming forward today. We knew Mabel Vickers killed her husband *and* Bradley Burbank but had no proof. Young man, if it is within my power, I will see that your mother gets the help she needs. Since you have been so forthcoming, I will tell you that I have George Baxter, my best detective, on his way to Italy. He will help get your mother into an institution in Switzerland that specializes in brain disorders. Mr. Brighton was adamant in his cable that he would make sure she be given the best care available."

The inspector assured Charles that he should not feel he'd betrayed his mother by confessing what he knew.

They had been on the water less than an hour when an explosion ripped through the air. It was deafening. The ship shuddered with the impact. A horn resonated, high pitched, splitting the air with a signal to its crew. Some of them began handing out life vests. Others ran toward the lifeboats, quickly lowering them into the water. People streamed up from the cabins below as women's screams pierced the air. Confusion reigned. Manning heard one of the sailors yell to another that a boiler had exploded. The ship listed as water poured into its hull.

Manning grabbed Mabel's arm in a tight grip. She'd started back toward the stairs to their cabin.

"Let go of me, Manning! Let go!" she screamed at him above the din around them, trying to wriggle out of his grasp. She beat at him with her free hand, but he held her tightly. "I need to get my jewels. I'm not getting off this ship until I have them and that's final." She pounded his chest, her hand balled into a fist.

"Forget the jewels, Mabel. I'll buy you some more. Come on! There's no time! We need to get into a lifeboat, or we'll go down with the ship."

The sailors, by now, had let down all the lifeboats so people could escape from the sinking ship. They were trying to calm the passengers as they helped them into the lifeboats now lightly tied to the main ship.

Manning held Mabel's arm firmly and headed for a lifeboat. Mabel leaned forward and bit him hard on the arm. Startled, his grip loosened. He immediately knew his mistake as she slipped out of his grasp and headed for the stairs. She pushed past people who were streaming up in droves.

Manning was left holding her life jacket, which she'd refused to put on. He took a deep breath and headed toward the stairs after her. Just then, the ship lurched and tipped aft, the stern dipping deeply into the water. The sudden sharp angle caused Manning to slip. He lost his footing and fell hard on the deck's wet surface. Sliding down…down…he grabbed, his hands flailing, but he could find nothing to stop the downward slide. He felt a hand grab his life vest and his descent slowed, but it halted suddenly as he hit his head. He was knocked unconscious by a steel bollard.

As Mabel descended the stairs to her cabin, the ship suddenly upended. Thrown backward against the metal steps, her head banged against the stair edge with a crack, her eyes glazed over, closing as she slumped against the steps. People wanting off the steamer scrambled over top of her body, their screams deafening.

A large man, purposely blocking those behind him, picked her up. He slung her over his shoulder as he crawled the few stairs forward, which were now canted sideways. Praying silently, he gained their freedom from the surge of bodies behind him. He stood, momentarily hanging on to the rail that circled the midship superstructure. He looked around and breathed a sigh of relief; he could see nothing that would stop a downward slide. He felt the steamer begin to slowly but surely sink, her hull upended and full of water. He felt the deadweight on his shoulder and knew the woman was still unconscious. Muscles straining as he held onto the railing, he slung the woman around to his front and quickly lined his body up to slip into the water without hitting a bollard. He let go. They slid down the steamer's plank flooring and hit the water. The woman flew out of his arms, the water not reviving her. He wondered if she was dead. As she started to sink, he grabbed at her floating hair and with his other hand grabbed frantically at the water, catching hold of a piece of masthead. He hooked one arm over the huge piece of flotsam and dragged the woman with his other hand. He felt the burn and abuse of unused muscles.

The man, with much effort, got Mabel's head up and over the top of the beam so that she was on her back in the water. He began to paddle, kicking hard with his feet. The added stimulus of adrenalin pumped through his veins as he paddled. He wanted to get away from the steamer as quickly as possible. He moved with the waves, which aided his progress, toward a distant shoreline. He looked back and saw the last of the steamer as it made its way to a new home at the bottom of the Mediterranean Sea. From his low vantage point, he couldn't see the vortex created by the ship, how it sucked in everything around it, but he felt its huge drag on his body. He was far enough away to escape its clutches. Once the water fully settled, he stopped paddling and let the waves push him toward shore, exhausted but thankful to be alive.

Charles believed he had done the right thing in speaking to the inspector. He felt so much better. He slept soundly through the night after telling the inspector about his mother. Since Mr. Brighton knew all about it, he would be on his guard and be safe. Charles was grateful, too, that his mother would be taken care of. The boy was beholden to Olivia, thankful she cared enough about him to have a talk and find out what bothered him.

Olivia gave thanks to the Almighty that she'd spoken to Charles. She made a mental note to tell Ralph all that transpired. Ralph was solid, and he would give thanks and pray for Charles and Manning.

Victoria enjoyed her classes. She was fortunate to be able to go to day school. Most girls were educated either at home or not at all. Manning, insistent she have an education equal to any boy's, had enrolled her in a reputable day school. She'd already mastered Latin and was passable in Greek. Her favorite study was history.

She'd written two letters to Maddie and had received one reply that painted boarding school in glowing terms. Her new stepsister seemed to have taken to boarding school like a duck to water. She wrote Tory and said every day was a fun experience.

Tory was thrilled to have both Henry and Charles, not to mention Olivia, live in her house. She couldn't remember ever having such a full agenda. Something was always happening. They'd gone to several small concerts and Henry, enraptured with the music, endeared himself to her so that her first impressions of him were fading from memory.

Charles, she observed, looked better. Although Tory missed her papa dreadfully, she was apprehensive about the reappearance of Mabel. The rest of her new family was perfect.

Most days, while the weather was still pleasant, she and Charles rode on the beach, or waded in the waves, having a fabulous time after school. Because Charles wasn't afraid of horses and wanted to learn, his competence grew at a rapid pace. He said he was thrilled to ride and enjoyed the time spent grooming and caring for Ebony. Tory frequently listened in when he talked with Ralph, and she could see Charles was learning much from him about the care of his horse.

"Do you know when your papa is supposed to come back?" Charles asked.

"No—supposed to be two or three more weeks, I think. Papa told me seven or eight weeks and it's been five. I've been marking it off on the calendar."

"Tory…I…I'm going to tell you something. I think it'll make you feel better. Aunt Ollie told me he's taking my mother to a hospital where she can get some help. He's going to leave her there for a while. I…I think she's a little insane."

CHAPTER X

Heaviness in the heart of man maketh it stoop:
but a good word maketh it glad.

PROVERBS 12:25

TORY'S HEAD JERKED UP TO LOOK at Charles in surprise. Her hazel eyes looked questioningly at him. "How do you know this? I'm sorry, and I suppose it's not nice to say so, but I have been dreading their return. Not because I don't miss my papa. I miss him every day. It's just, well, your mother looks at me with eyes that look like she could kill me. I'm not jesting. Her eyes give me the shivers."

"I know, Tory. I know. She's looked at me like that lots of times. It's because she is, in truth, insane. I've been afraid of her ever since I can remember, and she's my own mother. I reckon your papa began to notice it and cabled Aunt Olivia. It was through her that I found out he's going to try to put her into a hospital in Switzerland. Maybe there, she'll get help and become normal."

"Well, it's good news to me. I wish Aunt Olivia could stay here and live with us forever, but I know when Papa gets home, she'll go back to her normal life. She seems to like being with us, though, doesn't she?"

"Yes, I guess I never thought of her not being here. She's a wonderful person, and I love her," he responded with fervor.

"I do too. Oh look, Charles." She slid off Commotion. "Look here. Isn't this an unusual piece of driftwood?" The conversation returned to regular talk, but the two children had forged a bond between them, able to share almost anything with each other.

When Manning awoke, he was flat on his back aboard a freighter overloaded with passengers from the steamer. The man who'd caught him on his downward slide toward the ocean sat protectively over him. The freighter happened to be passing by when its crew heard the distress signal from the steamer. The captain pulled as close as he dared and ordered his men to haul people out of the water and out of the lifeboats. They weren't that far from shore, perhaps a mile or less out, but when a ship went down, the captain knew it sucked all that was around it down with it, so he stayed a safe distance away.

Manning sat up, his head spinning.

The man who'd saved him spoke in Italian. Manning knew the language, but his brain seemed clogged and he couldn't, for the life of him, make sense of what the man said. He started to shake his head but stopped immediately as it set up a thousand little hammers, each pounding its own rhythm. The man tried French, speaking to him rapidly. Suddenly, Manning's brain clicked into gear and he replied. "I am all right, thank you. I have *the* enormous headache, but that is to be expected. I want to thank you for saving my life. That sounds banal, just saying thank you, but in truth, what does a man say?"

The man answered back in English, with a British accent.

"It's enough. I would hope you would do the same."

All of the sudden memory came sharply into focus, and Manning said, "I have a wife, she was..." His voice trailed off. It sounded the utmost stupidity to go back for jewels when your life was in danger. He didn't care to disclose that information to this wholesome-looking man who'd saved his life.

Manning rose shakily to his feet and excused himself to go look for Mabel. He walked slowly through the entire freighter four times, but she was not there. His head pounded so badly, he felt nauseated. He wondered if he were concussed. His gaze swung toward the Mediterranean. Flotsam was everywhere. He would have to begin a search of survivors once the captain made port. He would travel up and down the coast. If she survived, she was a danger to whoever saved her. He went to speak to the captain, who related to him that all survivors of the wreck were on board his boat. They had circled and circled the waters where the steamer went down. He was most desolate, but there were no others.

Mabel regained consciousness. The day was pleasant, not too cold. The sun, beginning to make its way to bed, started to slip from a sky that would shortly be turning to dusk. The Mediterranean was warm.

"Wha...what happened?"

The man looked at her blankly.

"I asked you, what happened?" she repeated sharply.

"Lo non ti capisco." I don't understand you.

She rolled onto her stomach and hung on to the masthead, the salt water making it easy to float. The man felt relief at her becoming conscious. It eased his feeling of responsibility. He knew there'd be no communication between them.

"How irritating! This is going to be simply wonderful, just grand!" she exclaimed sarcastically. "I don't understand a word you're saying."

Her tone was disgusted and he looked at her in wonder. *Does she not know her close brush with death? I praise the Lord God Almighty that He has spared my life. Praise God!*

With no more conversation between them, they finally washed up on the shore. The woman had an ugly look on her face, and the man who looked down at her knew she was evil. Before she even got to her feet, he strode off as fast as his tired legs could carry him. He wondered if he had done the world a disservice by saving her life. He took no joy in it.

Mabel stood swaying on the beach and watched as the man strode off. She called after him, but he continued down the beach, walking at a fast pace. She screamed at him again but to no avail. She felt exhausted and incapable of coherent thought. Her head throbbed abominably. She began to throw up, losing the contents of her stomach. She lay down in the sand where she had washed up, the Mediterranean lapping at her heels. The air had cooled but didn't feel cold. Mabel lay for some time thinking of what she must do, but nothing made any sense to her. She fell asleep, her dreams tangled and filled with horrid apparitions.

The beautiful ship of the Cunard Lines came into port on a blustery day. George and Adeline descended the gangplank to the dock, making their way through the customs shed without a hitch. They didn't have much luggage. Adeline had packed light as she planned to do some serious shopping while in Europe. She was well aware that the newest styles came out of France and Italy, and she couldn't wait to buy shoes. She loved the stylish Italian brands, and her feet were always shod in the newest but most comfortable style of shoes.

Genoa was cool but pleasant; temperatures ranged in the high sixties. The wind had blown out a storm from the day before, and the city looked newly washed in an aura of bright light. The sun, reflecting off the rooftops and sides of the ancient marble buildings, sank lower over the early-evening horizon. It was that time of day when birds retired and silence permeated the air. This was not the case near the harbor, as parties were being met. Laughter and the activity of the unloading ship brought a cacophony of sound that seemed to energize rather than drain.

So much marble, Addie thought, *and in so many different colors. I'd forgotten how beautiful Italy is.* Adeline had traveled around the continent when she'd graduated from the Young Ladies Finishing Academy in Lucerne, Switzerland, years ago. She'd loved Lucerne and had, with several other girls, memorized many of its streets. Genoa gave her the same feeling as Lucerne, that of old culture mixed with modern living. It was a heady blend.

George had asked a customs agent where a good hotel could be found and hailed a waiting *carrozza di hansom*. They found a beautiful hotel just up and off the water with a superb view of the Mediterranean. After settling into a blatantly deluxe room, they dressed for dinner.

George helped his wife button up her elegant evening attire before turning her to face him.

"Madam Baxter, what is your pleasure? Italian cuisine, or Italian cuisine?" He laughed down at his Addie, the crease in his cheek deepening and his teeth even and white.

She laughed, her head thrown back to look up at him. She stroked the groove in his cheek and slid her fingers down to outline his well-shaped lips. Her chocolate-brown eyes sparkled with good humor and a zest for life.

George said, "You become more lovely every day, my dear." His hand traveled up her arm and behind her back, and he pulled her into his arms. With a passionate kiss on her lovely lips, he patted her hand, placed it on his arm, and led her downstairs. They were a very handsome couple, and heads turned when they entered the dining room.

It was a late dinner, and George wanted to enjoy himself this evening. He figured he'd have much to do in the morning. He'd need to check with the shipping line that Brighton had cabled him about and find out how often it ran and when it came into port. Perhaps Brighton had already passed through Genoa. If that were the case, finding him would be more difficult. It would take some ferreting out information. Not everyone spoke English.

Adeline and George sat at a table sparkling with crystal, and the glow was reflected in his wife's eyes. He smiled warmly at her.

"I'm so glad you wanted to accompany me on this venture. It'd have been boring without you by my side."

She smiled over at him. "What is your plan of action?"

He explained what he planned for the next morning, and she listened with a slight smile on her lips. George loved how her eyes glowed in the lamplight.

Mabel awoke on the sandy beach. She could feel her clothing stuck to her body. It was stiff and mostly dried except her front, which had lain on the wet sand. She stood, feeling nauseated, sick, and thoroughly chilled. Her head felt heavy on her neck and throbbed with pain. She looked up and down the beach, and it was all she could do not to simply sink back down onto the sand. It was dawn, the sun just breaking over the horizon. Fingers of light crept out from behind the dim skyline that stretched more and more to fill the world with bright light. Mabel stood there swaying. Her head seemed full of the sea, her ears felt stopped up, and she ached all over. She put her hand to the back of her head, and her fingers came away sticky with blood that still oozed from a wound.

I have no idea which way to walk. I'll go in the same direction that wretched man went. It must be north. I've lost my shoes. I have nothing. She began to walk unsteadily on the hard, wet sand. *Manning. Manning should have stayed with me. I'll make him pay for this!* She continued down the beach, hate filling her and giving her strength. Hate fed her.

George woke up early and lay still, not wanting to disturb Adeline, who slept snuggled up against him. Her beautiful hair, smooth as silk, was spread out over her pillow. Her softness and sweet temperament never failed to melt his heart. His love for her grew continually. It never paled. *How thankful to God I am for her.* He lay quietly and counted his blessings and prayed for more than an hour before she began to stir.

George had signed up for full service when he registered at the front desk. They wanted to breakfast in their room.

A waiter entered with a white tablecloth covering his serving cart. He quietly set the table until Adeline began to converse with him in Italian. He laughed at a jest she made, and because of her friendliness, he gave them the full benefit of all he had to offer. It was a veritable feast, and the coffee—delectable. It was one of the reasons George had fallen completely in love with Addie. She was friendly to everyone and did not look at class distinction as a thing to be countenanced but seemed to love others with the love of Jesus. George knew one of her spiritual gifts was edification. She encouraged others.

After breakfast Adeline said, "I'm going shopping, George." She grinned at him. "I cannot wait to begin. It seems as if everything that's new in the fashion world has been in Europe a year or two ahead of the United States. I think I'll find some shoes first." She went on to say, looking out the window at the shops, "I'll be right out there on the main street should you need to find me. Otherwise, let's meet back here at noon. Is that amenable to you, darling?"

He helped her with her corset and dress, unused to assisting her, but his fingers were nimble and he was adept at fastening the tiny buttons, having practiced unbuttoning them. "Yes, that sounds like a solid plan." He peered over her shoulder as he finished buttoning the back of her dress. "It looks to be a fine day. If it's warm enough, we'll find a nice little restaurant and sit outside for lunch. How would you like that?"

Adeline turned in his arms and he kissed her thoroughly.

When they were ready, they exited the lovely hotel and parted ways, George heading toward the docks and the steamship company about which Brighton had cabled him.

He found the company discreetly tucked in between two larger buildings, one a warehouse and the other an exporting firm. Petrolini Steamers was a sizable company, and as he entered the main office, people were in a flurry of activity. A small crowd stood in front of the reception desk, and others sat on benches or stood by the walls. The noise of chattering voices echoed loudly in the room. It took George a bit of time to get someone to help him and then to find a man who could speak English. He had the fleeting thought that he should have brought Adeline with him to save time, but she would be bored to death in a place like this.

The man asked with a heavy accent, "Yes, what can I do for you, sir? Are you looking for a loved one? We," he said and waved his hand expansively to include the entire building, "we just this morning received the manifest, but we have no way of knowing until the freighter gets here just who survived. I'm sorry I can't be of more help. The freighter should be here any time now. It's been slow, as it's overloaded."

George was shocked. He quickly explained what he wanted, sorry he had to bother someone who must be extremely busy. There was only one steamer out of Rome per week. George calculated that the steamer that went down was most likely the one the Brightons were on. The man showed him a copy of the manifest, which another man was copying. It had arrived from Rome, by cable, that morning.

George scanned the list hurriedly, finding the Brightons were, indeed, on the downed steamer. George thanked the man, handing back the papers. He thought back and remembered Brighton had said in his cable that they were heading toward Rome and would be leaving there after three days of touring.

He would wait for the freighter to arrive and pray Manning Brighton was safe.

CHAPTER XI

Blessed is the man whom thou choosest,
and causest to approach unto thee

PSALM 65:4a

MANNING WALKED SLOWLY throughout the freighter a fifth time, feeling an overwhelming sense of guilt. If he'd just held tighter, if he hadn't eased his grip. It was dusk, and the faces of people began to be difficult to see at any distance. He knew she was not aboard. Mabel was gone.

He made his way back to the man who'd saved him and said, "My name is Manning Brighton, and again, I want to thank you. I was on an unstoppable slide, heading for the water, and could find no handhold, nothing to stop me."

"You are most welcome. I'm Stewart Grenly. I was on my way to a lifeboat and had hold of a steel post when you came sliding down. I made a quick grab for you, and I'm afraid I drug you into the bollard." His eyes

105

were a gray-green flecked with brown and lit up while he talked. "I must say, 'tis a most gratifying thing to save a man...I..." He waved his hand

deprecatingly, clearly embarrassed by his feeling of self-worth, having saved Mr. Brighton from certain death. "I can't explain how I feel. Being English, I shouldn't anyway." He laughed at this confession, and people around him looked on in wonder that a man could laugh after what they'd just endured.

He sobered quickly embarrassed by his laughter. "I'm so sorry, sir, about your wife. Such a tragedy."

Another wave of guilt hit Manning. At the man's words, he'd felt a beginning sense of relief. No more problems with Mabel. Then the guilt of that feeling laid itself upon his initial guilt of not having saved her. He looked at Mr. Grenly with eyes full of misery.

Grenly and Manning stared out to sea. The horizon disappeared as a star twinkled here and there. The night sky, which became dark as ink, settled itself over the freighter.

Manning suddenly patted his waist. *At least my money belt is still with me. Guess I can be thankful for that. We should make Genoa by morning.*

George met the freighter. He stood outside the rope rail, carefully scrutinizing every passenger who came off the overloaded freighter, most of them looking disheveled.

There's so many. It's a wonder the freighter didn't sink with such a load. He espied Brighton in a line of people filing toward the gangplank that connected the freighter to the shore. George, with sharp eyes, gazed behind Brighton, but there was no Mabel.

Manning Brighton shuffled down the wooden gangplank as the mass of people moved slowly. He nearly walked straight past George, who immediately reached out to grab his arm.

"Brighton, so glad I found you." George looked into blue eyes darkened with misery. "You've had quite an ordeal." Manning nodded to the end of the rope rail, as if he didn't care to hold up people behind him. He walked toward the end and turned to shake a man's hand, thanking him as George waited for him outside the crush of people.

Manning stood still a moment, looking disoriented. He had no luggage, nothing to declare. He placed a palm on his forehead, as if his head ached. George watched as he made a U-turn around the railing to where he stood waiting for him. Having seen the wretchedness in Manning Brighton's eyes, George did some fast praying before they met.

George didn't shake his hand; he took Manning into his arms and felt the man's shoulders begin to shake. He didn't let go and prayed he could help lift the burden that weighed Brighton down.

"Let's go back to my hotel," George said. "We can talk there." George had walked down to the wharf but hailed a cab for the return trip.

"Are you in need of cash? Did you lose your money?" he asked suddenly as the thought occurred to him.

"N-no, I had my money belt on. I always wear it when I'm traveling, sometimes even in bed." Manning leaned back against the *cab carrozza's* seat and rested his head. He closed his eyes and swallowed. "George, I can't..." His voice trailed off.

"It's all right, Manning. It's all right."

"I..." His voice trailed off again.

George sat back and didn't say anything. *I'm glad Adeline is still out shopping. It will give Brighton some time to...to what?* George sat pondering, and he prayed for the man sitting across from him. *Lord, please let me be of some help to this man. Give me wisdom in what to say.*

George paid the driver, and instantly the door was opened before them by a hotel porter who bowed his head in polite acknowledgment of George.

He picked up his key from the front desk and asked that a pot of coffee and a breakfast be brought up to his room. The two men climbed the wide stairs together. Entering the room, Manning was obviously surprised to see female lingerie draped over a chair and shoes kicked under the table by the window.

George picked up the nightgown he'd thrown over the chair's back, and opening the bedroom door, he tossed it on the bed, closing the door behind him.

"My wife accompanied me and is out shopping," he said with more aplomb than he felt.

There was a discreet tap on the door and upon opening it, the same waiter who'd come earlier entered with his white-draped pushcart and set the table for one. He smiled but was silent, in contrast to his earlier chatter once Addie had begun talking to him.

The waiter asked, " *Devo versare?*" Shall I pour?

George, with no idea what he'd said, looked blankly at Brighton, who replied, "Please do."

The waiter looked curiously at the bedraggled man but made no other comment. George pressed some lire into his hand, and he bowed himself out with a *grazie* to the room in general.

"Do you take sugar and cream?"

Manning started to shake his head but instead sat abruptly on the settee, elbows on knees, holding his head in his hands. "I like it black. Sorry. I have hammers going off in my head." He rubbed at his temples.

George said, "I don't know what all happened. I only know the steamer went down, but I am sure a little food could help that head of yours, even if you don't feel like eating."

Manning rose slowly. "You're probably right." He sat at the round table but didn't make a move toward the food. He stared at the beauty out the window. "When something so traumatic happens, you wonder that life goes on the way it did before. The sun keeps shining, birds keep singing, but I seem to hear and feel everything through a haze, through a tunnel."

He picked up his fork as George whipped off the hot plate cover to reveal eggs, bacon, hashbrowns, and toast. Manning began to eat and as he ate, George sensed the man's appetite returned. He sipped his coffee, and George sat across from him, one leg crossed over his knee. When Manning finished, he wiped his mouth, drank down the rest of his coffee, and began to relate to George exactly what happened. His blue eyes were shadowed as he spoke. When he finished, George poured another cup of coffee for both of them.

Santa Marinella sits where the ancient Etruscan port of Latium stood several thousand years ago. Later, in 384 BC, it was plundered by Dionysius. Years later, in 191 BC, the Romans colonized the area, and it became well-known for Roman baths as well as a supplier of fish to Rome. Once magnificent, its ruins and a medieval castle gave reminder to what had once been a glorious locality but was now a small village.

It was in this community, purely Italian, that Mabel finally found herself. Hours before, she had come to the point of merely steeling herself to the misery. The sun beat down—a mild heat, but having no food or water, Mabel felt she could go no further. Grimly, she plodded on, placing one foot in front of the other. Finally, she saw in the distance a castle seeming to rise straight out of the sea.

A small village backed the castle and Mabel, finally reaching it, felt lightheaded from dehydration and exhaustion. She knocked on the door of a huge marbled edifice that looked the most promising. When the door was opened by an old wrinkled woman dressed all in black, Mabel thought for sure she had met death itself and fainted on the threshold.

Filled with consternation, the old woman, a nun, left her unconscious visitor lying on the threshold.

She walked swiftly to the rear of the abbey, calling out as she went. The abbot who'd been on his knees praying rose hastily and went to the front door. Mabel was lying over the doorsill, her face pallid, nearly bloodless. The head priest crossed himself and, speaking rapidly in Italian, told the nun to pick up her feet. He hauled her up by the shoulders, and they carried her to one of the cells in which visiting monks slept. They laid the unconscious woman on a cot-like bed.

The dwelling Mabel found was part of the monastery.

George was doing his best to console Manning.

"I know this sounds callous, but what happened may be for the best," George said. "Mabel would either wind up in an institution for the mentally insane or hung for her crimes, if she committed them. We've never had a witness come forward, but the Boston department is quite sure she killed her husband, Horace Vickers, and her friend, Bradley Burbank." George took another sip of coffee. "She was a danger to all with whom she came in contact. I read your detailed cable. Besides the fact that we're quite sure she murdered two men, the irrefutable evidence that she tried to destroy your daughter's locket and some of the behavior exhibited on your trip points to a demented soul. Also, her unhinged conduct is not solely directed at men."

"That's true," Manning said heavily. "I've gone over the scenario enough times to know I didn't want her to be in close contact with my Victoria. I simply don't see how I could have missed her erratic behavior before I married her. I can't begin to tell you how I have rued the fact that I married her, especially without a good conversation with my daughter first." He took another sip of his coffee and asked, hesitation in his voice, "George, can things like that run in a family? Can it be passed down to her children? It's something I've been wondering about, but I simply don't know."

"Neither do I. I believe you'd have to ask an expert about that, but what are her children like? Do they seem normal?"

"Yes, but then I thought Mabel was normal. I'm beginning to question my own judgment." He put his head in his hands again and said, "I feel so guilty. If only I'd not loosened my grip." He looked over at George. "I feel guilty, too, that I cannot mourn her. It's a relief to me she's gone. She was like a noose around my neck, getting tighter and tighter. Her displays of demented anger were frightening. She threw a tremendous display of out-of-control behavior at the captain's table. I didn't know what to do with her."

"As I said, this all may be for the best." Manning jumped as the door opened abruptly.

A porter entered, loaded down with the result of a huge shopping spree. Adeline Baxter followed him in.

She handed him a goodly amount for the gratuity, smiled, and said, "Grazie, Signore, grazie." She closed the door behind him. Turning, she said brightly, "Ciao." But as Manning's disheveled appearance sank into her consciousness, the smile faded, and concern spread itself across her beautiful face.

"What happened? George...Manning...what happened? Where's Mabel?" She could sense something was very wrong.

Both Manning and George stood when she entered the room. Manning looked over at George, clearly wanting him to answer her questions. Adeline had been a good friend of his late wife, Laura, and the Baxters moved in the same social circles as the Brightons.

George answered her. "There's been a terrible accident. The steamer they were on went down, and I am afraid Mabel went down with it."

Adeline gasped. "What are you saying? The steamboat you were on sank? Oh, how dreadful. Oh my, that's horrible. I'm so sorry, Manning."

"I don't know what all happened. I was unconscious. It's as I told you, George." He glanced at George, then back at Adeline. "Mabel started to go to her cabin to get her jewels. I grabbed her and told her I'd get her new ones. She beat at me and screamed as I began to steer her toward the lifeboat. People were streaming up from the cabins below and chaos reigned. When we got close to the rail, she bit me on the arm, and I relaxed my grip. She pulled away, starting for the stairs. I stared after her for a few seconds, not believing she would jeopardize her life for a few jewels. People were coming up, and she had to fight to go down. I started after her, when the steamer totally listed aft. I slipped, headed for the sea, and could find no handholds, but an Englishman reached out and grabbed me. I hit my head on a bollard and was knocked unconscious. And there you have it. He dragged me into the lifeboat, dragged me onto the freighter, and thankfully sat over me until I came to."

Adeline plopped onto the settee as if the wind had been knocked out of her. George and Manning both sat back down at the table. It was quiet for a few minutes. George drummed his fingers on the table in a silent rhythm, a habit Adeline was thoroughly familiar with. He was thinking out a plan of action.

He asked, "How would you like to go out again, Addie? Manning can give you his sizes, and you can get some things for him off the rack. I'll go down and see if I can get him a room on this floor. Manning, you can use our bath, and if Adeline gets back in time, you'll have some clothes. If not, there's a robe hanging on the back of the bathing room door. I'll have a maid come fill the tub for you."

George was used to giving orders.

Christopher Belden went to the rear of the building to get a cup of coffee. It was one of the things he enjoyed most about the setup at the bureau. There was a cook, Elsie, installed in the little kitchen at the back of the station's main floor. A maid, Daisy, served coffee, cleaned, and did overall light work that kept the department a clean, inviting place to work. Unlike his usual two steps at a time, he took the stairs at a sedate pace up to his office, holding a brief in one hand and his coffee in the other. It was a Monday morning and mail was stacked on his desk. A small fire burned in the grate as the weather had cooled dramatically in only a week. His office felt good after the chilly hallway. He sat and thumbed through the mail when a light tap sounded, and a delivery boy entered with a telegram. He thanked the youth, signed for it, and ripped it open as the young man left.

George Baxter had cabled him and gave a bare outline of what had transpired in Italy. Chris thought it quite cryptic and wondered at it. The cable was short, simply informing him that Brighton had been found. It also stated that his wife was dead. He sipped some of the hot coffee and leaned back in his chair. He closed his eyes and thought about the message. *Mabel Vickers-Brighton dead?* He prayed for wisdom and discernment, his heart full of misgivings. It was too easy. *Life is not so simplistic.* He prayed again for Brighton's protection. Not knowing any of the details, he knew, somehow in his gut, he knew Mabel Vickers-Brighton was very much alive.

CHAPTER XII

They that go down to the sea in ships,
that do business in great waters;
These see the works of the LORD,
and his wonders in the deep.

PSALM 107:23-24

MANNING ALSO SENT A CABLE to the Brighton residence. Tory was ecstatic. Her papa would be coming home in six or seven days. The house went into a flurry of anticipation. The cable indicated that Mabel would not be coming but did not elucidate. Mabel's children were full of questions, but Olivia tried to calm them. They would find out when Manning got home what, exactly, had taken place. Perhaps he had found a place for Mabel to stay where she could have good care and get well.

Henry was upset. Even though his mother had bigger temper tantrums than he did, he was the apple of her eye and he knew it. He liked being in the Brighton home and Olivia was wonderful, but he knew none of the Vickers children were a favorite; she treated them all equally. As he thought about it, she didn't even give Tory any more special favors than they received. Still, he missed his mother's doting attitude toward him.

"Where will she be living? Who will take care of her? Mama will want to come home and be with me." His voice rose. "She didn't even want to go! Mr. Brighton made her go!" His eyes teared up and he ran into the hall, slamming Tory's sitting room door behind him.

Olivia followed him down the hall. His door was still ajar, and she went in and sat down on the side of the bed. She watched him for a few minutes as he sobbed his misery into his pillow. Olivia scooped him up into her arms and carried him to the rocking chair by the window. He was heavy but complaisant. She didn't say anything to him. She just rocked him and rocked him. As his sobs lessened, Olivia began humming a hymn. It soothed Henry, who fell asleep.

Skies looked happily upon Charles and Tory the next afternoon. Balls of fluff skimmed across its blue expanse. It was Indian summer, and the weather was perfect. Henry was practicing on his violin, which he loved to do more than anything else. The two older children were riding on the beach, glad class had been let out a bit earlier than usual.

Walking their horses leisurely down to the strand, Tory and Charles talked about their subjects and the teachers who taught them. Once they were at the beach, the two children raced their horses down the sandy shore, neck and neck, but soon Ebony really stretched out her legs, and with sand spitting, Tory was left behind. When they came to the cove, they dismounted to walk back the way they had come.

"Ebony can really go when you let her all out, can't she?" Tory said, impressed with Charles' new horse.

"Yes, she's quite a horse. I love riding. It's exhilarating." Switching subjects abruptly, he looked guiltily at Tory. "I'm glad she's not coming home. Horrid isn't it?" He repeated his comment. "I am glad my mother is not coming home. It makes me feel awful that I don't want her here with all of us, but it's true. I don't."

"I'm very sorry. Perhaps she'll get well. Maybe the hospital will have someone who can find out what the problem is and treat it. I don't think you should feel guilty. Oh, Charles, it's not your fault she is who she is. She needs help, and you're not the only one to think so. Papa must think so too, else he wouldn't have taken her someplace to get her help. And please don't feel bad that you don't want her here. I don't either. She's not nice, and until she gets help, I hope she never comes here."

"That's true," he said thoughtfully. "I didn't think of that. Thank you for your words. I've been worried about your papa being with her every day. It's not safe."

"What do you mean, not safe?"

"Well, I think you know what I mean. I always wonder what she's going to do next." He didn't want to tell her what he'd witnessed. He had loved his father deeply, and he knew his own mother had killed him. Since sharing with the head of the Boston Detective Agency, he felt no need to tell anyone else about what his mother had done. There was no sense worrying Tory. She'd start worrying about her father. And besides, it sounded as if everything was going to be all right.

Tory looked down at the sand as they walked along. Glancing at Charles, she said, "I was scared too. Then I remembered to pray about it. I gave my worries to Jesus and He calmed them. I'm not saying I never worried about my papa anymore. What I'm saying is that I have a God who is bigger than any of my problems. Charles, I've seen what God can do. His answers aren't always what I asked for, but His answers are always best for me or what is best for someone else. I was really angry at God when my mother died. I prayed and prayed for her to be healed and she wasn't. While she was ill, she asked Jesus to come into her heart. It took a long time for me to understand what good there was in any of it. Now I know where my mother is forever and forever. If she had been healthy and lived a normal life, perhaps she'd never have asked Jesus into her heart. I know you don't know Jesus as your personal Savior, but I do. I have for over five years. I am never completely alone and I…" Her voice trailed off. Charles looked at her with a bit of wonder in his eyes.

"Ah, so that's what it is. Tory, I want Jesus in my life too. I'm tired of worrying myself sick and in my heart, deep in my heart, I want Jesus. I want what I know you have."

Right there on the beach, Charles allowed Jesus to take control of his heart and to cleanse him of all wrong. He repented of all his sins, known and unknown. Tory, obviously thrilled, got goose bumps on her arms. Charles became a Christ follower, giving all that he was or ever would be to the King of Kings.

Mabel awoke strained and tired in every muscle of her body. She looked around the small room and wondered where she was. There was a tiny window and the walls were whitewashed. She saw a large crucifix on the wall at the foot of the bed. Craning her neck to see above her head, a wave of nausea hit her, and the pain in her head beat a steady tattoo, like the pounding of drums. A small table stood beside a bare wall on her right, with several candles, two of which were lit. Closing her eyes against the pain, she took a deep breath and swallowed the sudden saliva in her mouth. She felt nauseated. All at once, conscious thought was regained, and her eyes flew open as she remembered Henry. *Henry! I must get back to my Henry! And Manning. I must get back to Manning. I'll be sure to get back to Manning.* She lay for a few moments, rethinking her wording. *I'll be sure to get back at Manning.* Agitated by her intentions, she lay for a time, her head pounding, not able to keep her thoughts coherent. Sometime later, she drifted off into nothingness again.

Guests invited to sit at the captain's table of the Cunard Liner bound for Boston were standing around but not yet seated. The captain had not yet arrived.

"My name is Stanley Gilbert," a tall, lanky young man said. He turned to shake Manning's hand.

"Nice to make your acquaintance. My name's Manning Brighton. This is Adeline and George Baxter." Adeline inclined her head and smiled up at Mr. Gilbert as he and George shook hands. Manning thought the young man looked vaguely familiar but couldn't place him.

Two women approached the group. One appeared to be in deep mourning dressed as she was in unrelieved black. Her lovely face was lined by the years she bore, but her eyes sparkled a greenish hazel beneath heavily marked brows. The other woman looked young and quite self-possessed. Dressed in stark contrast to her companion, her décolletage was cut low, exposing a slender neck encased in a diamond choker. Drop earrings and a huge diamond-studded comb in her shining black hair twinkled brightly in the lamplight. Wearing a dress of the brightest red Adeline had ever seen, the young woman looked exotically beautiful. She spoke to the group at large, introducing herself in a heavy Spanish accent.

"Good evening. I am Señorita María Fernando Esperanza de la Soto. Thees ees my mother, Señora María Alphonse Esperanza de la Soto. We are from Barcelona." She pronounced Barcelona in a Castilian accent, lisping the name as Barthelona. She and her mother seemed comfortable in the formal setting.

Captain Eldridge arrived and began making introductions all around. "This gentleman," he said as he placed his hand on the shoulder of a large, rotund man, "is Herr Bernhard Haas, and his wife, Marlene, on holiday from Germany. Herr Haas owns Haas and Sons Textiles. Perhaps you've heard of it?"

Adeline's face wreathed into a generous smile as she turned and shook Frau Haas' hand. "Oh, you produce some of the most marvelous fabrics! My seamstress uses fabrics from your company quite often."

Mrs. Haas looked at her blankly, and Addie suddenly realized she hadn't understood a word she'd said. She switched to German and repeated herself. "Oh, *Sie produzieren einige der herrlichsten Stoffe! Meine Schneiderin verwendet Stoffe aus Ihrem Unternehmen sehr oft.*"

Frau Haas' face broke into a beatific smile, and she replied, "What a wonderful thing. You speak my language. I have been nearly dying of complete boredom. Barney is a wonderful communicator. However, we've been on holiday for almost five weeks. Not understanding what is being said around me, believe me when I say, it is beginning to pall. Barney knows several languages, but me, none but German." The two women chatted for a few minutes.

Another couple was introduced to the group, the captain saying, "This is Meneer and Mevrouw Pieter Van Aalst. The Van Aalsts live in Den Haag and Meneer is in parliament there. Please be seated and enjoy comestibles par excellence, and it is to be hoped, stimulating conversation." He smiled benevolently around at his guests, looking forward to a pleasant evening.

Name cards had been place near the top of each plate, and the guests, without further ado, found their places.

Everyone sat down and Manning, seated beside Adeline, turned to speak quietly with her while rounds of French bread smothered in baby shrimp and topped with caviar were served as the appetizer. As they were removing the plates in preparation for the soup course, the captain began to speak about the sinking of the steamer. Word of that incident traveled like wildfire, especially among shipping companies.

"It was a huge tragedy and no mistake." The captain was a short man with heavy side chops becoming part of his mustache, and his chin clean shaven. "I knew one couple, dear friends of mine, who lost their lives in that catastrophe." He shook his head mournfully and began to excoriate the steamer's captain. "The man had no right taking that steamer out of port when he knew there was a problem with the boiler. Knowing it wasn't safe, the blockhead took a risk in sailing and thus lost so many lives, his own included."

Manning said nothing, his emotions still raw. George, who sat across from him, glanced hastily at him but said nothing.

Señorita de la Soto's chair separated George from Stanley Gilbert, who spoke up. "I was on that steamer."

Before he could say more, Captain Eldridge exclaimed, "You don't say! Why, you can tell us what happened that sad day better than anyone!"

"No, not better than anyone, sir," Gilbert said, and he looked across the table at Manning and nodded. "I recognize you, sir. I'm sorry about your own tragedy. I remember you quite clearly. As I reached the top of the stairs, I saw you begin to head my way. I wondered why. My mind was not quite so sharp at the time. I suddenly realized you were with the woman trying to go down the stairs. So, as I said, you were starting my way when the steamer upended. Everything happened so fast after that. I was picked up and thrown over the side by someone. I don't even know who. I was in the water thinking to drown when someone in one of the lifeboats hauled me in, and we paddled to the freighter that hovered a distance from the steamer. There were others, some definitely dead, but some, like me, holding on for dear life. It's not an experience I'll ever forget. The horror of it wakes me at night. I wonder, to what purpose did I survive? Why did I survive and not someone else?"

George replied, "Those are difficult questions no man can answer. Suffice it to say, you must ask the Almighty God why He spared you. Be grateful you have time to find His purpose for your life, young man. He has a plan for you. What you must do is all the good you know to do until God's specific call comes to you. Seek Him with your whole heart."

Mr. Gilbert looked at George with respect in his eyes. Manning could see the younger man believed George was speaking truth to him. Gilbert's focus switched back to Manning.

"What about you, sir? What happened to you?"

Manning said, "I was knocked out and don't remember anything until I awoke on the freighter."

All eyes at the table shifted from Stanley Gilbert to Manning. A distinct whisper of German could be heard in the silence as Herr Haas translated in sotto voce to his wife. Manning kept his eyes on Gilbert, ignoring the stares of his shipmates. George spoke to alleviate the tension and thus give Manning a reprieve.

"Yes, Captain, it was quite a tragedy. I'm sorry to hear about your friends. I waited for the freighter to come in, and I can tell you it was a forlorn and quiet bunch who descended the gangplank that day. Many people waiting were thankful to see their loved ones safe and sound." He turned to Gilbert and asked, "So, do you have any idea how many souls were lost at sea that day?"

Stanley Gilbert replied, "No, no I don't."

Before he could say more, Meneer Pieter Van Aalst spoke of a tragedy that occurred recently in the North Sea, and the conversation turned to other such incidents. Manning breathed a sigh of relief as the attention moved around the table. He needn't speak of his own personal tragedy and felt grateful for George's thoughtful intervention.

The starter was a French onion soup, and conversation turned to politics and on to the incident between Rutgers and Princeton over the stealing of a cannon by students. There was much laughter. The conversation then turned to Spain.

Manning looked over to Señora de la Soto and said, "These are interesting times in Spain, so I hear."

"*Si, es verdad*. It is true." Her eyes sparkled, rivaling her daughter's jewels. She spoke English with a British accent ladened with Spanish. "We have had Antonio Cánovas del Castillo as prime minister thees past year and now he ees terminated by King Alfonso." She snapped her fingers. "But it shan't be long and he weel again be in office. I have no doubt of it." Turning to Adeline, she inquired, "Have you veesited the Prado in Madrid?"

The evening was a huge success. Manning thanked George for his quick wit before going to his cabin, his eyes still shadowed by the trauma.

CHAPTER XIII

Thou art the helper of the fatherless.

PSALM 10:14b

MABEL AWOKE TO VOICES. She didn't open her eyes but lay quietly, wondering and on her guard as to whom those voices might belong. *Where am I?* she brooded. *Am I in some sort of prison?* Her mind cleared, and she slowly opened her eyes to see a young priest and the old woman who had answered the door. They were conversing with someone else. She turned her head to see in the corner of the room. Another man in a dark suit sat on a straight-backed chair. Her head throbbed with the movement. Furtively, she felt the back of her head where a large plaster covered her wound. The smell of liniment was strong in the tiny room, and she realized it was from whatever was on the gauze on her head.

The man sitting in the corner of the room got up and coming to the side of the bed, spoke rapidly in Italian.

Mabel blinked uncomprehendingly. Her brain seemed slow in comprehending what was happening around her, and she took a deep breath. Her head felt as if drumsticks were beating on a bass drum. Her ears heard the voice as if through a long tunnel.

Her brow wrinkled in frustration, and she replied in English. "I don't understand what you're saying."

The man switched to French, but Mabel had never had any formal learning and didn't know what he said.

"Didn't you hear what I just said? I don't understand you!" She spoke in an astringent tone of voice. She knew it was rude, but she didn't care. Her head hurt, and she felt an urge to hurl something at the man in the dark suit.

The priest and the old lady stared at her, clearly taken aback by her tone. Mabel looked fully at the priest and saw compassion and concern for her in his dark eyes, which glowed warmly at her. She perked up and gave him a tentative smile.

He smiled cordially and said something to the other two. He spoke directly to the old woman who, with lips pressed tightly together, took a tin cup and filled it with water from a small clay pitcher. She held it to Mabel's lips, but Mabel wanted to brush it out of the old hag's hand. Because of her overwhelming thirst, she was compliant, downing the cool liquid in one draught.

The old woman's inscrutable brown eyes stared into Mabel's with no curiosity. Mabel looked back at her coldly, her unblinking icicle-blue eyes staring at the old woman over the rim of the battered tin cup.

When the old woman straightened up, she crossed herself.

She turned away from the evil she'd witnessed in the deep-blue gaze. She spoke to the two men and left the cell with a slow, measured step. The abbot, clearly startled, followed her out, walking beside her as he spoke.

"Sister Amalia, can you truly see the woman is evil? I sensed something in there, but she has been through some sort of traumatic ordeal. It's been three days since the steamer went down. Perhaps she was on it." He shook his head. "So many souls lost that day." The priest was known for looking at the best in people and trying to help them develop that good to its full potential.

Sister Amalia spoke gently but firmly. "That soul in there," she said and nodded her head toward the monk's cell where the younger woman lay, "is lost too. The devil himself looked out of her eyes at me!" She walked, with stately, unhurried step, down the flagstone hall toward the kitchen.

Back in the monk's cell, the man in the suit went back to stand beside the woman in the bed. He spoke slowly in Italian, hoping she could understand him.

"*Sono un medico.* I'm a doctor—Dr. Luigi Aroni." He gently took her hand and felt her pulse.

Mabel lay quietly under his ministrations, unable to communicate, but she understood he was a doctor.

I need to get out of here. Somehow, I am going to find money and transportation out of this place and get back to America.

The doctor finished examining the woman.

But as he looked into her eyes, he knew what Sister Amalia said was true. He didn't know if it was evilness. He didn't know exactly what he saw. He did know he saw a disturbed mind in the depths of her eyes. It startled him. He too turned away and crossed himself.

The week sped by as anticipation rose to a fevered pitch in the Brighton household. All was in readiness for the master to come home. Janey and Lorna had polished the silver and cleaned every nook and cranny in the big manse. Cookie, her baize apron stretched around her formidable frame, made delectable treats and planned meals to tempt the most lagging appetite.

Frankie had the gardener cut the last of the roses. Flower arrangements now graced every room; the front foyer flaunted a huge bouquet of them in an elegant crystal vase. The housekeeper inspected everything, making sure all was in order, but more, looked warm and inviting for a weary traveler.

Ralph had the stables in shipshape condition, the stalls mucked out, and the horses groomed nonpareil.

Olivia began to pack her bags slowly and with much regret.

I have opened my heart to these children, and now it's time for me to go, but to what? More charitable work, more dinner parties, more soirées, more entertaining myself? I know, Father. I involve myself with other people and have many wonderful relationships, but oh Lord, how I shall miss these children! I love them as if they were my own. I don't remember when I've ever been so happy.

The Cunard Liner was due into port early on the morrow.

Tory was so excited she was sure she wouldn't sleep a wink. She was in the kitchen with Cookie, licking a spoon.

"Oh, Cookie, Papa will be so glad to be home and enjoy your cooking again! He always says no one in the whole world cooks as wonderfully as you, and I agree. What are you fixing for dinner tomorrow night?" Tory had smeared chocolate on her mouth, and her tongue worked hard to clean it off.

Cookie Roberts smiled. "Well, now, let me see. What do you think would be a good meal to welcome your papa home?"

"You already know what I'm going to say. Chicken fricassee is his favorite, I think, or your Indian curry dinner, or a roast leg of lamb. He sure likes that. What do you think, Cookie?"

Cookie waved a spatula toward Tory. "I think you'd best be a washing your face, little girl. No matter how hard you try, your little ole tongue ain't gonna reach that chocolate, missy."

Tory grinned at her. She was so happy she could scarcely contain it. Twirling around in the kitchen, she scampered to the little washroom under the back stairs and splashed some water from a jug onto her hand. She scrubbed at her face. *I'm so happy Mabel isn't coming home with Papa—so, so happy. I didn't want to let on to Charles exactly how happy I am, but I am! I am!* She dried her face on the towel and noticed a bit of chocolate on it. *Well, I guess my face wasn't clean, but it is now.* She laughed for sheer joy. *Papa's coming home!* Walking sedately back into the kitchen, she thought about the vast change in Charles. *No more dark circles under his eyes. Did realizing his mother wasn't coming home make that much of a difference? She's so wicked, and he's afraid of her. Well, now he needn't be!*

Frankie came through the large swinging doors into the kitchen and said, "There you are! Miss Olivia's been looking for you, missy moo!" Walking up to Tory, Frankie gave her shoulder a squeeze. "She's waiting for you in your mother's sitting room."

126

Tory skipped out of the kitchen on happy feet and then slowed as she thought about Olivia leaving. *Oh how I wish she could stay!* Tory was old enough to know that would not be the case, and she dragged her feet, knowing somehow that Aunt Ollie wanted to say a good-bye without onlookers. Although it was a day early, she knew they mightn't have time for a proper good-bye later.

She tapped on the door and heard Aunt Olivia's sweet voice say, "Enter."

Tory opened the door, peeking her head in first. She started to smile and said, "Aunt Ollie—oh, Aunt Ollie, I don't want you to go!" She ran straight as an arrow into Olivia's waiting arms.

"It's all right, Toralina Lou. Oh, how I do love you!" Olivia's arms tightened around the girl's shoulders, and Tory sobbed on her breast. "I'm not so worried about you now, Toralina Lou, since the new Mrs. Brighton isn't coming home with your father." She lifted Tory's chin to face her own eyes misted with unshed tears. She looked deeply into her eyes and said, "Tory, your father loves you very much. Every one of the staff adore you. You and I have a special connection because of your mother, but I love you as if you were my own girl. If ever something comes up and you need help, I'll always be there. In truth, we have a special connection because, in Christ, we're sisters. We're sisters for all eternity. Just think of that!" She smiled, her tawny eyes glowing with love for Tory.

Victoria brushed away her tears and smiled back at Olivia. "That's curious, isn't it? That we're sisters, I mean. It's true, though, isn't it? We *are* sisters. I love you so much, Aunt Olivia. And believe me, if ever I need help, I'll come running."

The next day dawned with pinks and purple streaking the sky in a glorious array of light. A few clouds stretched their way across the heavens in ever-changing configurations as a brisk breeze pushed them rapidly by. The wind off the water was cold, and the small group waiting for the de-boarding shivered in the early morning air. A Boston winter was just around the corner.

Manning scanned the crowd and saw Tory as she began to jump up and down. "There he is! Look, right there! There's Papa!" She waved frantically, and Manning smiled at his daughter as he descended the gangplank. *She looks just like Laura*, he thought. Noticing the rest of the group, the smile died abruptly as he looked away. *What in the world am I going to say to those children? How does anyone say—your mother is dead?* His head ached and his stomach began to churn.

George and Adeline were ahead of him, and the three headed for the customs shed before meeting their party.

Once through customs, George said, "I'd like to meet your family and say hello to Olivia, if that's all right with you."

Adeline chimed in. "I would too."

"It's fine with me. Come on and meet my little family."

The three weary travelers walked toward the group as Tory, with a glance at Olivia, flew across the cobbles and into her papa's waiting arms.

"Oh, Papa...oh, how I've missed you!" She hugged him tightly as he picked her up and buried his face into her clean-smelling neck. Tears started to his eyes, and he tried to hold them back, taking a deep, shuddering breath before facing the children. As he pulled away from Tory's neck, his eyes caught and held Olivia's.

She saw such misery in their depths and wondered at it. *Does he feel guilty for having Mabel committed? Oh my, this is something serious.*

Charles and Henry hung back behind Olivia's skirts, and Manning, seeing the two children, grabbed Charles and gave him a tight hug. He turned to Henry, scooped him up into his arms, and hugged him close to himself, as if by their closeness he could ease the pain that was sure to follow.

Henry, surprised by the display of affection, pulled back and grinned at Manning. He'd not been hugged by a man for quite a long time, but suddenly, he remembered his mother.

"Where's my mama? Where did you put her? I wanted her to come home. You made her go with you, and now you haven't brought her back. Where is she?" Henry's voice, full of rancor, pierced Manning's heart. He wriggled to get down, wanting out of Manning's arms. Manning gently set the boy down on his feet, but he didn't answer his questions.

Straightening his back, he glanced over at George and Adeline who were waiting to be introduced. He made the introductions.

"I know you both know Olivia. This young man is Charles Vickers, and this is Henry Vickers." Tory stepped forward and he said, "And this is my daughter, Victoria. Children, this is Detective George Baxter and his wife, Adeline Baxter, who is a great friend of Olivia's."

Charles looked into the clear eyes of Inspector Baxter.

He remembered what Chief Inspector Christopher Belden said, that he had his best man on the way to Italy to help Mr. Brighton get his mother some help in Switzerland.

The two boys sketched a bow, and Tory dipped a sweet curtsy toward the couple, a sweet smile on her face.

"How do you do?" they said in unison.

"I do very well, thank you, and so does my husband," replied Adeline. "What nice manners you have!"

Adeline loved children and had always felt a sorrow in her heart that she had none. She glanced at Olivia. "What a lark you must have had these past few weeks with these children!"

"Oh, I've had the time of my life!" Olivia exclaimed. "When did you meet up with Manning?"

Adeline looked taken aback for a moment, and George smoothly stepped into the lull. "We met in Genoa. It's a lovely port city." Looking over at his wife, he inquired, "Adeline, my dear, are you anxious to get home? Perhaps we can visit just a bit with Olivia and get to know the children?"

Manning, surprised the Baxters didn't wish to go straight home, suddenly realized it was because they wished to help him relate the events of the tragedy and be of support to him. He looked at them over the heads of children, thanksgiving in his eyes. Henry jerked on his frock coat and demanded again to know just where his mother was. Manning looked down at the boy and felt incredible sorrow for him. Turning toward Olivia, he gave her a quick hug of thanksgiving for watching the children.

Olivia pulled away and grinned at him, her cheeks reddened. "It's nothing, Manning. I probably had more fun than the children. But," she said as she waggled her forefinger at him, "should I ever need a favor, believe me, I plan to collect."

Manning returned her grin. "And I shall be happy to oblige you, dear lady."

Ralph waited with the wagon, and George and Adeline were able to have their luggage stowed on the flatbed as well. George tipped the young man who had trundled their bags out of the customs shed. Manning had nothing but a large satchel of things he bought before leaving Genoa, his new clothes, and what he had on his person.

CHAPTER XIV

Surely I am more brutish than any man,
and have not the understanding of a man. I neither
learned wisdom, nor have the knowledge of the holy.

PROVERBS 30:2-3

AS THEY HEADED FOR THE CARRIAGE, Tory asked, "Papa, where's your luggage? What happened to the beautiful set of cases Mama bought you?"

"Later, sweetie. I'll explain later."

Olivia said she had driven the carriage to the wharf. The boys climbed onto the wagon with Ralph, and he clucked for Glad and Glee to head home. Tory climbed up on the driver's seat of the carriage and sat snuggled up next to her papa, delighted he was finally home. George, Adeline, and Olivia entered the carriage; Olivia sat across from the other couple.

Once they were underway, Adeline said, "Oh, Olivia, the most tragic thing has happened. The steamer Mabel and Manning were on sunk." Olivia gasped as Adeline continued with her story. "Mabel, well, you know how she was, headed down the stairs after the boiler exploded on the steamer, wanting to get her jewels. Manning grabbed her and…and they started for the side where the lifeboats were, but Mabel bit Manning and he let go of her. She ran for the stairs to go to their room. Manning started to go after her, and suddenly the whole steamer upended. He lost his footing and thought he was a goner. An Englishman snagged his life vest as he slid down and saved his life, but his body swung over to the side. He hit his head and knew nothing until he woke up on a freighter. Mabel went down with the steamer. The captain of the freighter said he circled and circled the area, rescuing people in the water, and there were no others who survived."

"Oh, how horrible! So that's what I saw in his eyes! I wondered at his doleful expression. He looks absolutely miserable!"

George said, "Yes, he feels guilty that he let go of Mabel's arm. The guilt is compounded because he can't mourn Mabel. She was wicked, and he knows it. We, at the department, feel she may have murdered two men, her late husband and Bradley Burbank. You remember him, don't you?"

"Yes," Olivia replied. "I knew him. We were dinner partners at several functions. I know for sure Mabel murdered her husband."

"How do you know?" George, flabbergasted, stared at Olivia.

Olivia dropped her eyes to her lap. Lacing her fingers together, she looked back up at George. "I took Charles, the eleven-year-old Vickers boy, to see your Chief Inspector Belden. He…he saw his mother poison his father. He couldn't sleep from the horror of it and was afraid his mother would do the same to him."

"Well, I'll be jiggered!" George exclaimed. "We thought we'd never find a clue to prove Mabel Vickers killed her husband. How sad for the boy. What a burden that is for the poor lad to carry. I pray he's not guilt ridden for speaking up about his mother."

"No, no he isn't. He's become a believer. Tory has been a wonderful help, although I'm quite certain he hasn't told her about his mother's wickedness—didn't care to worry her, I suppose."

"Well, as we three know, there is nothing better in life than to know the intimate love of Christ." George spoke candidly. "How thankful I am to hear the boy has made a commitment. I pray Manning comes to believe too. Jesus is our source and resource and such a comfort when things go awry."

Adeline said, "Let's pray for Manning every day. Not only to get through this trauma without guilt, but more importantly, that he comes to a saving knowledge of Jesus Christ."

"I think we can all agree to do that. My biggest concern is Henry." Olivia frowned. "I haven't quite figured him out. He can be such a charming little boy, but he's subject to incredible displays of temper. I don't know if it's simply having been mollycoddled in the extreme by a mother who is insane, or a disorder passed down from her."

George and Adeline both looked nonplussed.

"Do you think he could be violent?" Being a detective, George had witnessed violent children before—not often—but in his line of work, he saw all manner of wickedness and degradation.

"I don't rightly know," Olivia replied. "He's beginning to play the violin, and perhaps it might be the key to settling him down. He can release a lot of emotion into his playing, but he bears watching. How do I relate that to Manning? I don't wish to cause a feeling of distaste for the little man. Henry needs attention, especially in light of what has happened to his mama."

George marveled at his wife's ability to find solutions to problems. He listened as she spoke to Olivia.

"I hesitate to ask, but would you be willing to stay on at the Brightons' house until all the furor has died down?" George realized that Adeline thought Olivia was the best solution for a household that needed a steadying influence. Adeline explained her suggestion. "What I'm thinking is, Henry is going to need special attention. He's probably alienated some of the staff, and Manning is not going to be able to break through to the boy when Henry considers him the source of his problem."

"Why, I don't know," Olivia replied. "That answer would be up to Manning, don't you agree? Of course I would be willing to stay on, if I can be of use."

"I think it's a splendid idea, my dear," George said. He patted his wife's hand and enfolded it into his own. "Let's see what happens and we can go from there."

When they arrived in front of the Brightons' manse, Manning jumped down to open the carriage door.

He reached for Adeline's hand and helped her out of the carriage. "Thank you for explaining," he whispered. She merely inclined her head, serious eyes belying the smile on her lips.

Scrambling down from her high perch, Tory said, "I'm going around the back with Charles and Henry."

She ran around the side of the house to the stables and halted abruptly at the scene in front of her. Ralph had gone into the stables, but Henry was pounding on Charles' chest with both fists, yelling at him.

"You don't love Mama the way I do. I think you hate her! You don't *care* that she's not here!" Henry yelled.

Charles took Henry's wrists to stop him from pummeling him. "Stop it, Henry! I mean it! Just stop! Mother needs help. You know as well as I do that she has temper tantrums...worse than yours! You've seen some of the mean things she's done to Maddie and me. Don't you want her to get help? Don't you know if she doesn't get help, she'll start on you too?"

"She won't...she loves me best!"

"She doesn't love you anymore than she does me. She only loves herself! You need to grow up, Henry!" He climbed down the wagon seat, not bothering to help Henry down, and walked up the steps to the back door.

Tory headed to the stable, ignoring Henry, to tell Ralph what her father had related to her about Mabel. She changed her mind, thinking it would be better coming from her father. She turned and walked past Henry, who now stood beside the wagon while he digested what his older brother said. He turned slowly, shoulders slumped, and followed Tory up the back stairs to the kitchen.

Frankie, Cookie, Janey, and Lorna had come out to welcome the master home. They lined up by the front door when Manning entered, and he greeted each one with warmth and affection.

"Meet me in the kitchen in a few minutes," he said to them. "I have something for each of you." He asked Olivia, "Could you please make George and Adeline comfortable for a few minutes while I run up to my rooms?" He started up the stairs, treading slowly up the steps.

Olivia was in her element acting as hostess.

"Certainly," she replied. "Cookie, can we have some of those delicious scones I saw you pulling out of the oven this morning?" She nodded her head and smiled at Frankie, who took over.

"Let's go to the kitchen," Frankie said to the staff. As they began to file out, Frankie turned graciously to the Baxters and asked, "Would you like coffee, or would you prefer tea?"

Adeline answered, "Coffee for George and tea for me, please." She followed Olivia into the parlor. George trailed behind.

Olivia was an extremely courteous hostess. The three sat chatting quietly about Mabel, but Olivia said nothing about her cut-up dresses or the bizarre behavior of Mabel Vickers-Brighton.

Adeline asked, "Will you have the girl who has gone off to France come home for the funeral?"

Olivia gave a small gasp. "I didn't even think of that. There must be a funeral even though there is no body, mustn't there?"

"Yes, one more ordeal for Manning to get through, poor man. He's had more than enough to bear these past weeks. You should have seen him, Olivia, when he first arrived into Genoa. What a disheveled, sorrowful looking man he was." Adeline's eyes were full of pity for Manning Brighton.

They could hear him run lightly down the steps.

He headed for the kitchen where Tory, followed by Henry, had come from outside into the back entry.

"Where's Charles?" he asked.

"He came in ahead of us, Papa. He's probably in his room," Tory replied.

"Could you get him please? We're going to have tea in the parlor. It's so good to see you, darling. I missed you dreadfully. We've never been apart for so long, have we?"

"No, I missed you too, but Aunt Ollie is wonderful." Tory headed for the stairs. She looked back curiously at Manning, who carried a large satchel. *My Papa sure is nice. I think he's bought gifts for Cookie, Frankie, and Ralph.*

She climbed the stairs two at a time and found Charles sitting on his bed, looking totally forlorn.

"What's the matter, Charles?" She walked into his room and sat down next to him on the bed, putting her arm around his shoulder.

"I should comfort Henry instead of yelling back. He's very upset that Mother didn't come home. And then there's that detective. Why is he here?"

"I heard Mr. Baxter say he met up with Papa in Genoa. I remember his wife. I think she was a friend of my mother's."

Charles stared at Tory. "Oh, I suppose I'm imagining things. I seem to have a habit of borrowing trouble instead of waiting until it rears its ugly head."

"I don't know what you mean, but Papa said to come get you. We're having tea with the grown-ups in the parlor. Come on—I think there are presents!" Tory grabbed Charles' arm and both slid down the bannister, Tory having shown Charles soon after he arrived at the Brightons'. Together they went to the parlor. The Baxters and Manning were there. Henry was sitting on the edge of the settee next to Olivia.

"There you are. I've brought home some presents for you."

Henry perked up, sliding to the edge of the settee as Manning handed each of the children a gift. There was even one for Olivia. Excitedly, Henry tore open the wrapping. It was a wonderful set of wooden horses. Each one was painted intricately, depicting true horse breeds.

"Oh, I love them, Mr. Manning. They're beautiful, and I love my new horse, Ivory. Thank you, oh thank you very much!" Henry was overcome and being an emotional boy, he ran over to Manning and gave him a hug. He turned back to Olivia and said, "Look, Aunt Olivia. Look at how beautiful they are."

Tory had torn open the paper excitedly. Beautiful ivory hair clips rolled into her hand. She looked up at her father.

"What a lovely gift, Papa. Thank you! Look at the carving on them!" She stood and kissed his cheek.

Charles opened his gift and was surprised. He looked up, his eyes shining into Manning's. "This is something I've wanted for a long time. Thank you, Mr. Brighton. I've wanted to whittle and never thought to have a knife of my own. Thank you, again." He stroked the smooth ivory handle of the penknife.

Olivia had opened her gift. "Oh how lovely, Manning! Thank you!" It was an exquisite silk scarf nearly the color of her eyes. She wrapped the beautiful length of silk around her neck.

"Adeline helped me. We had a few days in Genoa before our ship sailed."

He looked at the children and decided not to wait until the tea arrived. "Charles, Henry, I am terribly sorry to be the bearer of horrible news. Your mother and I were on a steamer heading from the middle of Italy to Genoa. The boiler of the ship exploded. Your mother, I am very sorry to say, went down with the boat. I was knocked unconscious and didn't know anything. I'm so incredibly sorry."

There was stunned silence. Charles stared at Manning in disbelief. Henry, after digesting the news, picked up his horse collection and threw it at Manning.

"You killed her!" he screamed. "You killed her, and it's all your fault. She didn't want to go...you made her—"

Olivia grabbed Henry and covered his mouth gently but firmly with her hand. She pulled him toward the settee and sat him on her lap. He started to kick his legs, but she held him tightly and began to croon into his ear.

"I'm so sorry, darling, but it's no one's fault. Remember how your mother wrote about sightseeing and the lovely restaurants they ate in? She enjoyed everything that she did. You read the telegram yourself. It was an accident, and you can blame no one."

Henry stopped crying as he wriggled off Olivia's lap. "I hate you! I hate you, Mr. Brighton!" He ran from the room, nearly knocking into Frankie as she carried the tea tray into the parlor.

Manning, shocked by the boy's outburst, started after him, but Olivia took his arm and shook her head no. She turned and took Charles into her arms.

Adeline said, "Don't, Manning. Don't go after him just yet. He needs a little time to assimilate what's happened. It's traumatic, but I'm sure he'll come around once he can think it through."

"Charles, oh Charles, darling, I am so sorry," Olivia said. "Manning didn't want to say so, but your mother could have made it to safety. She chose to go after her jewels, and as Manning started to follow her, the steamer upended. Manning was knocked out. He too nearly drowned but was saved by an Englishman."

Charles' teeth began to chatter as he felt chills crawling up and down his spine. Frankie set the heavy tray down and poured a cup of tea, added two lumps of sugar, stirred it, and added some milk. She held it out to Olivia, who put it to the boy's lips.

"Swallow, Charles."

He took the cup with both hands and obediently took a swallow. The cup rattled against his teeth. "She's not dead. You may think so, but she's not. I feel it in my gut—she's not dead." He turned to stare at the detective.

CHAPTER XV

Thou art snared with the words of thy mouth,
thou art taken with the words of thy mouth.
Do this now, my son, and deliver thyself,
when thou art come into the hand of thy friend;
go, humble thyself, and make sure thy friend.

PROVERBS 6:2-3

GEORGE BAXTER WAS TAKEN ABACK. He stared at Charles.

"Manning can tell you the details, son, but supposedly there were no survivors. That being said, I've learned to trust my gut. You could be right, but I don't think so."

Manning looked at the boy, his eyes full of misery. "Charles, I looked around the freighter five times and couldn't find your mother. I talked to the captain. He said there were no other survivors. He sailed round and round where the steamer went down. He picked up numerous people, some dead. I'm sorry, son. She really is gone." He pulled the boy into his arms and hugged him. He sat back down and pulled the eleven-year-old onto his lap as if he were Tory, and kissed his cheek. He held the boy closely.

Charles, his face muffled in Manning's chest, said again, "I'm telling you, she's not dead."

Olivia had taken Charles' cup, set it down with a slight rattle, and plopped onto the settee.

George spoke. "Manning, we had a discussion of the situation on our way here from the docks. Addie and I feel Olivia should remain here for the time being, at least until things settle down. She'd be a stable influence, especially since she has been with the boys these last few weeks."

Manning looked over Charles' head at Olivia. "How do you feel about that? Can you continue giving up your social life a few more weeks?"

"Certainly. My social activities are not nearly as fun as these children. I have developed a relationship with them. In truth, I love them. I'd be more than happy to stay."

Charles, curled up and snuggled into Manning's chest, drifted off. His eyes closed sleepily.

Frankie tiptoed from the parlor and made her way slowly up the stairs to Henry's room. She prayed as she went. She pushed at his door, which wasn't latched, and silently went to the bed. Henry sobbed into his pillow, his little shoulders shaking in anguish.

"Poor wee man, you are…losing your mama that way. Poor little man you are because you don't know the comfort of Jesus nor have an understanding of the Holy One. He loves you more than anyone else ever could." Sitting on the side of the bed, she rubbed his back and as she did, she prayed for Henry in a low voice, but out loud.

"Oh Lord, we don't know why some things happen. We do know we can trust Thee to know what is best. I pray for little Henry. Help him to be comforted, to know people here love him. Help him, Almighty Father, to know Thee as his personal Savior. May he begin to comprehend the depth of Thy love for him. I intercede on his behalf, asking for Thy wondrous love to envelope him. Thank Thee, my Jesus. Amen."

Henry's sobs quieted under her loving ministrations. He fell asleep, his emotional trauma resulting in total exhaustion. Frankie covered him with a blanket and went back to the parlor to tell them Henry was asleep. She glanced over to see Charles also slept. She was glad to see Mr. Brighton holding the boy on his lap. She left the parlor to fetch more tea and coffee.

Tory, sitting quietly next to Olivia, spoke up when Frankie departed. "Papa, do you think Mabel *could* be alive? I mean, is there any chance of it?" Her eyes looked intently at her father.

"No, there's no way she could have survived. The Englishman, Mr. Grenly, told me the ship went down soon after he pulled me into a lifeboat. He said everyone who survived it was fortunate to be alive, as the steamer went down quickly. It sucked everything around it down too. Mabel was determined to get her jewels. No, she couldn't possibly be alive. I feel very sorry for the children. Mabel said she had no relatives. I don't know whether that is true or not. I'll have my lawyer look into it. I'd like to adopt the children if I am able."

"Who is your lawyer?" George asked.

"Elijah Humphries. He's a good man, very astute."

"Yes, I've never met him, but I have heard of him. He has a good reputation," George replied. He reached over and patted his wife's arm. "Well, my dear, I think it's time we went home. I need to fill out some paperwork and report to my chief all that has transpired." He spoke to Olivia. "I'm certainly glad you're able to stay on here for a bit more. The two boys need special attention, and then, of course, there's the daughter at boarding school. She will need to be notified and arrangements made for her to attend the funeral, or at least give her the option of attending." He arose and Adeline stood, as did Olivia and Tory, but Manning remained seated, still holding Charles.

"Please excuse me for remaining seated," he said, "but I thank you. I thank both of you for coming to my aid in so many ways. I'm in your debt and if ever you need anything, and it's within my power to help, believe me, I will."

"You are welcome, sir." George laid his hand on Manning's shoulder. "You know that Olivia, Adeline, and I will be praying for you."

"I will too, Papa," Tory said quietly. "I'll be praying, and Frankie too."

A cold rain beat steadily down, whipped around by a wind that cavorted, not able to decide which way it wanted to blow. Windows rattled and were streaked, the downpour splashing against the glass. Fires burning in the grates of every room gave warmth and warded off the damp chill. Lamps were lit to cheer the library, casting a soft glow where Tory and her father were gathered, both dressed somberly.

"Papa, I'm so glad you're safe. Maybe it's because Aunt Ollie, Frankie, and I prayed for you. Charles began praying for you too. He was very worried about you because he knows all about his mother. He has become a believer like me." She hugged her Papa around his middle, and he hugged her back.

"Thank you, sweetheart. I am thankful to be alive." *And thankful not to worry about Mabel anymore.* Guilt pressed heavily upon him like a leaded weight because he felt no remorse.

Tory wore the same brown dress she'd worn to the wedding. She was explaining to Manning that she possessed many articles of black clothing hanging in her clothespress, having recently come out of mourning for her mother. But she felt to wear black would be a sham because she didn't mourn Mabel.

Manning agreed and said that was fine.

He had cabled Madeline's school to explain the situation to the headmistress, asking her to explain to Madeline about her mother. Madeline opted to not come home for the funeral; her telegram expressed her regret. She'd miss too many classes for the time it would take to sail. Charles had said he understood. Neither he nor Maddie had been close to their mother. Maddie's telegram also expressed her gratefulness for the schooling Manning was providing her. She asked if she might go home with a school chum for Christmas, saying that she needed his permission first.

The Brightons always held a modest celebration, although much of Boston still harbored the Puritanical influence, and Christmas celebrations were frowned upon as being heathen. Manning had not yet responded to Maddie.

Olivia joined Tory and Manning in the library, and the three waited for Charles and Henry.

"Your hat is beautiful," Tory said. Having just returned from Europe, Manning could see that Olivia's toque was the epitome of high fashion, and around her neck was the scarf he had given her. It made her eyes sparkle even more than usual.

"Thank you. You look quite charming, yourself." She gave Tory a little hug. "I believe it's nearly time to leave."

Manning heard the clock chime and figured they had a half hour before they needed to be at the church.

"Victoria, please scoot on up and get the boys," he said.

It had been a week since Manning had returned, and today was Mabel's funeral. He still felt an overriding guilt that he'd loosened his grip. He was not sleeping properly. As well, he kept thinking of Charles' comments about Mabel still being alive. He would tamp the thoughts down as soon as they arose, but the notion that she could be alive had begun to affect his dreams. Mabel had no living relatives, so Manning didn't expect there would be anyone at the funeral besides the Baxters, and of course his lawyer, who was taking care of the arrangements.

The two boys entered the library, followed by Tory. Henry and Charles were dressed totally in black. Olivia had taken the boys, the day after Manning's return, into the city to a tailor. They wore black knickerbockers and hose as well as black shirts and vests.

Tory studied the two boys closely.

She secretly thought Charles looked quite dashing. Although his face was solemn, his demeanor was peaceful. Henry, on the other hand, was keyed to a high pitch, and although he was now speaking to Manning, he had not forgiven him for taking away his mother. The little group put on their coats; the two boys donned flat caps and Manning his top hat.

Ralph had the carriage hitched and waiting for the little procession. Running up the walk, he held an umbrella for Olivia and Tory. The wind danced around, splashing rain on Olivia's skirts, which were nearly the same color as Tory's dress. The trip to the church took little time and they had a few minutes to spare. They entered the grand edifice and sat in the Brighton pew where less than a year ago, Manning and Tory had sat mourning Laura.

Before being seated, Manning nodded to the Baxters and Elijah Humphries, his lawyer, and looked curiously at the woman seated behind Mr. Humphries.

143

Waiting for the service to begin, Manning thought about life, death, and what he believed. He realized he'd never contemplated death before. He'd come very close to kicking the bucket on that steamer. He'd always been quiet about his beliefs, but the truth of the matter was—he didn't have any. He sat in the quiet of the church in stunned silence and realized that an important part of living was missing in his life. The service began but he didn't listen, because in truth, nothing remarkable was said.

My daughter has more knowledge of spiritual things than I do. I need to develop something—what, I don't know. I do know I want something more than what I have. I've been so buried in grief over Laura. I knew she shouldn't have any more children. To lose her was the worst thing that ever happened to me. Now I have another worst— Mabel. I thought she was the answer to my sorrow. Now I feel no grief over her dying. What kind of man am I? He closed his eyes and contemplated the entire affair and his role in it.

The minister, not knowing Mabel, said a short eulogy, but before it was over, George had to leave.

A boy came in quietly with a short missive. George had been summoned, by his chief, to investigate a murder down on the east end. Adeline stayed, wanting to hear what the minister would say, but also because she wanted to support Manning. As she sat during a musical interlude, she prayed for the Brighton children, and especially Henry.

Olivia also sat praying. *Lord, help me to be of some help, especially to Manning and Henry. Manning needs You, Lord Jesus. I pray Your Holy Ghost will woo Manning to Your great self.*

The minister gave a perfunctory talk on the meaning of life, which seemed to bear no depth of reflection, nor did it enlighten the listeners in any way. With another song played by the organist, it was over.

Elijah Humphries exited his pew and walked forward, wanting to speak to Manning.

He was unusually short for a man and had the beginning of a paunch. His black hair was sparse except where it grew thickly around his ears. What was left hadn't yet grayed. His bright blue eyes looked with warmth into Brighton's eyes, conveying support and genuine goodwill toward his client.

"Good morning, Mr. Brighton."

"Good morning, Mr. Humphries. Thank you for being here." Manning drew Mr. Humphries forward and said, "Miss Olivia Anderson, this is my lawyer, Mr. Elijah Humphries. Mr. Humphries, Olivia Anderson, a good friend of mine, is acting temporarily as a nanny for my children, but she—"

"Normally keeps herself quite busy with charitable work." Mr. Humphries finished the sentence. "Mistress Anderson, it is with great pleasure that I make your acquaintance." His blue eyes looked with curiosity into her tawny ones and liked what they saw.

Olivia proffered her hand. "I am pleased to meet you. I don't believe I have had the pleasure of meeting you before, sir. May I ask how you know of me?"

"My wife is quite active in charitable work, and although she hasn't made your personal acquaintance, she is quite impressed with your selflessness and generosity of spirit." He smiled amiably.

"Charles, Henry, Tory, please meet my lawyer, Mr. Elijah Humphries. Mr. Humphries, my children."

"I'm not your child, Mr. Brighton." Henry spoke in a low, curt tone. "I'm Henry Vickers."

Manning was embarrassed by Henry's comment and looked at Elijah helplessly.

Mr. Humphries said, "Yes, yes you are young man. It's a pleasure to meet you, Master Henry Vickers." He held out his hand. "I am sorry about your mother. You must be quite grateful to have a benefactor such as Mr. Brighton to care for you. Being a lawyer, I know children who are left to the streets to fend for themselves, or they are put into the poorhouse to work." He turned and said pleasantly, "And you are Charles, a pleasure to meet you." As he shook the boy's hand he said, "I've heard you are an exceptional young man. And of course, you must be Mistress Victoria Lynn Brighton. I am pleased to make your acquaintance also." Tory made a sweet curtsey. Henry merely stared at the lawyer, as if thinking about what he had just said.

Manning looked gratefully at Elijah Humphries, who continued to talk. "Mr. Brighton, I have been looking for—"

"Excuse me." A woman pushed into the little group of people and continued. "I need to leave as I have an appointment elsewhere. My name is Mrs. James Hadley. I am sister of the late Bradley Burbank." She looked at Manning. "I read in *The Globe* about the steamer going down. It listed the Americans who died in the tragic accident. I need you to know, Mr. Brighton, that steamer did you a great favor. You are still alive. Had the steamer not gone down, I doubt you would be. Mrs. Vickers was a murderess!" She turned before anyone could make a reply and hurried out the great doors of the church.

CHAPTER XVI

Enter not into the path of the wicked,
and go not in the way of evil men.
For they eat the bread of wickedness,
and drink the wine of violence.

PROVERBS 4:14,17

"**WELL MY GOODNESS!**" Adeline had heard Mrs. Hadley's harangue and was clearly upset by it. "I don't think that was appropriate at a—"

"What did she mean by that?" Henry interrupted.

Olivia remonstrated. "Henry, it's not polite to interrupt—"

"I want to know what she meant!" He interrupted again, his voice rising to his old whiney pitch.

"Henry! I'll tell you what she meant!" Charles grabbed Henry by the shoulder and spun him around.

"No, Charles! Please, don't say anything!" Olivia turned to the older boy, who was obviously incensed by his younger brother's appalling behavior and beyond hearing. Manning was grateful Olivia seemed to know how to handle the children so well. He felt helpless to stop the unfolding drama.

"Tell me! I want to know what that woman meant!" Henry yelled, his voice echoing around the empty cathedral.

"What Mrs. Hadley meant," Charles replied in a low, clipped voice, "is that our mother killed our father. I saw her do it, and evidently she killed that woman's brother! Now, are you happy? You need to grow up, Henry, and not think the world revolves around you or your wants! Did you hear Mr. Humphries? We should be on our knees thanking the Almighty God that Papa Manning wants us! Would you rather go to the poorhouse? You certainly wouldn't have your precious violin there!"

Henry, the blood draining from his face, looked at Olivia, his countenance shocked beyond all measure. He crumpled to the stone floor in a dead faint.

"Oh my goodness!" Adeline was on her knees before Olivia could even react. She picked up the unconscious boy into her arms. Elijah Humphries stood next to her and helped her rise to her feet. She sat down on the nearest pew and stroked the young boy's brow, hoping he hadn't hit his head when he went down.

Olivia said, "I'll get some water." She hurried off in the direction of the minister, who was still standing at the podium, witnessing the drama from a distance.

Charles looked stricken with remorse. "I'm sorry. I seem to have no patience with Henry. He...he..."

Manning went to the boy and hugged him to himself. He was upset with the drama but liked the name Charles had given him. The two seemed to have a connection, a close bond between them since the first time Manning had stood up to Mabel, at dinner, the evening of the wedding.

"It's all right, son. You reacted honestly. Henry will be fine. It's simply that your mother doted on him. You know that better than I do. He misses it, that's all. He misses her dreadfully, I'm afraid." He hugged Charles to his side again.

"Oh, Charles." Tory had tears standing in her eyes. "That's why you had the dark circles under your eyes, isn't it? I'm so sorry for what happened to your father. What a horrible, horrible thing for you to see. Oh, I'm so sorry."

"It's all right. Aunt Ollie and I went to the police station, and I told the chief detective the whole story. After that, I didn't have any more nightmares. I didn't want to tell you because you would worry about Papa Manning, and it wouldn't have helped, except maybe to make you sick with worry."

Olivia returned with a wet cloth and laid it over Henry's brow.

Elijah said quietly in an aside to Manning, "I've looked extensively per your request. I can find no other living relatives for the Vickers children."

"I could have told you that," Charles said, overhearing the lawyer speak. "Our mother was an only child and her parents died when she was seventeen, unless she lied to us about that too." He continued. "Our father was one of three children, and they were orphans by the time he was ten. He had two brothers who died shortly after he married mother, so we don't have any relatives."

Henry began to come around. He moaned a little as he sat up.

He looked disoriented for a minute and as realization sunk in, he began to cry huge, wracking sobs as the truth of what his older brother said pierced his mind and heart. He knew it was true. He knew every word Charles said was true. He felt so empty, so alone.

Olivia said, "Oh, Henry, I love you and I'm so sorry about your father, about your mother. It's a lot for you to bear, but you are loved more than you know."

Charles was full of remorse. "Henry, I'm sorry I blurted out to you like that, but our mother was wicked, and I can hardly stomach you racketing on about her. I'm sorry I talked to you the way I did. I love you very much." He leaned over, taking Henry out of Adeline's arms. He sat rocking his younger brother back and forth as silent tears coursed down Henry's cheeks.

Manning took a deep breath and spoke quietly to Elijah Humphries. "Thank you for looking into all that for me. I should sit down with the boys and see if it would be all right with them for me to adopt. I need to get a cable off to Madeline and ask her too."

"You are certainly welcome," said Elijah Humphries. "I'll be on my way then. Oh, and Mr. Brighton, I'll be praying for you. Both my wife and I will be praying for you." He left, walking with echoing footfalls down the long aisle to the double doors.

Because there was no one attending the funeral besides the immediate family and the Baxters, no repast had been arranged. Manning offered to take the small group out for luncheon and everyone accepted—everyone being Adeline Baxter, Olivia, Charles, Victoria, and Henry, who was unusually quiet. The group went together to the French Hotel and Restaurant, a popular establishment. The French element of Boston could be seen dining there as the food was haute cuisine. The owner, a client of Manning's bank, always had special seating for Monsieur Brighton when he dined there.

The family, following Luis Lebeau, the owner, made their way to a large table.

When Olivia entered the restaurant, she looked around appreciatively. She'd heard about it but had never dined there. Looking over at another table as she walked by, she caught the glance of a woman she appreciated but didn't know. Madam Bouvier nodded to Olivia, a slight smile on her face. Olivia nodded back but saw the younger woman dined with her husband, and looked away. The Bouviers were dining with another couple. Olivia detested Armand Bouvier and wondered what had possessed the beautiful woman to marry him. Olivia had a close friend whose husband had been befriended by Monsieur Bouvier and then put out of business by him.

Manning saw Olivia's nod and looked over, but his lips tightened at sight of Monsieur Armand Bouvier.

Manning was aware that Bouvier was a lawyer. They moved in the same social circles, but Manning also knew the man was a cheat. Manning remembered Mabel saying she knew him quite well, but she never divulged how she knew him. Manning had several men who'd applied for lines of credit at his bank after Bouvier put them out of business. The man was unscrupulous, and Manning wondered how he could even sleep at night.

After seating them, Monsieur Luis Lebeau clapped his hands and a waiter appeared out of nowhere. A wonderful dining experience ensued.

Adeline said she had been to the restaurant several times with George and spoke highly of Luis Lebeau. "I saw an article in *The Globe* recently that Monsieur Lebeau has applied for a license and been approved to expand this restaurant. I don't think you could find more authentic cuisine in all of France. My George has a penchant for the food here."

Tory said, "Monsieur always gives me a special little treat at the end of the meal. You'll see what I mean." She nodded her head knowingly at both boys. "Henry, you do like to eat chocolate, don't you? I love it!"

Henry shook his head and saw her shocked face. "I'm jesting with you, Tory. Who doesn't like chocolate? I'll save room for it."

As the adults began to talk together, Charles asked quietly, "Are you all right, Henry? I'm sorry for belting out to you like that. I hope you know you can trust Papa Manning. I want him to love you. I already feel loved by him. He's a kind man and he cares about people."

"I don't want to talk about it right now. I need to think about everything." Henry spoke quietly but determinedly.

"Well," Tory said, "if you can't be with your own papa, you'll not find a better person to act as father for you. I am willing to share him. He's always wanted a passel of children, and I know he really likes boys."

There was a lull in the adult conversation, and Olivia happened to glance over at Madam Bouvier.

She was aghast to see her nearly in tears. Her face looked incredibly sad yet embarrassed at the same time. The other woman at the table was sobbing.

Suddenly, the man—not Armand Bouvier—stood, his chair scraping back loudly on the flagstone flooring. He clutched at his chest and went down like a ton of bricks, with nothing to break his fall. Armand never rose from his seat. He looked down, his lip curled in disdain at the man on the floor. The two women fell to their knees in an effort to help him. One of the waiters ran out of the restaurant for a doctor. Many of the other diners looked on with compassion and sympathy.

Manning rose and went over to help. He tried to make the man comfortable. Folding his frock coat into a pillow shape, he carefully placed it behind the suffering man's head.

Gasping for breath, the man's lips were turning blue, and anyone could see he was in an agony of pain. Nothing more could be done, so Manning, not wishing to intrude or stare, went back to his own table and sat down. He turned his chair toward the other table so if either woman called or signaled to him, he'd be able to see. The children at the Brighton table were silent, their eyes rounded in fear.

In a short time the waiter returned with a doctor. The woman was weeping copious tears as she and Madam Bouvier stood to give the doctor room. Madam Bouvier held the sobbing woman in her arms as the doctor shook his head sadly.

"He's gone, Evangeline. I'm so terribly sorry. He's gone." The woman looked at the doctor in stupefaction.

She turned to Armand and said, "Murderer!" The woman spoke in a low voice but because of the silence in the dining room, she may as well have yelled. She said it again in a vehement, accusatory tone. "Murderer!"

Adeline knew about Armand Bouvier and despised him. She watched the scene unfold in horror.

Armand, who had nonchalantly been cutting the end of his Havana cigar, stood up. He was not much taller than the deceased man's wife, and with lip still curled, replied sardonically, "Good day, madam." He slowly lit his cigar and when it caught, drew on it and blew smoke into her face. He nodded at his wife to accompany him. "Come, my dear," he said as he started for the door.

Liberty Bouvier grasped the other woman's hand tightly and said, "I'm so sorry, Madam Beaumont. Oh, I am so very sorry. Your husband was a good man." Tears stood out in her green eyes, and she followed her husband out the door.

Adeline went to the distraught woman as the doctor rose to his feet. He was giving directions, arranging for the body to be taken to the Beaumonts' residence. Two waiters quickly removed the dead man from the dining area to the back of the restaurant.

"Can I help you in any way?" Adeline spoke in a quiet tone to the sobbing, grief-stricken woman.

"No, no thank you. You've been kind. I must accompany my husband's body home."

The doctor spoke up. "No, Evangeline. You need to go with this woman. She'll see you home." He nodded his head gratefully to Adeline. "Thank you, ma'am; I appreciate your help. Madam Beaumont lives on Essex Street."

Adeline said, "I'll get a hansom for us, and we'll ride together to your home."

The poor woman took a shuddering breath and replied, "It won't be my home for much longer. That crook," she said, beginning to cry, "that crook, Armand Bouvier. I don't know how he did it, but he's ruined us. He took my husband's mercantile store right out from under him. He's responsible for my husband's death. I'm fortunate my parents can take care of us. They've a huge house on the Neponset River. I've seven children, poor fatherless bairns."

Manning walked over to the two women and said quietly, "I own Brighton Bank. If I can be of any assistance, please let me know. I know many individuals in this city, and if you have need of people to help you move, I can lend you a hand with that, also."

"Thank you. I have a good lawyer who told my husb—" She stopped speaking midsentence, her eyes filled, and her voice choked on the words.

"Manning, I will see her home. Thank you and rest assured, I'll be praying for you and for little Henry." Adeline took his hand and pressed it briefly. She hurried to her chair to retrieve her reticule and shawl and returned posthaste to Madam Beaumont's side. "Shall we?" She took the distressed woman's arm, and the two ladies went out the door of the famous restaurant.

CHAPTER XVII

I am the LORD, and there is none else,
There is no God beside me:
I girded thee though thou has not known me

ISAIAH 45:5

LIBERTY BOUVIER STARED STONILY out the window. She'd bitten the inside of her cheek to keep from crying in front of Armand. She could taste the blood. *Poor Madam Beaumont. Such a sweet woman and now a widow. Oh Lord, I pray for that woman. I lift her up to You. Father, wrap Your wondrous comforting arms around her. Help her as she tells her children what has happened. Give her wisdom that only comes from You. I pray the family knows You and the comfort You can bring to sorrowing hearts. Father, again, I lift Armand to You. May Your convicting Holy Ghost soften his heart and help him, dear Lord, to find You as his personal Savior. And Father, please help me to remain as You would wish. Help me not to become bitter over Armand and his evil ways. They are his, not mine. I ask this in Your precious, peerless name, the name that is above every other name, Jesus. Amen.*

155

Liberty Bouvier had been married to Armand for six long years. Married off to him at sixteen years of age, she'd been a bargaining chip to keep her greedy father out of debtors' prison. Her mother, saddened and ill, had died within a year of her marriage.

Liberty's father, Jacques Corlay, became Armand's business partner after the hasty marriage. The two concocted schemes to put business owners out of their companies and take over themselves. They managed to walk a thin line, and the police could not find enough evidence to arrest them.

Their carriage pulled up in front of the Bouvier manse. Armand hurriedly climbed down, taking long steps up the walk, not bothering to help Liberty out of the carriage. Jean-Paul Colbert, their driver, jumped down, umbrella in hand, and held out his other hand, which Liberty took gratefully. *"Merci beaucoup,* Jean-Paul." She made no excuses for Armand's lack of manners to Colbert; he was well-aware of them.

He smiled into Madam Bouvier's green eyes. *"Ce n'est rien,"* he said. It's nothing.

Liberty made her way up the walk and into the dark, depressing house that was her home. Armand had commissioned the interior done by a man Liberty was convinced must have lived in a mortuary. The interior colors of the manse were dark and heavy. Even her own rooms were cheerless.

She made her way slowly up the stairs, still thinking about poor Madam Beaumont. Annie, her personal maid, met her at the top of the steps. Her cheery countenance was a boon to Liberty, and together they went to Liberty's suite of rooms. Annie had become Liberty's best friend and confidante.

Armand controlled everything, and all her acquaintances were of his choosing. She was not allowed to entertain nor indulge herself in tea parties or any personal pursuits. On Tuesdays, because Armand was away from the house from early morning till night, Liberty volunteered her services to the Boston School for the Deaf. She'd learned to sign and felt fulfillment in helping out wherever she was needed. Armand had no knowledge she did this. He did know and approve that she regularly attended a small church on Rice Street. He felt, in some small way, that it gave him credibility to have a church-going wife.

Once Liberty reached her rooms, she had Annie help her disrobe. Although it was early afternoon, she donned a nightdress and crawled into bed. She was depressed and tried to fight it.

She lay there thinking about the article she'd read in *The Globe*. Mabel Vickers had drowned in the Mediterranean Sea. The woman had been, for a time, one of Armand's paramours. He'd even brought the Vickers woman into their home a time or two while she was still married to her poor husband. Libby knew he'd died. *Probably of a broken heart, finding out about his wife's perfidy. There's so much evil in this world.* She fell asleep, her heart full of sadness.

As the quiet group left the restaurant, lightening streaked the sky and thunder boomed. Besides the downpour, a storm had worked itself up, a real nor'easter, as the locals would say. Little rivers ran down both sides of the streets, the cobbles polished to a high shine by the driving rain.

Ralph scrambled down from his wet perch, umbrella in hand to cover the ladies' progress to the carriage. He held it over their heads and suddenly realized no one was talking. He wondered at their silence. It was a different group than the one who'd chattered together going into the restaurant. After seeing everyone inside the carriage, he climbed back to his thoroughly wet seat and drove the family home.

The rain beat an uneasy rhythm on the carriage top as wind dashed it sideways. Ralph, sitting on the hard seat, was soaked through and through. He'd be glad to get the horses into a dry stable and give them a good rubdown. Once that was accomplished, he planned to spend the rest of the day with a good book in front of a toasty little fire. He felt drenched and chilled to the bone.

Inside the carriage the silence was heavy.

Tory felt incredibly sorry for Madam Beaumont and prayed silently for her as the carriage wheels turned, rumbling on the wet cobbles. As she thought about it, she decided to pray for the beautiful woman,

Madam Bouvier. *Her husband is wicked…it seeps out of him. He reminds me of Mabel…evil. Poor Madam Bouvier. She has to live with him day in and day out.* Tory continued to think about what she'd just witnessed. *How horrible and ungodly to sit and not even care that a man is dying at your feet. Oh Father, I pray for the Beaumont family. I pray You would be close to them. Jesus, if there are any children, comfort them the way You comforted me when Mama died. Lord, I never thought about it before, but it would be better to have a dead husband than a wicked one.*

Manning sat thinking about Armand Bouvier.

Such a base man. I've seen him and his wife at various social functions. At least I did before Laura died. Mabel knew him quite well, I know that. What a cold fish the man is, to sit there when a man is dying and then simply walk out. I feel sorry for Bouvier's wife. She has to live with that wretched excuse for a man—such wickedness. I know, too, Madam Bouvier's father isn't any better. She is to be pitied.

Charles sat and prayed. His heart was full of remorse for his outburst toward Henry.

Lord, help me have patience with my little brother. He loved Mother very much. I am sorry for losing control and telling him she was a murderess. Protect this family, Lord. I just know Mother isn't dead. She'll be back to try to harm Mr. Brighton or Tory, or maybe even Aunt Olivia. I pray again, Father, please protect us. Protect all of us.

Henry was devastated.

He knew what his brother related to him in the cathedral was true. He'd enjoyed the attentions of his mother so much that he'd turned a blind eye to the things that were said and done to Charles and Madeline. *I remember her purposely spilling boiling tea on Madeline's hand. I saw the whole thing, and yet I didn't care about anything but having her cuddle me. I'm wicked not to care about others. I don't want to be like Mama. I don't want to, ever again, turn a blind eye to any evil around me. Am I like her? I believe I've had enough of temper tantrums. I don't want to be like Mama.*

Olivia sat praying for Madam Beaumont, Madam Bouvier, Manning, the boys, and Tory. There was a heavy feeling of unease in the carriage, and she prayed the Lord Almighty would dispel the gloom and bring joy to each heart. *Going to a funeral is bad enough, but over and above that, to witness the death of someone is a shock to the senses. Lord, help me be of comfort to the children.*

When the carriage arrived at the back of the Brighton house, the children clambered down and ran up the steps of the house quickly so as to be out of the rain. Manning started to get up, then sat back down heavily as Olivia looked at him, bewildered.

"What is it, Manning. What's the matter?"

"Nothing, Olivia," he replied, looking seriously into her eyes. "It's simply that I've been thinking, really thinking. I deal in money, but what you have given to this household cannot be measured in greenbacks. I want you to know I appreciate all you've done and I thank you from the bottom of my heart." His tone and eyes spoke from a sincere heart.

Olivia's face colored up, her peaches and cream complexion reddening under the compliment. "Oh, Manning, anyone else would have done the same."

"No, no, I don't believe they would. You have given the children stability and laughter. It's a priceless commodity in such times as these."

"Well," she said lightly as she tapped her forefinger against his chest, "I'll be sure to charge for my services, Mr. Brighton. I don't come cheaply!" She smiled, and he laughed up at her jest as he climbed out of the carriage.

Ralph stood holding the umbrella for Mistress Olivia. Manning, his hazel eyes warmed with laughter, turned to help Olivia down. She looked into his eyes and blushed again as he took her hand.

The rest of the week passed quickly. *The Globe* carried an article about the passing of Monsieur Beaumont. It was detailed and spoke of the many things the man had done to benefit the city of Boston.

Manning and Olivia both prepared to attend the funeral. Olivia wore a dark forest-green dress with a matching toque that sported a little veil. All was trimmed in black velvet.

Ralph drove them to the church, and Manning took Olivia's arm as they walked up to the huge doors. They had arrived a bit early and there was a press of people.

Manning was surprised to see Madam Bouvier there without her husband. She sat by herself, so Manning ushered Olivia into the same pew to sit with her.

Liberty smiled briefly at the woman who sat beside her. She was miserable.

She had a terrible row with Armand about her attending the funeral. Armand yelled and then spoke in a cold, hissing voice. She hadn't wanted to attend. She'd only met the Beaumonts at the restaurant, and to have her husband precipitate the attack that had caused Monsieur Beaumont's death... No, she hadn't wanted to come; she felt it was an affront. Armand insisted she attend. By her outward appearance, no one could know how shattered Liberty felt. She sat praying, sitting in the long pew by herself. She had no one to confide in besides Annie, her maid.

When Olivia and Manning entered the pew, she looked up in surprise, her green eyes swimming with tears even as she smiled. The color rose into her cheeks, knowing these two knew exactly what had occurred at the restaurant. She nodded slightly, shifting sideways to make more room as she reached into her reticule for a lace-trimmed handkerchief. Liberty dabbed at her eyes and looked forward, embarrassed beyond measure.

Liberty knew Mistress Anderson by reputation, but they'd never attended any of the same social functions.

She was surprised when Olivia leaned over and spoke gently in a whisper. "It's all right, Madam Bouvier. Please calm yourself. We know you had nothing to do with this. I want you to know, I've been praying for you."

Liberty looked at Olivia with wonder, her eyes filled with more tears that began to course down her cheeks, unchecked. Trying in vain to control herself, she sat, emotionally exhausted. The concern she saw in the other woman's eyes was like a gift.

"Thank you," she said unsteadily. "You are a breath of fresh air. I have felt so desolate about the passing of Monsieur Beaumont. I too am a Christian. I...I love the Lord with all my heart. It's His love for me that is my very sustenance. I'm s-so sorry for what happened. I had no idea my husband planned to tell Monsieur Beaumont that he had taken his business away from him." She took a deep shuddering breath as she continued to whisper. "I've not been able to communicate with Madam Beaumont. Will she be all right? Is there someplace she and the children can go?"

Olivia answered and gave Liberty's arm a gentle squeeze to reassure her. "Yes, Madam Beaumont has parents with a large estate on the Neponset River. They will be all right. It must have been difficult for her to tell the children. But, *you* need to know, it's not your fault, and I feel so impressed to tell you that I'm praying for you. In truth, I pray for you every day."

Liberty looked fully into the woman eyes, a bit startled by their beautiful tawny color, but more, the love of Jesus emanating from them. She said gratefully, "Thank you. If I didn't know Jesus as Savior, I don't know what I'd do. I appreciate your prayers. Your saying that is an encouragement to my heart from the Almighty, and I really do need it. Again, I thank you."

Olivia replied, "You are very welcome."

The service began, the organ's pipes soaring their beautiful music into the walls of the cathedral. The pews were packed with people who had cared about Monsieur Beaumont.

Manning listened carefully to what the minister had to say.

He spoke of the love of Christ and how each human being needs a personal relationship with Jesus Christ. He told the story of the prodigal son and how Jesus is always waiting with arms open wide to forgive us of our past and make us a new creation. Manning didn't understand all of it, but he stored the information in his heart where he would be able to ruminate on it later. He thought the message intelligent and not the garble of nothingness that he'd heard at Mabel's funeral.

The minister continued with his message. "Monsieur Girard Beaumont lived a life that testified to the love of God. His generosity to the poor and the donation of his time and talents to help others is one of the ways he showed the love of Jesus to others. He was a believer in

Christ and it showed in all he did. Monsieur Girard Beaumont lived his beliefs and once told me that he wanted nothing to deter him from pleasing the Lord. He said, and I quote, 'I want to be like the great revivalist Jonathan Edwards, who used to pray, "Oh God, stamp eternity on my eyeballs."' Well, my friends, Monsieur Beaumont is now in eternity with the Lord Jesus Himself. May God rest his soul."

He continued with his eulogy, extolling the life of Girard Morel Beaumont.

CHAPTER XVIII

*A word fitly spoken is like apples of gold
in pictures of silver*

PROVERBS 25:11

MANNING RETURNED TO WORK. He was glad for the mound of paperwork he must wade through as it took his mind off the events of the past few weeks. He threw himself wholeheartedly into the workings of his bank, determined to help more people who were ruined by Armand Bouvier and his father-in-law, Jacques Corlay. He had one of his clerks check on Madam Beaumont and arranged her move to her parents' house.

The days seemed to speed by, and Olivia decided she'd better begin to make plans for Thanksgiving.

The holiday had been observed since November of 1863. She thought about the proclamation issued by Abraham Lincoln, who was then president. He had proclaimed it a day to give "Thanksgiving and Praise to our beneficent Father who dwelleth in the Heavens." Olivia always thrilled to the many things President Lincoln had said and the way he said them. *Such a godly man*, she thought. Now Ulysses Grant was president and serving his second term. Olivia didn't know what to think of this president. More

163

than 110 people had been arrested for being involved in the infamous Whiskey Ring, and one of those arrested was a private secretary to the president. More than three million dollars had been recovered in tax revenues that had been diverted to government agents, whiskey distillers, politicians, and whiskey distributors. *It is a disgrace that so many men have abused their elected office. What is this world coming to*, she wondered disgustedly, *when man can lay aside his convictions and take bribes and live for dishonest gain?* She shook her head as she made her way to the kitchen to talk to Frankie and Cookie.

"Good morning, Cookie. How are you today?"

"Fine. I'm fine and fit as a fiddle, Miss Olivia."

Frankie came in through the swinging doors that led to the back entry and hall for the back stairs.

"Oh, there you are, Miss Olivia. I had a question for you. Should I lay Tory's locket out on the chiffonier? I think Mr. Manning has forgotten about it, and it does need repairing."

Olivia thought for a few moments before answering. "You know, Frankie, I think that would be fine. It has probably slipped his mind, and he knows you go through his socks periodically. Certainly, lay it out for him to see. He's not going to be able to have the locket itself repaired. The chain perhaps, but the locket will have to be custom made. It's beyond repair." She shook her head a bit ruefully. "I'm thankful the daguerreotypes weren't damaged." She felt a little down in the dumps and decided that after talking with Cookie and Frankie about Thanksgiving dinner preparations, she would see if Ralph would go with her for a ride on the beach. Perhaps it would clear her head. She knew part of the problem was Henry. He was too quiet, and she didn't quite know what to make of it. As she discussed a festive meal with the other two women, she wondered if she should leave it only a family affair or invite a few guests to celebrate with them.

Henry had been doing some serious thinking for a seven-year-old boy. He thought and thought about what Charles had told him about their mother. He began to think about the way his mother had treated Maddie and Charles. *I know I would have hated her. I would have hated everything about her, but Charles doesn't seem to hate her. He just didn't want to be around her. Too scared, I'll bet. I wonder if I am like her. It frightens me to think I could be. She really was wicked. The things she did to Charles and Maddie were very wicked.* The young boy spent a considerable amount of time in his room thinking. Or after school he could be seen, chin in his hand, sitting in the parlor or the library, if it was vacant. Henry thought and thought.

He hadn't played his violin since he found out his mother was dead. He had honored her by giving up what he enjoyed best in the whole world. But now, the more he thought about it, the more he realized his mother didn't deserve his loyalty. She had not been a good woman. She'd been mean and did horrible little things to Maddie and Charles.

If she had really killed his papa, and he had no doubt Charles told him the truth, his mother could have been hung. *No wonder Papa Manning had been going to put her into a hospital. Maybe it is better that she's dead.* The young boy went to his room and gently closed the door. Tightening his bow and stroking it with resin, he picked up his violin and began to play, pouring his little heart into his music.

The Brighton household teemed with excitement. Guests had been invited for Thanksgiving dinner. Sending out beautifully scripted invitations, Olivia, with Manning's permission, had invited the Blacks, the Leonards, and the Bouviers for dinner. Olivia was quite gifted in calligraphy, and the invitations were beautiful. The Blacks and the Leonards had children, but the Bouviers did not. Responses were received from the first two in a speedy manner, but the latter had not responded and Olivia wondered at it. *I'd like to know Madam Bouvier better and be some comfort to her, but it's likely her husband controls all her dealings.*

Frankie answered the door, as a young man had come to deliver a note from Madam Bouvier. The missive was sealed with a purple wax and Olivia broke it open.

My dear Mr. Brighton and Mistress Olivia Anderson,

It is with sincere regret I must decline your generous invitation of partaking in a celebration of Thanksgiving repast with your esteemed persons.

Circumstances prevent us from attending, but we are honoured you would think of us in such a worthy manner.

Kind Regards,
Armand and Liberty Bouvier
Monday, November 22, 1875

"Drat that man!" Olivia exclaimed, obviously startling Frankie, who turned sharply to face her.

"The Bouviers will not be attending our dinner, and I have no doubt it is because that Monsieur Bouvier controls everything his wife does. He's simply not civilized. I don't suppose the man has a genial bone in his body! I had hoped to establish a friendship with Madam Bouvier, who is quite young—early twenties, I should think. Her husband is a veritable beast. Believe me, he's evil. I know that he is."

"Well, it's a shame they can't come. You are a balm to one's soul, that you are, and no mistake!"

Olivia looked up in surprise. "Why thank you, Frankie. I appreciate that." She looked at the housekeeper with affection in her eyes. "We are sisters, you know."

"Yes, yes we are, and a joy that is too!" Frankie replied with a twinkle in her own eyes. "Well, my dear, I best be getting some chores done but mind you, I do understand. I will begin to pray for Madam Bouvier."

"Thank you, Frankie. I appreciate that; she would be too, if she knew of it. She needs it, that's certain."

Liberty had been excited about the prospect of spending Thanksgiving Day with people other than her husband's acquaintances. It wasn't that she was a snob. It was simply that as a general rule, his friends were social climbers. Most were people wanting to be recognized as having the best of everything. It was of utmost importance to put up a good front. Armand himself was a prime example. He hosted lavish parties. That he could afford it, Liberty had no doubt. Armand and her father, Jacques Corlay, were business partners. Although she prayed daily for their souls, Liberty knew neither man had an honest bone in his body, and they were wreaking havoc among businessmen who were enticed into taking out loans from them. They thought she didn't know anything, but she knew enough. She knew they kept a close ear to the ground. When the businessman had spent the money, they had a banker who was also a forger draw up fake contracts and call the loan in long before it was due. Thus, these men were losing their companies to a couple of scoundrels.

Liberty spent a majority of her time either in her suite of rooms on the second floor or in her sitting room on the main floor. She was an avid reader and could embroider, do tapestry, and tat lace as well as anyone, but her most enjoyable pursuit was to ride. Her horse Peanut had died a couple years back, and she had a new horse that was a joy to her. He was a gelding named Breeze because he could run like the wind. She was sorry for the inclement weather, as it kept her indoors.

Libby was in her sitting room thinking about Manning Brighton. *What could have possessed the poor man to marry Mabel Vickers? He seemed so chivalrous, putting his frock coat under Monsieur Beaumont's head. I suppose some men only look at the exterior, and she was well–put together. Still, was he happy with her? I know Armand introduced her to Bradley Burbank because she had become a noose around his neck. He doesn't like his women to cling to him. Oh Lord, I pray from the bottom of my heart that Armand would turn to You. He needs You and to know Your wondrous love. And Father, please help me. I feel so smothered by this house, and I know neither my father nor my husband love me. I thank You for Your wondrous love. May it flow through me to others.*

Thanksgiving was wonderful at the Brightons. The day dawned crisp and cool. White, fluffy clouds scampered across the heavens at a dizzying rate. A fresh wind blew, reminding kith and kin that winter was on its way. It was a grand, fair morning and the three children, with Ralph's help, saddled up to go for a ride on the beach. Olivia strolled into the stables, a beautiful suntan-yellow riding outfit gracing her small frame. Tory thought she looked quite smart and eyed her appreciatively.

"What a beautiful riding outfit, Aunt Ollie. I love the velvet trim. Brown looks good with yellow, doesn't it? Is it new?"

"No, not new, but thank you for your compliment. When I collected Lucy, I gathered up quite a few clothes I'd left at my house. I am so glad Lucy is now ensconced here. I missed her helping me dress."

"Are you going riding with us?" Henry had immediately gone over to Olivia and hugged her, knowing she would give him a big hug back. He smiled up at her, a gap-toothed smile.

Smiling down at him, she didn't answer but posed a question of her own. "Did the tooth fairy come last night?"

"Oh! I forgot to look!" He dropped his reins and ran out of the stable yelling "Don't leave without me. I'll be right back!"

Ralph laughed. "Do ye ken that custom has been around for a mighty long time? I remember as a laddie meself, a getting a pence or two for me tooth. Used to be, in th' olden days, folks would go a burying the tooth thinkin' it helped the next tooth ta' be a growing in. It," he said and nodded at Tory and Charles, "it also kept th' witches from gettin' a holt of it and be castin' spells on the child."

"Oh, Ralph! Don't scare the children with your stories!"

"I'm not scared." Charles spoke up.

"Me neither," Tory said, "but I am ready to go riding!"

Henry came back with Manning in tow. "Look what I found! Oh, look what I found!" He held out his hand for all to see, and there in his palm was a shiny new gold dollar.

"Aw, that's great, Henry! You have expensive teeth! The tooth fairy must love your music!" Charles patted him on the back, and Henry grinned.

"Well, it sure hurt coming out. I don't think it was quite ready. I tied a string to it and the other end to the door knob. I kept waiting and waiting for someone to come through the door. Finally, Frankie opened it and pulled my tooth right out!"

Everyone laughed.

Manning joined the group just as Henry had started his story.

He looked at Olivia with pleasure and asked, "Mind if I join you all for a ride?"

"Oh, Papa, how fun. A Thanksgiving ride with all of us. Ralph, you need to saddle up and come too!"

Ralph, who had been busy getting Olivia's horse, Sandoval, ready, smiled his thanks to Tory.

"Not today, wee one. I be a getting ready for guests ta' be a comin' ta' your grand party taday. I'll come wi' ye another time."

Manning saddled up Midnight and soon everyone was ready. Henry led the way down to the beach. This was Manning's first ride out with the boys, and he was amazed at what Ralph had been able to teach them in such a short time.

"You boys ride as if you were born in a saddle! I'm impressed!" He looked the two horses over and was glad he'd had Ralph pick them out. They were fine specimens of horseflesh.

Tory turned her horse and so did the other two children. Manning and Olivia started out in the opposite direction.

With a flick of Olivia's whip, her horse was off and flying down the sand. Midnight began to stretch out his legs. Manning held the big black in check, not wanting to leave Olivia behind, eating his sand. The two sped down the beach neck and neck, Midnight wanting to go full out. When they reached the rocky outcrop, they pulled up and Olivia laughed over at Manning, her cheeks reddened by the crisp air.

"Ralph had no such scruples. He's left me, many a time, letting your horses go full tilt." Her eyes gleamed with pleasure at the day and at her companion. "I'd love to ride astride as you men. It takes a lot more effort to ride sidesaddle than ever it did when I was allowed to ride astride."

"Well, why don't you?"

"It simply isn't done, Manning. You know that as well as I."

"Riding with a leg hitched up and both of them dangling on the same side of the horse seems an unnatural posture to me. I certainly wouldn't care about the conventions. After all, you have no man to dictate to you. Be eccentric and do as you please!" He smiled widely at her, wondering to himself how he'd ever thought her plain. He stared, taking her measure.

Bright, tawny eyes looked warmly back at him. Her mouth, lips full, was too wide but laughed and smiled often. Her demeanor was sweet, and Manning knew it wasn't faked but her true nature. Gleaming black hair shone from under the small riding toque perched on her head. His heart melted as he stared.

Olivia felt her cheeks redden under his intent gaze.

CHAPTER XIX

*In the lips of him that hath understanding
wisdom is found: but a rod is for the back
of him that is void of understanding.*

PROVERBS 10:13

"**WELL, IT LOOKS LIKE** the children will join us." Olivia glanced down the beach to break away from the warmth that surged up within her at his continued perusal. "I am so pleased with Henry." She spoke lightly. "He seems to have finally come to grips with his loss and has settled down. Have you noticed?"

"Yes, I have. Last night he called me Papa Manning for the first time. I am glad he seems to be more content. Perhaps the blowup of Charles telling him about his mother was a good thing. I know he's not wholly content, but most of his behavior is innocuous."

"Yes, and I agree with you. Sometimes, instead of beating around the bush, we need to be direct and honest. I suppose I worry too much about hurting one's feelings, but to allow someone to continue to behave poorly is empowering them to continue that behavior."

Manning merely nodded his agreement as the children rode up to join them.

Olivia laughed. "Your father thinks I should ride astride instead of sidesaddle. What do you think, Tory?"

"I'm never going to ride sidesaddle. It's such a horrible way to ride a horse. If I have to—why, I believe I'll move west! I've read that the women there don't ride sidesaddle, at least most of them don't."

"Why did women ever start riding sidesaddle?" Charles asked.

"I don't believe anyone knows," replied Manning. "Have you ever seen an antique Greek vase depicting a woman riding sidesaddle? I have, and riding that way has been around for a long, long time, but a few of the greats have rejected it. Almost a hundred years ago, Catherine the Great of Russia had a picture painted of her riding astride wearing a man's military uniform. Even though conventions deem it appropriate to ride sidesaddle, there are good reasons to ride astride instead."

The group rode back to the Brighton stables, glad for the ride and the camaraderie they were enjoying.

Henry, thinking about it later, decided his life had never been better.

The dinner party went without a hitch. The turkey was moist and done to perfection. Cookie had a special recipe for a wonderful stuffing. The conversation sparkled and was sprinkled with much laughter.

Olivia asked all at the table to name something they were thankful for the past year, and they shared their stories.

The Black and Leonard children were well-behaved. After the meal, they trooped off to Tory's sitting room and played Parcheesi.

Manning decided he'd better send a cable to Madeline. The Christmas season was fast approaching, and he hadn't responded to her telegram asking if she could spend the holiday with a friend. He sat in the library at his huge desk and leaned back in an oaken desk chair. He thought about the past weeks and knew he hadn't been this happy since Laura died.

Olivia has brought not only stability to the children, but she is like a breath of fresh air in this house. Not having children of her own, where does this wealth of wisdom in dealing with them come? She's brought laughter and a presence of wholesomeness and—and what? What are you thinking, Manning Brighton? You're attracted to her, are you not? He tamped the feeling down, not trusting his discernment to be quite so accurate as he'd once thought. *I feel so guilty being glad in my heart the problem of Mabel has been solved so conveniently, but it's what I think, isn't it? To be shackled with a crazy woman who murdered her own husband and one of the board members of my bank would have been a bleak way to live out my life. I feel so guilty, weighed down by it. It would be catastrophic if Mabel survived the steamer, but there is no possible way she could have if she went to her cabin to get her jewels. Oh, I feel so guilty for the relief. I feel so very guilty but glad nonetheless.*

He strode to the kitchen. "Cookie, I have an appointment with my lawyer early this afternoon, so I'd like to have an early luncheon, please."

"Certainly, Mr. Brighton." She nodded her head, not missing a beat in her chopping of potatoes. "You want the family to eat with you or to wait for their usual time?"

"Oh, I'd prefer them to eat with me if they are available. I thought the children were in school."

"No, there's some sort of special program, and they have the entire day as a holiday." Cookie nodded her head.

Manning trusted her. She knew just about everything that went on in the Brighton household.

"Mistress Olivia—she took them for an outing this morning. I 'spect they all thought you'd be a going to the bank today."

"No, not today. I needed to get caught up on some correspondence, and then I have the appointment with Mr. Humphries. I have a couple errands I've set for myself, so I'll be away the rest of the afternoon."

"Well, luncheon will be ready in half an hour. I do believe Miss Olivia'll be back with the children so's they can join you."

"Thank you, Cookie. I have a few things left I need to do." Going back through the dining room, he heard the children come noisily into the kitchen from the back door. Hearing Olivia's cheerful voice, he stopped to listen but couldn't make out what she said. Laughter rang out from everyone in the kitchen. *It's not just me*, he thought. *She makes everyone who is around her cheerful.*

Manning entered the front door of the modest office building Elijah Humphries shared with his partners. These lawyers held a reputation of integrity and genuine care for their clients. Mr. Humphries' office was located on the second floor.

Manning approached the front desk to tell them he was there for his appointment. A young clerk ushered him up the wide stairs and down the hall to a heavy door with Mr. Humphries' name painted on the door's glass window.

Tapping lightly, he opened the door and ushered Manning in. "Mr. Brighton to see you, sir." He quietly closed the door behind him. Elijah Humphries rose from his desk with a welcoming smile. He shook Manning's hand, greeting him with warm cordiality.

"Good afternoon, Mr. Brighton. I'm glad you could make it. Please," he said as he gestured to one of the heavy leather chairs that faced his desk, "be seated."

"Good afternoon, Mr. Humphries. I received your missive. I'd like to thank you for setting up this appointment. As you well know, the children have no living relative, and I don't wish to merely be their guardian. I want to adopt them."

"Yes, yes, I know that is your intent. As far as I can ascertain, you are correct, there are no other living relatives." He walked back around the desk and sat in a comfortable oak office chair. He continued. "Neither Mr. Horace Vickers nor Mabel May Weldon Vickers had any living siblings, although Mr. Vickers had two brothers who died shortly after his marriage to Mabel Weldon. Strange that his brothers died within months of each other. Neither was married, although the younger one was affianced at the time of his death. The coroner ruled it heart failure."

"Yes, I remember Charles saying his father had two brothers who died."

"Yes, yes, he did. It was a modest estate the parents left the Vickers boys, but it all went to Horace once his brothers died. Shame. I knew the younger one—such a nice young man."

Manning spoke frankly to Mr. Humphries. "I'm going to share something with you that I don't wish to go any further." His eyes bored seriously into Elijah's. "Mabel may be deceased, and I know it goes against the grain to speak ill of the dead, but she murdered her husband, and it is believed she murdered one of my board members, Bradley Burbank, as well."

Elijah Humphries, the shock visible on his face, was stunned. "I had no idea. Horace Vickers, murdered! He was a good man. Very quiet, but he had such an air of peaceful patience about him. I knew him personally, you understand. He adored his children. I never had any direct dealings with his wife. My, oh my. What a horrible circumstance."

"Yes, it was a tragedy, and I cannot begin to tell you how horrific the trip to Europe was, with Inspector George Baxter giving me a heads up just before we left port. I'm sorry I ever met the woman. The Inspector had told me that although they were quite certain Mabel was a murderess, nothing they knew could convict her in a court of law. There was no evidence. Turns out, Charles saw the whole thing, poor boy. He was petrified his mother would find out he knew and kill him too. He loved his father deeply. It's been a heavy burden on the boy. He was having nightmares, night after night, and began to lose weight. He finally told Olivia all about it. She took him to see Chief Inspector Christopher Belden. To be able to share that horror with a person who is an authority helped the boy mightily. He is sleeping better than he has for quite some time, poor tyke. I can't imagine the horrible nightmares he must have had."

"And no wonder! My, it is always a shock when one hears such a story. I don't know where you are spiritually, Mr. Brighton, but I don't know what I'd do if I had to carry the burden of knowledge of such things by myself. I am thankful I can lay things at the feet of Jesus and know He will take the burden, instead of me carrying things I was never meant to carry."

Manning stared at the lawyer for a full minute. He had no such balm for his soul. He yearned for more than what this life could offer him. With Laura alive, he'd felt no need of anything outside himself. He had been content with the way his life played out. Now things were different.

He was tired of carrying the load of life by himself. He dropped his eyes, sure his lawyer, with his shrewd blue gaze, could see into his very soul.

He didn't respond to Elijah's comment but instead said, "Well, do you have the paperwork ready for the adoption?"

"Yes, yes, I do. I understand you wish to bequeath to each child the same amount of monies as Victoria, that you want your estate divided equally to all four children, except the house and all its environs will go solely to Victoria. Is that your desire?"

"Yes, absolutely."

"Well then, I believe these to be drawn up correctly, and it is simply a matter of you signing these papers. I've drawn them up so as the house and grounds and a hefty sum will go to Victoria, as you requested, and an equal amount monetarily to go to the other three children. You are a very generous man, Mr. Brighton. It's not many men who would give to someone else's offspring an amount equal to their own child. Frankly, I only know of one."

"And who would that be?"

"Why, the Almighty God Himself. He gave all of us the benefit of being joint heirs with Jesus Christ, His only Son. Yes, it says so in the Good Book—Romans, Chapter Eight." He smiled pleasantly at Manning, who wondered if Elijah could discern the misery he carried in his own soul. He knew Elijah to be astute. It was one reason he was his lawyer. Manning was riddled with guilt and felt Elijah knew it but not its cause.

Manning didn't care to share with this man just yet, but he reckoned when the time was right, he would be coming to this man to talk about spiritual matters. Elijah Humphries had an impeccable record of integrity and an unsullied reputation in all of Boston. *Yes*, he thought, *today is not the day, but I need to make a commitment to Jesus Christ, and soon. And I want this man to show me the way.*

The two men sat and chatted about the adoption and what it would mean for the Brighton children. When Manning had cabled Madeline about her mother's death and funeral, he had asked her to think over being adopted by him. She, having made known her wishes about the funeral, had responded in the affirmative about the adoption.

Manning signed the necessary documents. They had been drawn up in duplicate form. There was one for Elijah Humphries to keep in his office on file and one for Manning to keep in his safe at the bank.

Leaving the law offices, Manning went to the train station and sent off a telegram to Madeline. It stated that he was now considered her adoptive father and as such, certainly she had permission to go with the girl to England for Christmas. He also let her know she would be welcome to come to Boston any time she'd like to visit. He sent a similar telegram to the headmistress of the boarding school and wired funds to Madeline's account.

He had a few other things he needed to do. He stopped by the jewelers, having paid a hefty sum to procure Victoria's locket in an exact replica of the one Laura had given her only a year ago. It startled him to realize it was nearly Tory's birthday. Laura had been the one to remind him of such things—birthdays, anniversaries, and so forth.

I wonder when Madeline's birthday is, or the two boys, for that matter. I need to ask Charles. I don't believe I've ever written myself reminder notes before, but I think I'd better start. I suppose I could look on these adoption papers to find those dates. It would then be a surprise to Charles that I know his birthday. I sure love that boy as if he were my very own.

Manning looked around the shop at the beautiful jewelry and thought he should buy something else for Tory's birthday.

He heard the tinkle of the bell over the door announcing another customer and turned to see George Baxter enter the shop.

"Good afternoon, Manning. Nice to see you. I happened to be passing by and saw you in here. Thought I'd say hello to you."

The two men shook hands warmly and Manning replied, "Nice to see you too. I thought of you and your lovely wife this very day and wondered if the two of you are tied up for Christmas. We would be honored if you would come join our little family for dinner. We're having a Christmas goose." He said it almost as if it were a bribe.

"That is, indeed, a most welcome suggestion. Adeline and I were mulling over what we should do for the day. Unless she's made other arrangements, I'll gladly accept for both of us."

George smiled with pleasure at Manning, happy the decision of what to do for the special day had been taken out of his hands. Adeline enjoyed Olivia Anderson, and it would be something for her to look forward to.

Manning turned back to the case full of beautiful pieces of jewelry and asked George what he thought he should get for Victoria's birthday.

The proprietor, hovering hopefully, didn't say a word, knowing this customer liked to make up his own mind.

"She'll be twelve on the twelfth of December."

"Well," George said, "how about a locket?"

"I just had a replica made of the one Mabel destroyed. Laura bought that for Tory last year just before she became so ill. It's in my pocket."

"Look at that, right down there in the corner." George pointed. "It's a charm bracelet, and you could add charms for different occasions. I'd get her that. Or perhaps instead of a bauble, you could get her a new saddle."

"Now that is a good suggestion! Think I'll save that one for Christmas." He grinned at George and added, "Perhaps you need to get something for Adeline. There's nothing so endearing to a woman as a gemstone and telling your special lady her own eyes outmatch the shine of it."

His heart constricted in guilt as he remembered the sapphires he'd bought Mabel and telling her just that same thing. He turned abruptly back to the glass case, and swallowing down his guilt, he said to the shopkeeper, "I'll take the little gold charm bracelet and would like to look at the charms there in the box."

George, his mind diverted by what Manning said, stared into the case to see if there was anything his wife would like. He missed the fact that his friend's hand shook a bit as he lifted the box to select a couple of the charms for Tory.

Manning was riddled with guilt.

CHAPTER XX

These six things doth the LORD hate:
yea, seven are an abomination unto him:
An heart that deviseth wicked imaginations,
feet that be swift in running to mischief

PROVERBS 6:16, 18

MABEL FELT MUCH BETTER. It seemed as if she'd been at this monastery for months. She had lost all track of time. She now ate at the communal table with all the inhabitants of the abbey, and it galled her to think that after having been married to Manning, she was now reduced to this. There was little conversation, and it suited her because she didn't understand a word being said anyway.

The back of her head had been shaved to clean the wound, and she wondered how badly it looked. Even after all this time, it still oozed slightly. The headaches were beginning to subside but her temper had not. She felt as if she could scream.

After the main meal, which was at lunch time, she had taken to wandering into areas she'd believed were off-limits, but she didn't care. She entered a room that was quite austere but empty of people. Stained-glass windows brought a feeling of peace to the room, which Mabel did not feel. There was a large desk, and behind it from floor to ceiling were shelves lined with books. Two walls held cupboards instead of shelves, and a couple of these had locks on them. There was a leather padded bench against the wall with a blanket and pillow on it. A half-dozen hard-backed chairs and a calendar and map, both pinned to the wall, completed the sparse accoutrements.

Mabel glanced at the map but was drawn to the calendar. The days had been marked off with black ink and she realized it was mid-December. Mabel began to study the old map. It was in Latin and took her a while to figure it out. Finally, she found Italy. She studied the old map carefully and thought she must be in Santa Marinella. It was the only thing that jutted into the sea, unless she was on Elba. If she was correct about being in Santa Marinella, by land she was only a few hours north of Rome. As she thought about it, she figured it was most likely the case. They'd only been on the water for about an hour when the boiler exploded.

I feel so helpless. I hate this feeling of not being in control. I have no one to talk to, no way to get out of here—nothing. I don't even really know where I am. Well, I'll find a way. I shall get back to Manning. It's all his fault I'm here. Mabel's thoughts began to eat at her like a cancer. *Yes, I'll get back to him!* She suddenly had a horrible thought. *What if he died on the steamer? What if Manning didn't make it? Oh, I must find a way to get to America and get my Henry back.*

The door opened. Startled, Mabel saw the priest and realized she must be standing in his private office. She turned eyes on him that glittered and wondered how he could not sense her mood.

Smiling pleasantly, he gestured for her to be seated, but Mabel brushed past him and went back to her little room. *I may as well be in prison.* Wanting to upend the little table with the water ewer, she restrained herself. *I must make plans. I must get out of here. This place has to have to have money somewhere to keep it operating. I'll find it and I'll get out of here.*

Madeline received a long telegram from Manning Brighton. She sat at her desk in her dorm room and read it over a second time. It granted her permission to go with her friend Claire to England for Christmas. Mr. Brighton had communicated the information to the headmistress. Glad that Mr. Brighton had given his permission, she planned to stay with Claire Lambert over the holidays. She'd been invited, but the headmistress had said she must have parental permission before she could go, or she would have to stay at the school over Christmas.

That Mr. Brighton wanted to adopt her was very comforting. She thought that since her mother was dead, perhaps he wouldn't want to be shackled with her children. Madeline had been through a few weeks of nearly biting her nails wondering what would happen. She was old enough to understand the ramifications if his support was to be withdrawn. She and her two brothers would be put either into the orphanage or into the Boston poorhouse on Charles Street. Madeline knew where it was because Mabel had threatened several times to put her in there. One time she'd hired a hansom cab and taken Madeline to the front of the poorhouse. Maddie had been paralyzed with fear, her whole body shaking. Her mother had simply laughed and told her she'd better behave and do as she was told, or that would be her fate. Sitting in her dorm and pondering, she actually felt a shudder go through her body. *I'm glad I never have to see her again!*

Christmas had been formally declared a United States Federal Holiday just five short years earlier by President Ulysses S. Grant. This year, Louis Prang introduced the Christmas card to Americans, and Victoria had been saving her coins to buy one for each member of her family. At school, the teacher had told the students that many Bostonians frowned upon celebrating Christmas. Tory decided they were just old-fashioned. She was a Christian and didn't see anything wrong with celebrating the birth of Christ, even if He had, in all probability, never been born in December, like Frankie told her.

"Does it make any sense to you, dearie, that shepherds would be out watching their flocks when in all likelihood, the flocks were penned up for the winter? Israel is way north of the equator. No, I don't believe Jesus was born in December. Some folk believe He was born in the fall during the Feast of Tabernacles, and others believe He was born in the spring around Passover."

Tory didn't care when Jesus was born. She was happy to celebrate His birthday and tried to figure out what she could do to make the day special for Jesus.

The sky was heavy with snow and the air cold. It was the damp kind that cut through clothes and made goose bumps appear. Tory and Charles were walking to the city center of Boston. Their breath came out in puffs of vapor, vanishing as soon as it entered the atmosphere. Both had some shopping to do, and they walked on happy feet. The wind blew and snatched at the words they spoke to each other.

"I sent a card to Madeline with a Christmas card stamp on it." Tory spoke to Charles as the two walked. "Papa had Frankie put a box together and I shipped my card with it, although I still paid for the stamp. It was lovely. And the box was filled with things Olivia picked out with Frankie. Maddie will love it!"

"I sent her a card too, but I didn't buy a stamp. And I wrapped up some money and put it into the box for her Christmas present. I wish she had wanted to come home for Christmas. She's probably so happy to be at boarding school, she'll never come back!" He smiled. "Madeline and I were always very close. My father, Maddie, and I made a pact that whenever Mother did something that hurt us, we would call a meeting and comfort each other. I think it kept us sane through the bad times. I believe it is even in the Bible that we are to comfort one another in our sorrows and rejoice with each other in our joys. Today, I'm rejoicing with you, Toralina Lou!"

Tory laughed. "Are you going to start calling me that too?" She giggled. "I think from now on I'm going to call you Charlie."

Grinning over at her, he lightly punched her on the shoulder. "In truth, it's what my father called me, and sometimes Maddie calls me that too."

"Well, it's what I'm going to call you too. Now, what shall we look for first, Charlie?" The two had decided to pool their money and buy presents for everyone together. Both had been making paper gifts. Charles had made a year calendar, one each for Frankie and Cookie. Tory had made decorative paper stacks for reminder notes and doodling. She had made little boxes out of heavy paper to stack the decorated sheets in and was proud her finished product looked so neat and efficient.

"Let's get some sweets for Janey and Lorna."

"Brilliant idea! Janey has a real sweet tooth, and maybe we could find some of those thin wafer cookies that Lorna enjoys eating. That would take care of those two. I have no idea what should we get for Ralph."

Charles thought for a moment, and his eyes lit up with an idea. "How about we get him some dried fruit? I know he loves apricots in season. If we could find him some dried ones, bet he'd be really happy with that!"

"As I said before, you are brilliant, Charlie me boy, simply brilliant!" Tory laughed at her accent, trying to copy Ralph's but knowing she fell short. Charles joined in. Their eyes sparkled with the excitement of gifts to be bought and secrets to be kept.

Viola decided it was time to visit Father Stenali again. She smiled at Sister Amalia as she opened the door wide. Contessa Viola Stella di Amalfi pressed Amalia's shoulder in a gesture of love. Wearing all black, she had been a widow for seven years but had no thoughts of ever being married again. In her secret heart of hearts, she had given her love to Father Lorenzo Stenali. Visiting him on a regular basis and making sure he was well, she contented herself with being his friend. She would die before ever confessing her love, but it remained pure and unsullied by any desire other than to be of help to him.

Sister Amalia chattered on, telling the contessa of their newest inhabitant and how she sensed a deep-rooted evil in the woman. Viola looked closely at Sister Amalia and knew her speech was not stemming from jealously but from an all-consuming concern for Father Lorenzo. The old nun loved Father Lorenzo as much as anyone ever could.

"He doesn't see it, Contessa. He thinks I am imagining it, but I tell you, even Dr. Luigi could see a troubled mind in her eyes. She frightens me!" Sister Amalia crossed herself and whispered a prayer of protection for the monastery.

"Will I meet her at luncheon?"

"Sì, Contessa, you will meet her."

Viola pressed Sister Amalia's shoulder once more with a gentle hand. "So, let us see Father Lorenzo then."

The two women walked the long hall back to Father Stenali's office. Tapping on the door, Sister Amalia opened it before he said anything. To their surprise, he was not there, but the woman was. Viola appraised the other woman carefully. She could see the bandage of gauze on the back of her head, but the woman held herself regally and turned slowly to face the two women, her poise surprising Viola. A pair of deep-blue eyes, innocent of anything sinister, gazed back in a questioning manner. She had been studying the map pinned to Father Stenali's wall.

"Good morning," the contessa said quietly.

"I don't understand you," the woman replied in English.

Viola spoke rapidly back in kind, with merely a hint of accent. "I said, good morning."

Someone who spoke English!

"Oh! Oh, you speak English!" Mabel exclaimed. Her pleasure at being understood nearly overwhelmed her. "Where am I? I nearly drowned when the steamer went down, and I haven't been able to talk to anyone since I arrived. No one speaks any English."

"I am Contessa Viola Stella di Amalfi. I have the pleasure of speaking with?"

"I'm sorry. I am Mabel May…uh Vickers." Mabel decided she would not use the name Brighton. *I am planning to see that man in the very near future, and using his name would not be wise for what I have planned for him.* Now that someone could speak English, she'd have a better chance of finding out a few things. *This woman is my ticket out of here. She is beautiful.*

Viola remained quiet and allowed the injured woman to assess her a moment. What other people thought of her did not concern her. What God thought of her did. Viola's beauty lay not only in her physical attributes but in her heart as well. She had an abundance of thick, glossy black hair swept up and away from a perfect neck. A lace snood held her hair in place, fastened with jeweled clips. Her eyes sparkled as if with a hidden secret and were an unusual light brown ringed by an almost violet color. Her voice was cultured and smooth. She wore a beautiful black silk dress that seemed to shift in differing shades as she moved.

"Father Stenali sent for me. I have been in Rome for the past fortnight and have just returned. He knows I speak English and wished that I should come speak with you. I hear by your accent you are not British, but American. Am I correct?"

Mabel thought she'd better play this woman for all she was worth. Perhaps she could get some money from her.

"Yes, yes, that is correct. I was on holiday and...and"—she dabbed sorrowfully at her eyes—"my poor husband has died...drowned in that horrible accident on the Mediterranean." She peeked up at the other woman to see if she believed her story and was relieved to see the contessa had swallowed it hook, line, and sinker.

Viola believed the woman but saw Sister Amalia did not, as her lips were thinned in disgust. In Italian, the nun said, "It is a lie, I tell you...I see it...it is a lie."

"Shush, Sister. Can you not see the poor woman mourns her dead husband?"

"I tell you, Contessa...it is all a lie!" She turned on her heel and left the room just as Father Stenali entered.

"Good to see you, Contessa." He spoke warmly. "I am so glad you are back. This poor woman has not been able to communicate with any of us. Perhaps now we shall find out her story."

"Good to see you too, Father." She reached out a hand and grasped his in a warm gesture of friendship. "Her name is Mabel Vickers, an American. She says she was on the steamer that went down and that her husband was killed in the accident."

Father Stenali turned to Mabel, his eyes full of compassion. "You poor woman. If there is anything we can do to help you, please let us know."

Viola translated for him.

Mabel became even more convinced the contessa was her ticket out of this nightmare.

"Tell him thank you." Mabel looked demurely down at her hands. "My biggest need is to get back to America— to Boston. My poor little boy will be beside himself with worry, not knowing what has happened to us. He will, most likely, be told of our deaths."

The contessa translated with ease as the priest responded. "That is a tall order, but we will certainly see what we can do."

"Thank you. It's all anyone can do." Mabel smiled pleasantly. "Now if you'll please excuse me, I'd like to go back to my room and wash up for lunch."

Strolling past the two Italians while Viola translated, she walked smoothly with no self-consciousness at all.

Mabel had discovered, only that morning, that she could cut across the courtyard and halve the time going to her cell. She opened a heavy wooden door and glanced at the huge bush beside the door. It was heavy with overripe black berries, many having already dropped to the ground. *It's belladonna. How fortuitous! Poison right here—right here beside the door.* Smiling to herself, she crossed the courtyard, the cobbles smooth under her feet.

CHAPTER XXI

A stone is heavy, and the sand weighty;
but a fool's wrath is heavier than them both.

PROVERBS 27:3

"**NO AND NO, WE SHALL NOT BE** accepting any of the invitations you have received, my dear." Liberty watched with an even countenance as Armand tapped the end of his cigar into the ashtray on his desk. He leaned back into his chair, which swiveled slightly. Taking another deep draught of his cigar and lifting his chin up, he blew it into the air.

"Liberty, my dear sweet little wife. Correction, my dear sweet little *Christian* wife." He sneered. "*I* shall pick our friends, not you." Armand had sent a message upstairs, by way of Annie, to have Liberty join him in his study.

"Will that be all, Armand?" Liberty did her best to conceal her fear of him. *Lord, please help me—give me strength, give me wisdom, and most of all, help me to not hate him. Please help me to remain pleasing to You in all my attitudes. Help me to remember he is bound by Satan, a man lost and without hope the way he is now, and that my struggle is not against flesh and blood but against the spiritual forces of evil that bind him.* She stood before him looking for all the world as if she were comfortable, her head held high, her carriage straight. But she could feel goose bumps popping out on her arms and tried her best not to shudder.

Armand looked angry. "No, it is not *all*. We will be dining here with the Honeywells and others for Christmas dinner. I want you to do me proud, madam. You shall wear the emeralds and dress in a manner befitting my position. None of those high-necked choker dresses you're so fond of sporting, is that clear?"

"Yes, Armand, it is perfectly clear." She turned to leave, but his words stopped her.

"By the way, I am very sorry to say, your horse is quite ill, and I'm having him put down." His eyes bored into hers with contempt for all that she was.

Facing him with horror on her face, she said, "N-no, Armand, there's nothing wrong with Breeze. I rode him only this morning." Eyes filling with tears, she pleaded. "Please, Armand, no." She despised herself for begging, but for her horse she would do anything. *Oh Lord, he is so evil. I bind this evil from me in the name of Jesus!*

"Well then, I'll think about it. You now have my permission to leave." Armand loved wielding his power over her.

"Oh, how amusing!" Adeline was enjoying the Christmas feast and the camaraderie around the Brighton table.

Henry had just told the story of losing his front tooth.

"The other front one is loose too, but I'm not going to tie a string around it." He lisped as he spoke. "It was scary, sitting there waiting for someone to come through the door. It took too long, and I almost gave up." He smiled at the Baxters, giving them his best smile. Today would be the first time he performed on his violin in front of people other than the family. He was excited, knowing his skill far surpassed most children his age. He practiced every single day and never tired of playing.

George was an astute detective, always aware of what was happening around him.

As he sat there, he sensed an undercurrent of electricity flowing between Olivia Anderson and Manning Brighton. *Now that would be an excellent combination,* he thought. *Manning is too serious by far, and Olivia has the ability to make lighthearted jests and get the man to unwind. She must be a breath of fresh air to him.*

Olivia, eyes sparkling said, "Can you imagine, Henry, if you had tied your tooth to the string and to the doorknob, but it wasn't ready to come out? You'd most likely have gone flying right into Frankie's arms." She laughed at the word picture and everyone else laughed too.

Tory said, "Maybe you could tie a strand of Ivory's tail around your tooth and give her a swift flick of your whip. That'd pull it out without having to wait!" She giggled.

"I've never had goose. This is delicious!" said Charles. It seemed he was always hungry. "Look at all this food. I'm very thankful to have so much!"

Manning looked at his children and felt blessed.

"We are very fortunate. There are many families who have nothing," he said. "My bank donated baskets to the needy and to the poorhouse, but I often wonder if any of the people in the poorhouse ever see what is given them. I suppose some of the people who care for them still have a soft heart."

Charles spoke, clearly without thinking. "Mama said she was going to put Maddie and me int..." His voice trailed off. "Sorry, I didn't mean to say that. I wasn't thinking."

"Where *was* Mabel going to put you, Charlie?" Tory asked. "She wasn't going to put you into the poorhouse, was she?" She looked horrified at even suggesting it.

Henry said, "Yes, that's what she said. I heard her tell them that's what she planned to do. She said they ate too much and cost too much."

"Let's talk about things that are happy, shall we?" Olivia interjected quickly.

She was disgusted with some of the things that had surfaced about Mabel from the two boys, but she didn't want them dwelling on the bad things. "I shall have to get Cookie's recipe for the gravy. It's simply scrumptious!" She smiled around the table, but as she looked over at Manning, she saw his eyes looked troubled. "You do realize it's been said, the way to a man's heart is through his stomach. If that holds true, every man should be madly in love with Cookie! I know I am!" Her eyes were bright with laughter.

"Back to food." Manning smiled over at Olivia, whose cheeks became rosy. Turning to his daughter, he asked, "Do you remember Frankie telling you to eat your food, Tory? That what was left on your plate could keep a child in India alive for a day?"

"Yes, and I told her to box it up and ship it to India. I'd much rather keep a child alive than to eat what was left. It shocked Frankie." Tory grinned as laughter ensued.

Cookie had outdone herself, and the table was ladened with delicacies to delight the palate. There was a yam dish, potatoes and gravy, salads—both sweet and green—and a dressing that tasted wonderful. Her homemade rolls with the strawberry preserves she'd put up last summer were delicious.

Charles couldn't seem to stop tasting things. He'd never in his life had such a wonderful meal. He was thankful and voiced it.

"I would like you to know, Papa, this is the most wonderful meal I've ever had in my entire life." Charles looked at Manning with serious eyes.

Manning felt his heart turn over in humility as the boy addressed him without the Manning attached to the Papa.

"It *is* a wonderful meal, but what is more wonderful is that I love you. I love you as if you were my own son."

The table became quiet as the import of his words sank into the hearts of those gathered there. Charles looked at Manning with eyes warmed by love and spoke with no sense of embarrassment.

"I love you too, and I have never in my entire life been happier."

It had been decided earlier that dessert would be appreciated more if eaten later.

Lingering after dinner, George and Adeline were entranced with the children. George wondered, not for the first time, if he and Addie had made a mistake when they'd decided not to adopt children.

Olivia stood and said, "Now it's time for some charades. We shall be split into two teams. I've asked Frankie to join us. Cookie has made up the phrases from books, plays, and of course, Benjamin Franklin quotes as well as other sources. Frankie has put four ones on strips of paper, and there are four strips that are blank. The ones will be team one, of course, and the rest on team two."

Adeline said, "Oh, I do hope I'm not shackled with only adults!" She laughed at the children's looks of surprise.

"Oh, I think we'll most likely be evenly divided." Olivia clapped her hands. Manning, Henry, Frankie, and Adeline drew ones. Team two was Tory, Olivia, George, and Charles.

"Now for the rules," Olivia said. "I know there are several ways to play. We have a sand hourglass timer that is perfect. It lasts five minutes."

The children all chattered, showing each other gestures they used to identify the category.

"I put my hands together, like this"—Tory held her hands flat together—"and then I unfold them like this if it's a book title."

Charles said, "If it's a play, you do this." He pretended to pull a rope that opened theater curtains.

Henry folded his hands in front of himself and mouthed silent words. "And if it's a song, you pretend to sing, right?"

Liberty sat quietly, listening to the conversation flowing around her. It was Christmas day, and she'd arisen early and gone to church to celebrate the birth of Christ before anyone else was up. She and Annie had exchanged gifts before breakfast. Liberty had given each of her staff a thoughtfully chosen present. Annie had apparently saved her money, and she bought her mistress a beautiful comb for her hair. Libby had given

Armand a beautifully tooled money belt, but he never gave her anything for any occasion unless other people were there to witness it.

She had dressed to please Armand and wore a stylish black brocade with sleeves slashed every few inches from her shoulder to elbow. Green silk peeked out from the slashes. From elbow to wrist, the brocade was embroidered with a matching green thread. The skirt matched the lower arms, and her emerald necklace and earrings completed her attire. Her coppery curls were swept up and cascaded down her back. She looked ravishing.

She felt tired as the men on either side of her kept vying for her attention. She caught Armand's dark, inscrutable eyes on her more than once and was doing her best to entertain both men. Her father, Jacques, was there with his latest paramour on his arm, a lovely blonde woman with more than average intelligence. Armand had seated Mrs. Honeywell on his right, which was a place of honor, and Mr. Honeywell on Liberty's right. She wondered if the man had any clue that Armand garnered information from his wife about his company, which would land the couple most likely penniless when he finally performed his *coup d'état*. As she sat there thinking and nodding her head at the man who leaned over to converse with her, she wondered if there was any way she could warn him.

"Sir," she said quietly, so quietly he had to lean closer to hear what she said. "Since you have been talking extensively about plans for the expansion of your company, I believe I should tell you that now is *not* a good time to borrow against your company, unless it is through a bank. My husband *owns* several companies he has newly *acquired*. I understand Mr. Brighton's bank has been generous in lending for expansions and the pay back rate is quite reasonable." She smiled into his eyes and could only hope he was astute enough to listen to her and not think her some witless female.

His gray-green gaze stared into her green eyes with a look that was at once startled and then comprehending. He looked as if a light bulb had gone on inside his head. He glanced down to the end of the table where Armand Bouvier monopolized his wife's attention.

"Thank you. Thank you very much," he said quietly.

She inclined her head slightly and replied, "Thank you for listening, sir." She was thankful to see Armand still busily engaged, talking to Mrs. Honeywell. He had not seen the intimate exchange between herself and Mr. Honeywell. Liberty took a deep breath and felt she had done well to save a man from destitution or worse. She knew she walked a fine line, but now the dinner had been worth it.

"Bravo! Bravo!" Frankie clapped her hands and the others followed suit. The staff were seated in a semicircle behind the Baxters and the family, listening to Henry play his violin.

He'd played several other pieces but saved his favorite one for last.

Standing erect beside the pianoforte, Henry grinned and with an exaggerated bow said, "And now for my favorite as a finale to my program, *An der schönen blauen Donau*, or you may know it as the popular *Blue Danube*, by Johann Strauss the Second. It was composed only eight years ago but has become so popular, it's crossed continents already." He lifted his bow and began to play.

Manning was dumbfounded the boy played so well. He'd only been at it for little over two months. His eyes met Olivia's, hers bright with unspoken excitement.

She mouthed "Child prodigy!" He nodded and turned back to give his full attention to Henry Horace Vickers, soon to be Brighton. He sat in awe listening to the music, pure and lovely, pouring forth from the violin. He glanced over at George and Adeline. They too were clearly stupefied that such a young boy could play with the heart and talent of a great artiste. It would not be long before the boy would be performing on the stage in front of a huge crowd.

Mabel tried to be patient, but she felt as if she were spinning her wheels. The days ran into each other, and it brought her up short to see the date on a calendar in Father Stenali's office. *It's nearly Christmas! I've been in this wretched little village for nearly two months. I must get out of here! The contessa said she would help, but it seems nothing is being done. I shall do things myself. I shall take things into my own hands and make things happen for me!*

She walked around the little village and met all kinds of people. Fishermen clogged the docks in the early mornings with their nets, floats, and all kinds of paraphernalia spread out so passersby had to watch where they walked.

Mabel, going by the same boats day after day, had met one man who spoke a guttural English. Every morning she spoke a bit to him. One morning she decided it was time to find out if he could help her.

"How can I find someone to sail me north to Genoa?" she asked. "I must find someone who can do that."

"It take money, mees. *Molto* monies."

"And if I have it, what then? Who do I talk to? I must get to Genoa by cover of night without anyone knowing. Can you do this?"

"*Sì, posso farlo.* Yes, I can do it." His eyes shifted around. Lowering his voice still further, he said, "You must let-a me know in a morning of day you wheesh to sail. I take-a you myself. I tell-a no one." He pointed to his chest. "Me, I work alone."

CHAPTER XXII

Give ear to my words,
O LORD, consider my meditation.

PSALMS 5:1

MANNING AWOKE EARLY, HAVING had only a couple hours of sleep. He groaned. It was quiet and he lay quite still, hoping for the elusive dream to come back. Drinking heavier than he ever had, it brought him initial sleep that lasted, at the most, two hours. He spent his nights tossing and turning, hoping to sleep but knowing he wouldn't. Sometimes at dawn, he'd get another half hour, but his thoughts kept jumping to Mabel and how glad he was that she was gone. He went over and over in his mind the whole scene of trying to get her into a lifeboat. Had he relaxed his grip on her hoping she'd go after her jewelry? He didn't think so, but he'd rehearsed the scenario so many times in his mind the truth had become jumbled with scenes that had never happened. He groaned again, flipped his pillow over, and punched it. He lay and thought about his own life and where he was headed. *I now have responsibility not only for Victoria, but for Charles and Henry as well as Madeline.*

Shall I become a sot and make matters worse? Riddled with guilt, he decided to make an appointment with Elijah Humphries. He lay thinking about the new year. Many of his acquaintances made New Year's resolutions. *I've never put much credence in that. I need something a lot more substantial than do-gooder wishes or wishful thinking that things will get better. In truth, I think things for me are getting worse.*

The day dawned cold, the air crisp. Smoke from fireplaces wafted their scent of burnt wood and coal into the wintry air. Skies were a glorious blue, but the ground was covered in a thin blanket of white. Boston was finally experiencing its first snow.

Charles, Tory, and Henry made their way toward school, excited to be back in class and to share their experiences from over the holidays with their friends. Taking their time, there was much laughter as they threw snowballs at each other. Henry was quite accurate, which surprised Tory.

"Look out!" Charles yelled at Henry, whose back was toward an empty field. "Look out behind you!" A filthy dog headed straight for Henry.

Henry thought Charles yelled because he'd thrown a snowball, so he paid no attention.

Tory was closer and ran full tilt to deflect the cur if it jumped at Henry, getting between him and the dog. The animal came to a screeching halt about four feet from Tory, who stood protectively in front Henry. The dog didn't seem mean but sat down on his haunches in the cold snow. One ear was torn and bloodied, his coat matted and filthy. He was skinny, and his tail didn't wag as Tory approached him with a gloved hand.

"Be careful, Tory. He could be one of those dogs who bite without warning," Charles admonished.

"I don't think he's going to bite," she said as she advanced even further. The dog kept his eyes glued on her but stood warily, starting to back up. He wouldn't let her get close.

"Come on, little dog...come on...I won't hurt you." She spoke soothingly, but he wouldn't let her near.

Henry said, "We'd better go, or we'll be late for school."

Charles agreed. "You're right, Henry. Let's get going!"

The three children left the dog and started walking rapidly toward the school. Tory looked back to see the dog still sitting there.

"Where do you think he came from?"

"I don't know, but it sure looks like no one's taken care of him. He's just a stray."

Henry said, "I sure am glad he didn't bite you. Thanks for protecting me."

He'd not missed the protective stance Tory had taken. She was becoming a real sister to him.

Olivia had begun her day as usual, early. She awoke and said, "Good morning, Lord. Thank You very much for another day!" She lay there for a few moments in the dark and sat up to light a taper. Leaning back against pillows, she thought about what needed to be done. She looked around the beautiful room. It was papered in the most beautiful wall paper she'd ever seen. Creamy, it had sprigs of rosebuds ranging from light pink to hot pink that covered two of the walls. One wall had been painted the lightest pink shade and another a medium shade. The duvet cover, pillow shams, and chairs were all covered in matching shades of pinks, cream, and splashes of green that gave the room an inviting, elegant look. A Turkish carpet woven in the same tones, but mostly the creamy shade, met her feet as she swung her legs over the side of the bed. She stood and stretched.

Pouring coal from the scuttle into the grate where embers glowed slightly, she took the small bellows and pumped them gently to give the coals some air. Finally the new coal caught, flickered, and grew brighter as flames began to lick their way up from the embers. She shivered and slipped into a lavender silk robe lined with cashmere. Making her way down the stairs and into the kitchen, she saw Cookie already hard at work preparing breakfast. Greeting the cook, she helped herself to a cup of coffee and went back upstairs to sit in a chair by the fireplace in the bedroom. She read a chapter in her Bible every day, going through it methodically. Next, she read a scripture that the minister had preached on, and she would meditate on it. She sat quietly and fell into prayer.

Lord, how I praise You for this day, this day in which I can live, breathe, and have my being. I will rejoice and be glad in it. Holy, holy, holy is the Lord God Almighty, who was, who is, and who is to come. I give You praise from my whole heart. You are a compassionate God, slow to anger and abounding in loving-kindness. You also give wisdom, Lord, and I need a bit of that today.

You know I am very attracted to Manning. Only You know I have loved him since before he married Laura. I only share it with You because You know all things already, and I need help. You also know I have loved Victoria as if she were my own daughter. Father, I do not wish to be unequally yoked, and that is why I have not pursued a relationship with Manning. Now I can scarcely think of anything else. I think of him all the time! What am I to do? I know he needs help with the children, but it's becoming unbearable to be near him. Should I go home? Lord, please give me an answer. She continued to pray for each child, Manning, the house staff, and especially for Liberty Bouvier. She prayed too for Madam Beaumont and her fatherless children.

It was time to get dressed. She rang for Lucy, who was, as always, ready to serve her mistress. Olivia chose a yellow satin dress, one of her favorites. Her black hair was swept back and held in a loose bun with decorated combs. In a short time she was ready to deal with whatever the day had in store for her. She kissed a surprised Lucy on the cheek and exited the room, humming to herself.

Mabel sat in the darkened corner of the priest's office and speculated. *How in the world can I get my hands on some money? I wonder if the contessa has money she could lend me? Once I left, I'd never have to pay it back.* She had been checking every day with Brugali, the fisherman. He would tell her when the moon would be good for sailing at night. He planned to sail up the coast, keeping land in sight. Mabel thought the price he was asking was far too much. *Somehow, I must get back to my little Henry and also to my dear, dear Manning.* Her eyes glittered in the darkening room.

Charles looked for the fifth time at the big regulator clock on the wall in the classroom. He wanted to be outside and headed home. *I want to take Ebony out and exercise her, and I want to write to Maddie, and I promised to listen to a song Henry made up for his violin. Will the hands on that clock ever move?*

Finally, the schoolmaster said it was time to go home. Charles looked over at Victoria to see if she planned to stay and help the schoolmaster or go straight home with him. He wondered if Tory was sweet on the schoolmaster. He was young and to Charles' way of thinking, quite good looking.

Tory caught his eyes on her and mouthed, "Let's go!"

Earlier, at recess, most of the snow had melted off, but as Charles, Tory, and Henry left the schoolhouse, they could feel the air was already beginning to cool and the sky was heavy, laden with a burden of snow that looked to be more than what they'd had the night before.

"I think it's going to snow again." Henry snugged his scarf tighter around his neck as he felt the wind's icy fingers dipping into his coat. They walked swiftly down the road toward home.

Tory felt the lace on her boot come untied and asked, "Would you please hold these?" She shoved her books into Charles' hands and bent down to tie her boot, pulling the lace tight and tying it. Out of the corner of her eye, she saw something move. She turned to see the poor dog with the chewed ear.

In a quiet voice she said, "Look behind us. Poor little guy. Maybe he'll follow us home. Peculiar that he waited all day and didn't follow any of the other students home. C'mon, let's see if he follows us."

The three children headed home. "He's following us, all right, poor little tyke." Charles felt his heartstrings sadden for the little dog. "Perhaps we could keep him." The children turned into the Brighton residence and went around to the back.

Charles said, "You two stay here. I'll be right back!" He disappeared into the house and shortly was back with a piece of meat. "Here boy. C'mon, no one's going to hurt you, little guy. You're all right here, c'mon." Despite the steps being wet, Charles sat on the lowest one, bribing the dog. Slowly, step-by-step, he came closer. Tory and Henry were almost holding their breath, not daring to move for fear of frightening the little dog. They needn't have worried. For some reason unknown to the three, the dog had decided he belonged to them. He was quite dirty and wasn't wagging yet, but he didn't act too frightened either, since the meat peace offering went down with hardly a chew.

The snow that had threatened earlier in the day began in thin, tiny flakes, turning to huge puffs of wetness.

Tory said, "It's getting cold. Do you think we could just put him into the back entry and then bathe him? What if he has fleas?"

"Dogs that have fleas are always scratching, and I haven't seen him scratch. At least, not this morning and not this afternoon."

"That's true, Henry. Good observation!"

"Shall we ask? Aunt Ollie mightn't like it with her little dog, Snuggles."

"You go ask, Tory. Maybe you should ask Frankie first. After all, she'll be the one to have to let him out and care for him when we're at school."

"All right, but Frankie would most likely listen to Henry. She seems to have a special place in her heart for him."

Henry spoke up, knowing what Tory said was true. "I'll go. I'll ask Frankie first. I'll get on my knees if I have to!" He grinned at the other two and climbed the steps to the back door.

Tory tried petting the dog again, and this time he let her. She and Charles stroked him.

While Henry was inside, Manning rode up on Midnight. He'd been to visit his lawyer.

Looking down at the children as Ralph came out of the stable to take his horse, he asked, "What's that you have there?" he swung off his horse and Ralph, looking a bit surprised at the dog, took the black stallion and led him into the stable to brush and feed him.

"Thanks, Ralph," Manning said as the groom took the reins from his hand. "Think we're in for a bit of snow...wouldn't you say?"

"Yes, sir, by my way of thinking, we're in fer more than a bit o' snow an' no mistake!" He grinned at his boss.

Manning crouched down. "Hey, little guy," he said to the dog. "You've found yourself a home and a good one at that." He reached out to the little dog that almost seemed to snuggle into his hand. "He looks like some kind of terrier, doesn't he? Here you go. We need to get in out of the weather."

He picked the filthy dog up, his arms outstretched, and carried him into the back door.

Charles and Tory trailed behind him, grinning at each other behind his back.

Placing the dog on the little rug used to wipe feet, Manning peeked into the kitchen and saw Henry heading toward him with Frankie at his heels. The children were busily taking off their wet things and hanging them up, unlacing boots and pulling off wet stockings. The dog began to shiver uncontrollably.

Frankie, hands on her hips, said, "Well, Mr. Brighton, looks as if you've got yourself a dog. I wonder what kind it is?"

"Yes, Frankie, I believe I do. Some kind of terrier, I believe. Could you please see to it some water is heated? I'll run up and change my clothes, and we'll take a good look at what we have here."

Frankie had been looking down at the dog, but as Manning spoke, she looked up and into his eyes.

His voice sounded better than she'd heard it since Miss Laura had died. His eyes looked clear and untroubled. A wide smile creased her face into crinkles around her eyes, and there was an answering smile on Manning's face.

He took the stairs two at a time and strode down the hall. Turning the corner, he nearly ran into Olivia.

"Sorry." He put his hands on her shoulders to steady them both. She felt warm and yielding under his hands, and he removed them as if he'd touched a flatiron.

Olivia asked, "Is anything wrong?"

"No, in all truth, everything's all right! I'm hurrying to change, as the children have brought in a stray dog. He's horribly filthy, and I'm going to clip his coat and get him cleaned up." His blue gaze smiled into tawny eyes filled with confusion, and he proceeded to his room, the door banging shut behind him.

Olivia spoke softly to no one. "Now, what is different about that man? Something is, I can tell."

CHAPTER XXIII

Give ear to my words,
O LORD, consider my meditation.

PROVERBS 2:10

MANNING CHANGED HIS CLOTHES and ran posthaste down the back stairs.

Frankie poured hot water into a large tub that already had cold water in it.

Olivia donned a large baize apron belonging to Cookie, and with Manning, she was down on her knees trying to comfort the dog, which shivered and looked terribly forlorn.

The children talked in hushed voices, trying not to scare the poor little animal.

Frankie, looking upon the scene, came in with more water. Sensing a warmth flowing between Mr. Brighton and Miss Olivia, she smiled to herself as she poured the water into the tub.

The children were all down on their knees, and the little dog wagged his tail for the first time, that is, until Manning, shears in hand, began to clip the huge mats off him. He began to wriggle, backing away, so Manning sat full on the floor, his legs stretched out with the dog between them. It took some time, but finally all the huge mats were lying on the floor. The worst part was combing out the dog's ears and face, and he trimmed off much fur there too.

Frankie laid newsprint on the floor and the children gathered up the mats of fur and dropped them on the paper. She wrapped it up and placed it in the rubbish bin.

"Whew! He stinks, doesn't he?" Victoria had been stroking the dog until her father started in on his head.

"Yes, right now he does, but after he gets bathed, he will be smelling much better. He's filthy, but wet dog fur, even clean, doesn't smell the best."

Olivia asked, "Is he terrier or part terrier?"

Charles said, "That's what Papa said. What shall we call him?"

Henry spoke up for the first time. "I think we should call him Mozart. Isn't that a good name for a dog?"

He hoped everyone liked his suggestion. Music was now his passion and he liked Mozart's music. "We could call him Bach, but that seems like a name for a big dog."

"I don't know. Mozart seems like a big name too, for such a little dog. I like Muffin or even Snowball now that we see he's white under all that dirty, matted hair, and we did find him in the snow." Tory didn't really like the name Mozart.

"Muffin is a sweet name, but I don't think Snowball fits. He's not all white, either. I like the name Mozart and then we could call him Moe," said Charles.

"I like that too," said Manning. "Is that all right with you, Tory?" Manning grinned at his daughter. "Let's name the dog Mozart and call him Moe for short." He lifted the dog into the warm water, which the dog didn't seem to mind one bit.

"I don't particularly like the name Mozart, but I like Moe. It's short and fits him, I guess," Tory replied.

Olivia said, "Manning, do be careful. He'll shake unless you hold his muzzle. Dogs shake from the nose down, and if you hold his nose steady, he won't be able to shake water all over you."

"How'd you learn that?" asked Charles.

"By trial and error, I suppose. My little Snuggles used to shake water all over me, and one time when he started to shake off, I grabbed his nose and he stopped. It truly does work." She laughed. "I have been wetted more than once by my sweet little Snuggles."

Manning was scrubbing Moe with soap. It was amazing how dirty the water was. Frankie had more water boiling on the stove, so the dog was lifted onto an old blanket. Olivia held his muzzle as Manning took the tub, with Charles' help, and dumped it beside the steps outside. The snow fell fast and furious and had already piled more than an inch on the stair railing.

Charles lifted his face and caught several snowflakes on his tongue.

Manning said, "If this keeps up, son, there will be no travel tomorrow. It'll be a day at home for the Brightons. Perhaps we could get some sledding in." He smiled at Charles, his face illumined by the light of the sconce outside the back door.

Charles grinned back at him. "I'd like that. I know we have had our Christmas break, but you worked almost every day except the twenty-fifth. I like spending time with you, sir." Manning clapped the boy on the shoulder and gave it a squeeze.

They went back inside together. Manning washed the dog, shampooing and scrubbing his fur, and repeated the process of dumping the water. Finally, after two rinses, the dog looked clean. His coat was a bit choppy, but it was curly, so it didn't look too bad.

"We can trim him up a little, later. I think he's been patient enough. He sure is winsome. Look at that little face. We've got ourselves a sweet-looking dog," Manning said.

Although the pup was wet, it wagged its tail at the warm tone in Manning's voice. Manning was proud of his handiwork. "I didn't see any fleas in the water. Did any of you?"

Olivia responded right away. "No, I didn't either, and I looked for them. I do not want a dog with fleas in the house. They are too difficult to get rid of once you have them."

"I wonder who owned him."

Henry was a bit worried someone missed his dog.

"Well, whoever it is, this little guy has been out on his own for a while," Olivia said.

"Do you think he's trained?"

"Yes," Olivia responded, "for some reason, I do."

Mabel sat on the floor in the corner of the priest's office, nearly invisible in the dim light. It was early evening and she'd just finished her Spartan meal. Wondering how to get her hands on some money, she thought of impossible schemes, such as robbing a jewelry store or breaking into some rich people's house and stealing their money. As she sat there, Father Stenali came in, apparently unaware of her presence, and went straight to one of the locked-up cupboards.

Father Stenali was thankful for the donations the monastery received and kept all valuables locked up in his office.

He reached inside his clerical collar and pulled out a large key on a heavy chain. Opening one of the locked cupboards, he placed money— and some loose jewels a priest from an outlying district had given him that day—into an intricately carved box. It was a large sum of money and had been collected over a period of months. Sensing someone else in the room, he straightened up and looked around. In the dim light he saw no one.

Father Stenali left his office, grateful the parish would be able to begin the needed repairs on the orphanage. It was an old edifice that housed many children and was close to being condemned as a building unfit for habitation.

Mabel made no sound sitting in her darkened corner. She now knew how she could get money for her trip.

The next morning she visited Brugali, who was her passport out of Santa Marinella. She walked the docks often. At first she caused quite a stir among the fishermen, but now they were used to seeing her day in and day out. She spied Brugali sitting with his feet hanging over the side of the pier, repairing a length of rope for his anchor.

"If-a you have-a za money. In *sette giorni la luna e perfetta.*"

Ah, she thought. *Next week the moon is perfect, and that is perfect for me.*

"Grazie," she said. "It is perfect for me too." She smiled brittlely at the fisherman, who didn't look surprised. Mabel had been learning basic Italian and could understand more than she could speak. She returned to the monastery and took a brightly colored ceramic cup from her room. Retracing her steps down the long corridor, she looked around and saw no one observing her, so she entered the courtyard and picked some of the black-colored berries from the belladonna bush. Nightshade.

Manning, teeth brushed, lay in bed. He'd taken no spirits this night. He wondered how long it would take him to fall asleep. He thought back to his luncheon appointment with Elijah Humphries earlier in the day.

He'd asked the lawyer to meet him at his club, reserving one of the private rooms, and they were served a wonderful luncheon of grilled salmon, asparagus, and baby red potatoes. He'd drunk a white wine; the lawyer had apple cider. They had chatted over the meal, and Manning could see Elijah was curious as to why they were meeting.

Talking together over Black Forest cake and coffee, Manning asked Elijah questions about God and salvation. After the first question, Elijah's bright-blue eyes had turned from a questioning look to one of understanding.

Manning, stretched out on his bed, reflected on what happened next. He had prayed a prayer of repentance. He'd asked the Lord God Almighty to forgive him of all his sins and to come into his heart. He didn't feel a bit different when he had finished praying and told the lawyer so. Elijah said it wasn't about feeling. It was about faith. *God has forgiven my sins. Do I believe it? Yes, I do. What's strange is, I didn't feel any different when I first prayed but I sure do now. I feel as if a weight I've been carrying has been lifted off my shoulders. It wasn't my fault Laura died. She'd wanted another baby. And I tried to save Mabel and I failed. Now, I must leave the past behind and with God's help do the best I can for the future. Elijah said I must live one day at a time and make it the best day, in thanksgiving to God who gave it to me.* His thoughts turned into sweet sleep.

Waking the next morning, Manning sat up and lit a taper. As he turned up the wick, he touched the flame to it. The wick caught and the lamp next to his bed filled the room with light. He shivered. He saw by the mantel clock it was nearly six. *I slept the whole night through,* he thought in surprise. It seemed earlier as it was still so dark.

He pulled back the heavy drapes, and he could see by the streetlamps still burning that snow covered the city in a virginal blanket of pristine whiteness. *There will be no school for the children this day.* He stretched and smiled in wonder at the uninterrupted night's rest he'd enjoyed.

Carefully, he laid wood and a few coals in the fireplace and lit it. He crawled back into bed and pulled the feather duvet around his bare shoulders and lay with one arm curled around the back of his head. He thought about what he could do to make this a memorable day for the children. Then, as his thoughts seemed wont to do lately, his attention swung to Olivia. *I love her. I have been with her enough to realize she is a beautiful woman. They say beauty is in the eye of the beholder. I don't think I thought much of her looks when I was married to Laura, and I reckon that's as it should be. Now I see the goodness in her, and her beauty seems almost overwhelming. I don't want to live without her. I wanted companionship and a family, and as a result, I married Mabel in a hurry. I knew, even when I married her, that it was too quick, but I didn't see the harm in it.*

I thank You, God, for taking away my guilt. I still long for companionship, but I feel free. If Olivia will have me, I want her to enjoy a courtship, outings, the theater, time to know for sure if she wants marriage too. She'd have to give up quite a bit of social life, but she's already done that and seems perfectly happy foregoing it. He lay there for quite a time thinking about some of the things Elijah Humphries had told him. Manning was grateful his lawyer wanted to mentor him and teach him the way of living a Christian life.

The room was finally warming up. It was still cold but not frigid. He threw another log onto the grate and began to dress. As he picked up a bit after himself, he began to hum. He belted out the phrase of a song he'd not thought of in a long time and left his room, happy and ready for the new day.

The week seemed to have dragged along, but finally the day arrived that Mabel had been waiting for. She had laid careful plans. She crushed the berries and extracted the liquid, straining out any of the pith. The juice was a rich dark-red color, and she knew it was sweet to the taste. She wrapped the pithy pulp into a handkerchief and went out to the outhouse to throw it down the hole. She stopped by the pump and washed her hands, rubbing them thoroughly to make sure none of the residue remained. Even the leaves of belladonna were extremely poisonous. She was quite sure what she'd just thrown down the toilet was deadly. As she walked back to her room, she wondered why anyone would plant such a poisonous bush where there was human habitation.

She wrapped the few belongings she'd been given into a brightly colored scarf and looked around the stark cell. Mabel was glad to be leaving the austere surroundings that had been her home for more than three months. *I cannot wait to be gone from here. I deserve to be gone. Wonder, should I go see Maddie first?* Mabel placed her scarf with the few meager things she needed—a comb, extra stockings, and a shawl—under her pillow, ready to grab when she was ready. Feeling quite satisfied that she was prepared, she also decided she was famished. Mabel headed toward the dining hall to eat dinner.

CHAPTER XXIV

Give ear to my words,
O LORD, consider my meditation.

PROVERBS 2:10

OLIVIA COULD TELL SOMETHING WAS different about
Manning. She'd sensed it the evening before, but this morning he fairly
radiated charm and good humor.

It wasn't as if the old Manning didn't charm me, but this…this is overwhelming.
She had gone down the stairs, as was her habit, to get her coffee. Manning
was already seated at the kitchen table and looked at her with eyes that
were warm with admiration. He stood as she entered the kitchen, but she
waved him to be seated. She was in her lavender robe and felt embarrassed
that he should see her thus.

"Good morning, Olivia. You're looking lovely this morning." He
smiled. "Are you usually up so early?"

"Good morning, yourself." She smiled in return. She could feel her
cheeks growing warm under his perusal. "Yes, I usually come down for a
cup of Cookie's delicious coffee and then return to my room to read."

"What do you read?"

"Oh, I read the Word of God daily. I also pray before I begin to live out my day. If I didn't do this, I wouldn't be able to hear God's voice. I wouldn't know His guiding hand in my life, and He does guide me, Manning. Please believe me. He does."

"I believe you, Olivia. Believe me, I do." He smiled up at her. "Would you please sit down a minute? I'd like to share something with you."

Cookie had been watching, surreptitiously, the exchange between the two and was smiling to herself. She was in the process of making crab eggs Benedict for breakfast. She saved making the hollandaise sauce for last. It was tricky, and Cookie was a perfectionist when it came to cooking.

Olivia sat down a bit apprehensively. *He's not going to tell me everything is under control and I can go home now, is he?* She wrapped her fingers tighter around her coffee cup as if its warmth could travel up her arm and thus warm her heart. She sat on a chair across the table and looked over at him. Her calm stillness belied the thumping of her heart. She felt this to be a momentous moment. Time seemed suspended as she waited for his words.

Oh Lord, she prayed, *please, whatever he's going to say, don't let it be that I should go home now. I...I love the children and I love him. I don't think I could bear it.*

"I'd like to tell you something that happened to me yesterday."

Manning noticed she was shivering. "Are you cold? Let's go sit by the fire in the library. It's quite warm in there." He got up and led the way out of the kitchen.

Cookie was disappointed. She wanted to hear what had happened to him yesterday.

Olivia took a seat near the fire and Manning handed her a knitted blanket. "Thank you." She wrapped it around her shoulders like a shawl and curled her legs up underneath her.

He went over to close the library door to avoid any drafts. He smiled and took the chair across from her. Crossing his long legs, he sat staring at her for a long minute to gather his thoughts. His eyes on her brought the color to her cheeks.

"Yesterday, I'd made a luncheon appointment with my lawyer, Elijah Humphries. I believe you met him at the funeral? Yes, well, he's a very intelligent man." He turned his head to stare into the flames and watched them lick at the wood and then swung his gaze back to Olivia.

"We had a delicious meal at my club, but the whole purpose of talking with him is because I've been very dissatisfied with my life. Yes, extremely dissatisfied ever since Laura died. I kept thinking there's got to be more to life than this. I thought Mabel could help me get past the pain and be a companion and mother for Tory. As you well know, she was a sick woman, or insane, or both. I think anyone who takes the life of another must be insane. I call it insanity of the heart."

Olivia murmured something that sounded as if she was agreeing, but Manning continued to talk. "Mabel's funeral eulogy was a farce. I almost fell asleep listening to the man, but Beaumont's was a different matter altogether. It caused me to think about my life and the path I've been taking. I've been so riddled with guilt...guilt that Laura got pregnant and died. We both knew the doctor said no more children. Then there was Mabel. I kept wondering if I let go of her hand purposely—knowing she'd go for her jewelry—and perhaps I'd be shed of her. I know Adeline told you she bit me on the arm and I loosened my grip. I cannot say I felt the least bit sorry over her death, but the lack of remorse brought with it its own form of guilt." He took a long drink of his coffee as Olivia sat, visibly mesmerized by what he was telling her. Her eyes were warm with sympathy.

He continued. "So night after night I've lain awake, not able to sleep. I pondered over and over again what the rector said about Beaumont and his life of service, his many charities, and the relationship he had with God. I've tried to help people, and I believe I've done many things that are good, yet I still felt this emptiness within me. Yesterday, I asked Elijah Humphries a lot of questions. We sat and talked for the longest time about spiritual things. It led to me asking the King of Kings into my heart. God has forgiven me, and Jesus has taken all my sins away."

By this time in his narrative, Olivia was smiling through her tears of joy.

Manning had become a Christian. She realized that the Almighty had answered her prayer as well. Her heart felt near to bursting with joy.

Manning continued his narrative. "Last night was the first night since marrying Mabel I've had a full night's sleep. I've made many mistakes in my life, and I know I'll make many more, but I cannot begin to tell you the joy that has entered my heart. Not a rush of joy or feeling different when I finished my prayer yesterday, but a slowly growing knowledge that I am His and He is mine, and both of us are in this together. I have much to learn, and that brings me to the second part of my narrative."

Olivia looked questioningly at him, still wondering if he wanted her to stay on here at the Brighton residence.

"Olivia." He slipped out of his chair and got down on one knee. He took her hand in his and said, "Olivia, I've grown to love you. I can't stop thinking about you, and I know who you are is not a front but the real you. Will you please do me the honor of becoming my wife? I love you, and thoughts of you have invaded my every waking moment. I want to marry you and grow old with you. You make me laugh and feel alive. Olivia, I don't want to go through the rest of my life without you."

He looked at her face streaming with tears and wanted to gather her up in his arms. The wait before she answered him seemed interminably long.

Olivia stood and so did Manning. She put her hand to his chest and he grabbed it, holding it there.

"Yes, oh yes, Manning. I will marry you tomorrow if you wish it."

He pulled her into his arms and felt her body pliant and yielding. His lips came down on hers.

She'd never, in her thirty-one years of life, been kissed before and didn't know what she had expected, but it wasn't this. She felt the flame of desire pierce through her and kissed him with all the ardor she had stored up within her.

Manning couldn't remember the last time he'd been kissed like that. He set her back, shaken, and stared into her eyes with passion darkening his.

"I love you, Olivia. You, of course, know I'm not mourning Mabel, but observances must be made. Gossips will talk. They talked about me marrying Mabel before a year was up after Laura's death. I've never held much to the conventions, but for your reputation's sake, I wish to do so now. I wish to court you and give you time to really know this is what you want, and I want you to enjoy a time of cherishing, which I plan to do for the rest of my life. Oh, my dear girl, I do love you." He kissed her again, releasing her reluctantly. "I didn't mean to ask you so abruptly. I had thought I should have some special event planned and then ask you. I have a ring that was my mother's that Laura never wore. It's a garnet set with diamonds, and I'd thought I would give it to you when I asked you. I'm sorry. I should have asked you in a fancy restaurant or after the theater or something special."

"This *is* special." Manning started to interrupt her, but she continued. "Since I walked into this house, it has been special. You've given me hope that it will continue. I love you and I love the children. I don't think I could have borne it if you'd told me it was time for me to go home. Thank you, Manning. I thank you from the bottom of my heart. I've never, not in all my life, enjoyed myself as much as I have here with you and the children. Each day feels like a gift to be unwrapped throughout it."

His looked deeply into her tawny-colored eyes and saw nothing but love shining back at him. He said, "I've watched you and Tory and Frankie, and even Charles. I want you to help me learn about faith and God's goodness an—"

Just then, Frankie entered, tapping on the door but not waiting for a response. "Excuse me, but breakfast is ready," she said. She looked at the two of them, who looked at her almost befuddled, as if they didn't know what she just said. She grinned. "The children are at the table waiting for you. No school today. The drifts are too deep and everything outside has come to a screeching halt. No milk or eggs delivered this morning. Cookie has made crab eggs Benedict and wants you to eat it right away."

She left, bustling out the door in a hurry to go tell Cookie they'd be right there. She also wanted Cookie to know that most likely there'd be another Mrs. Brighton before long. Smiling from ear to ear, she hurried back to the kitchen.

It was Tuesday and Liberty sat in her dark sitting room. She wished she could have this one room painted a light, airy yellow or a creamy white, but Armand would not permit it. The curtains were pulled back but the sky was heavy with snow yet to come. It was a beautiful site, but the snow kept her from going out. Tuesdays she always volunteered at the Boston School for the Deaf. The children had started back to school the day before, having a bit of a holiday to celebrate Christmas and the New Year. She was eager to communicate with the ones she worked with and to see their joy as their hands flew with excitement, relating their holiday adventures by signing to her.

She sat crocheting a table runner. *Lord, how grateful I am for Your company. I feel so stifled in this house, especially on days like this when I can't ride or get out at all. Lord, I pray for Armand. I'm thankful Mr. Honeywell listened to my warning. Armand has been livid that the man didn't borrow any money from him, and he hasn't been able to seduce Mrs. Honeywell. They've not attended any of the social functions we've been to of late.* Liberty smiled a little to herself. *My prayer is that no one would borrow from my father or Armand again. Please soften their hearts and help them see their need of You as their Savior.*

Her sitting room door banged open and Libby nearly jumped out of her skin. Armand was never home on Tuesdays, but of course, the snow had kept him in too.

"Dinner at the Ovingtons' has been cancelled, my dear. We shall be dining in." He left as abruptly as he had appeared, leaving the door wide open behind him. The fire sputtered in the draft, and Liberty rose to close the door, but Sigmund, Armand's butler, was there before she reached it. He nodded solemnly at her and closed the door.

Oh Father, is this to be my life for years to come? Please help me. Thank You for the church I found on Rice Street. Oh Father, I love singing hymns and being with other Christians. Thank You for a minister who preaches Your Word. Help me obey it. I ask again for me to respect Armand. Your Word doesn't say I must love him, but that I should respect him. I don't. You know I don't. Please give me an image of him to respect. I wish to be obedient. I love You, dear Lord. Amen.

Hard rolls, cheese and cheap wine…I feel that's all we ever eat. Well, never again! I am finished here. Mabel brushed some of the remains of bread crumbs off her hands and onto her skirt as she strode down the echoing cloister. *Brugali said tonight is the night. It's the eleventh of January and a full moon. I am ready!*

Her mind was set on one thing and one thing only. *I shall leave this godforsaken, cold, stone place tonight. I cannot wait to be away from here and on my way to Boston. That contessa, sitting there talking to that visiting priest as if she were a prima donna herself. I hate her. She and that old hag. I hate them both! The contessa is rich and could have given me money to go home. Well, I will hurt her with the deed I do this night!*

She entered her cell for the last time. Once she had the juice she'd placed under the bed and her roll of belongings, she headed toward Father Stenali's office. She hummed a ditty to herself as she walked down the long corridor.

Sister Amalia, standing in a deep recess of the corridor, watched the woman called Mabel as she passed by. She had been keeping close watch on the woman since Christmas. Sister Amalia could feel in her heart something was up; she sensed it. Something bad was going to happen and it concerned this evil woman.

CHAPTER XXV

An high look, and a proud heart,
and the plowing of the wicked, is sin.

PROVERBS 21:4

SISTER AMALIA REMEMBERED a conversation she'd had with the contessa several years back when sharing a cup of tea together. The contessa had told her that God's people were bestowed with different giftings from the Holy Father. She'd laid her hand on Sister Amalia's shoulder and said that certainly she, Sister Amalia, had the gift of discernment.

The contessa had also cautioned her. "Don't waste the gift the Holy Father has given you. Many people who have this gift end up a gossip and tell the things they discern about people to others who have no business hearing it. It saddens our Father when we abuse what He has so readily given us. No, dear Sister, the gift is for you to see and then pray for the person or situation you perceive. Yes, that is how the gift of discernment is to be used." *So, now I am using the gift; I have been obedient and have told no one of my feelings except the contessa. I have been praying for protection for Father Stenali and all who abide or visit within these walls. The Holy Father Himself has shown me the evil this woman can wreak upon people.*

Sister Amalia saw Mabel enter the office of Father Stenali, as she so often did after the evening meal. She breathed a little easier, knowing the pattern was not broken. She walked briskly down the long corridor and around the dining hall to Mabel's cell, wishing she had cut across the courtyard. She entered with a soft step, making no sound. Looking around, she immediately realized that all the woman's personal effects were gone. It frightened her, and she headed back down the corridor to the doors that cut across the courtyard toward the Father's office.

Mabel had entered Father Stenali's office and quickly poured the priest a glass of wine, adding a hefty amount of the dark belladonna from the cup. She opened one of the heavy drawers, placed the poisoned cup inside, and closed it quickly. She turned back to the desk and poured herself a glass of wine. Holding it carefully so as not to spill, she went over to her usual place to sit. Her scarf full of her things lay under the chair in the darkened corner.

The priest entered and Mabel stood as he walked to the desk, seeing the wine poured there. Hearing her step, he turned to look at her.

"I have good wine. You join me." She gave him her best smile and spoke haltingly in Italian, but she made herself understood. She'd practiced the phrase.

He picked up the red wine and took a sip. "It's sweet," he said. He took a hefty drink and set the glass down. Starting to say something, he grasped his throat and staggered. The priest crumpled to the floor in an agony of pain as sweat broke out on his forehead.

Mabel yanked the chain from his neck, opened the box, and scooped the money and jewels into a drawstring bag that had been sitting on the priest's desk ever since the donation for the orphanage had come in. Stepping over the priest, who was still cognizant but not able to talk, she grabbed her scarf and made her way down the hall as far as the side door. She ran across the courtyard and out of the monastery.

By now it was dark, but the moon was not as bright as the fisherman had said it would be. The air grew cooler as she approached the water.

Mabel ran, filled with the dread of knowing she could be apprehended. She ran as fast as her feet could carry her to the dock and the fisherman. Brugali waited for her. He helped her onto his craft with a sense of urgency, and taking the oars, they shoved off and were on their way. Mabel's eyes glittered in the darkened night.

The priest, still aware of his surroundings, couldn't control his body. His heart raced, pounding so hard that he couldn't hear anything but its beating. All was a blur and his mind could not function. Nausea hit him, but it was unproductive retching, arching his body. He lay exhausted.

Sister Amalia knocked on the heavy door and, receiving no answer, pushed it open. She walked swiftly to the priest's side and fell to her knees. His pupils were dilated and he sweated profusely.

Sister Amalia could no longer run, but fear put a swiftness to her feet she hadn't experienced in years. She went to the dispensary and grabbed a bottle of a poison called Calabar. Carefully, she put a few drops into some water and hurried back to Father Stenali. She knelt beside the unconscious man, and opening his mouth, she administered the liquid, knowing it was the only thing that could save him. She also knew it could hasten his death if she hadn't used the correct amount. By itself, it was perhaps more deadly than belladonna. She massaged the priest's throat as he seemed unable to swallow. Finally, a bit of the liquid went down, and she gave him a little bit more.

The contessa, who had come for the evening meal, lingered to talk to a visiting priest who had stopped on his religious pilgrimage to Rome. The man was a balm to her soul, and she enjoyed discussing things of spiritual import. The contessa, unlike most men and women, was an avid reader and well-versed in the scriptures. The visiting priest stood and bade her an early good night, saying he was worn and weary from his long journey.

Contessa di Amalfi approached Father Stenali's office, surprised by the opened door. Usually, the door was shut as the Father spent much time in his office praying. She entered with a quiet step and was horrified by what see saw.

"What has happened? What is wrong with him? Will he be all right? Oh, Amalia, I couldn't bear it if…" Her voice trailed off. "Is there anything I can do?" Going to her knees, she stroked Father Stenali's sweating brow. He seemed unaware of her presence.

Sister Amalia stood slowly, her aged body tired from the emotional crisis. Looking down at the contessa and the priest, she replied in a hushed but bitter tone.

"I told you that woman was evil—how evil, only God in heaven knows. She poisoned him, Contessa. That viper poisoned him! I have given him the extract of the Calabar bean. I have always kept it because of that cursed bush out in the courtyard."

As she spoke, the contessa had taken her shawl and balled it up, placing it gently behind the priest's head. Sister Amalia took a blanket from the bench and handed it to the contessa.

She continued to speak. "It is the only thing I know as an antidote to belladonna, but it too is deadly. I have no reason to believe that I gave him the right amount of the Calabar. I don't know if the Father will recover, and perhaps I have hastened his death." She began to cry huge, wracking sobs.

"Hush, Sister, hush." The contessa stood, taking the old woman into her arms. "You have done the best you could and whatever the outcome…well, it is that blonde-haired witch who is at fault. No one but her."

Her thoughts raced ahead of her words. *I shall follow her and have her arrested if it's the last thing I do!* "I will go now and send for Luigi. Get another blanket and cover him. He may be sweating now, but it won't last." She left the room in feverish haste, crossing herself and praying as she ran down the corridor. Yelling, which simply isn't done in the monastery, brought help in several forms.

The contessa gave directions quickly and succinctly. One of the kitchen boys ran to get Dr. Luigi Aroni, who lived only a few houses away from the monastery. Two other men came to help put the priest into his bed, and another went to rouse the inhabitants of the monastery to meet in the chapel to pray. Yes, they would all pray.

It was beginning to snow again, and light fluffy flakes whirled their way down from a pure white sky. There was no wind, but it was quite cold.

Charles was having the time of his life. They rode in a sleigh pulled by horses. It was almost as fun as sledding down a hill. Some of the hills were too steep, and Olivia had told the children they were to be careful. Accidents could happen, even on a sled.

Tory bounced with excitement. "I think this is one of the grandest days in my life!" she exclaimed. "I'm sorry it's time to go home."

Henry chimed in. "I'm sorry too, but my feet are so cold I can't feel them anymore. Wasn't that the funnest hill you ever sledded on? I've only ever been sledding one other time, and it wasn't so much fun."

His breath looked as if he were smoking and Charles laughed, but he changed the subject. He didn't want the day spoiled by talking about his mother sledding into Maddie on purpose.

"How many hills did we try out today?" he asked. "I lost count after the third one, I think."

"Wasn't it seven?" Tory asked. "I'm pretty sure it was seven."

Olivia said, "I think you're right, Toralina Lou. It was seven. When we get home, we'll gather in the kitchen and have hot chocolate, but first you must change out of your clothes, even your knickers. I want the wet ones hung up on the pulley in the back entry, please. We don't want to cause more work for Frankie than we have to."

"Mmm, that sounds good, and I'm going to sit by the hearth and warm my poor feet," said Henry. "I can wriggle my toes, but I can't feel them."

Manning said, "We certainly don't want anyone getting sick. We'll be home in just a few more minutes. It was fun, though, wasn't it?" He held the reins lightly in his gloved hands. He had thoroughly enjoyed himself. He hadn't gone sledding for years, and the added knowledge that the woman sitting beside him would one day be his wife was an incredible feeling. He wondered how long the euphoria would last. *I think it's going to last until I die. I loved Laura deeply, but the added bond of having Jesus Christ be the center of our relationship is going to magnify the love we have for each other. It will help us over the hurdles that can separate a couple.*

Olivia replied, "It was exciting for me. I haven't been on a sled since I was about eleven years old. I must look a fright, but I don't even care." She was bundled up from head to toe in a long coat, a scarf around her neck, and a woolen hat that had seen better days. It was Manning's, and to his way of thinking, she looked darling in it, with her cheeks rosy from the cold.

He looked over at her and grinned. "You look like a street urchin, and I love it!"

"What's a street urchin? Is it like a sea urchin?" Henry pounced on the word, wanting to increase his vocabulary.

Charles replied, "It's a child of the streets and usually poorly dressed. An urchin by itself is just a poorly dressed, mischievous child. I reckon it could be just a mischievous child without being poorly dressed." He ruminated over the word, thinking he'd like to be a lawyer when he grew up. He wanted to be like Mr. Humphries, or maybe he should be a banker. He didn't know yet and kept wondering what he'd like to do best. He didn't want to get caught up in something he hated and have to do it the rest of his life. He had no idea he would inherit enough money that he'd never be stuck doing something he didn't like. Manning Brighton was a wealthy man.

The snow began to fall in earnest, and before long they were covered in white fluff. The family arrived home, and shedding themselves of coats, hats, scarves, boots, and socks, they each headed to their own rooms to change. The house felt warm in contrast to the out-of-doors, and they were glad to be inside. Dusk fell early, and the day faded to pitch-black night.

Father Stenali rested quietly. The little group that had surrounded him made their way to a side room where a fire burned warmly in the grate, taking the chill out of the heavy stones that made up its walls. It was early morning and both Sister Amalia and the Contessa Viola Stella di Amalfi collapsed into chairs. They were worn out from the emotional upheaval they had suffered through the long night.

Viola, her light-brown eyes such an unusual color, stared intently at the doctor. "Luigi, oh Luigi, please tell me he's going to be all right. God in heaven above, show mercy and let your healing touch cover the Father. Oh, please God…"

"I don't know yet," the doctor replied. "I truly don't. There is no set formula for knowing exactly what a poison will do. Sister Amalia, you must know that what you did was the right thing. To do nothing was sure death. If you know your history, you know the wife of Emperor Augustus and the wife of Claudius both used belladonna to murder some of their contemporaries. Even before that, it was used to make poison-tipped arrows. Yes, it has been used throughout the ages."

He shook his head at such wickedness and continued to talk. "You were so right, Sister Amalia. That woman not only has a disturbed mind, she is evil. Wicked beyond the scope of our imagination to poison a priest."

"But what do you think, Luigi?" the contessa asked again. "Will Father Stenali recover?"

"I think, perhaps, he just might have full recovery. One really good sign is that there is no paralysis of the muscles. It might have affected his sight, but I believe that he would be dead by now had it not been for the Calabar that Sister Amalia administered to him. We can thank the Lord Almighty she was so quick to give him the antidote. He seems to be doing quite well for what he has endured. An older man or a man with a weakened heart would not have survived the trauma placed upon it. We must also realize that only time will tell, my dear. Only time will tell."

CHAPTER XXVI

Discretion shall preserve thee,
understanding shall keep thee:

PROVERBS 2:11

THE MOON, A BRIGHT FULL ORB in the sky, lit the way for
Brugali. It had grown so bright it seemed almost early morning or dusk.
He could see clearly, but he kept a close watch on his passenger too. He
didn't trust her and could sense the feeling was mutual. The fisherman
kept the coastline within sight. He didn't want to steer too close for fear of
reefs, but because the moon was so brilliant, he didn't have to worry about
being able to see his way forward.

Mabel said nothing.

Since they pushed off from the pier, her mind was focused on what she
should do next. *I don't think it wise to let Brugali return and tell anyone where I've
gone. If I get rid of him, I won't have to pay him either. I'd literally kill two birds with
one stone. Hmmm, seems like a good plan. Now, how do I go about it?*

Viola Stella di Amalfi couldn't seem to settle her thoughts. "Will Lorenzo, er, Father Stenali awaken at all this night?"

"I don't think so, Contessa. He is worn out from retching and the drug on his body. I assume it pretty safe to say he will sleep through the night. At any rate, I'm having a cot put into his room, and I'll sleep there just in case he awakens."

"I shall tell those who are praying in the chapel they can go to bed, and then I shall go home." She turned to the old nun, who looked exhausted. "Get some rest, my dear Sister Amalia. I think you will be quite busy taking care of our priest on the morrow. I have already decided to follow this woman, Mabel. I want her arrested for what she did. I will pack and make preparations for all that needs done. I believe I can hire a coach to take me up to Livorno, and I will book passage from there. I am quite sure this Mabel will go back to Boston. Wherever she goes, I will find her and make sure she pays for her crime."

"Ah, Contessa, remember 'Vengeance is mine; I will repay, saith the Lord.' Don't harden your heart, my dear. Whatever you do, don't harden your heart."

"No, Luigi, I will not do that. I do not hate her. I simply want justice. She tried to kill our priest. Did anyone look to see why? We've been so concerned about Father Stenali, we didn't even look in his office."

The three of them trooped back to the priest's office, and it was Sister Amalia who discovered the large key on the desk where Mabel had dropped it.

"Oh no! This thing she does is wicked. The father was so delighted to have the money to renovate the orphanage..." Her voice trailed off. She pulled open the heavy drawer and saw its contents had been emptied. "So this is why she poisoned him. She wanted the money to buy her way out of here." Tears stood out in the old woman's eyes and ran down her wrinkled cheeks. The contessa pulled Sister Amalia into her arms to comfort her.

"Don't tell him it's gone," she said. "I will replenish it myself. Please do not worry him further." The contessa looked apprehensively at the other two. "I mean it—please do not tell him. He has had enough to bear. He will forgive the woman and so must we, but I still want her to pay for her crime. I will telegram the Boston Police Department of her attempted murder and robbery. But I must go myself to make sure justice is served. I must!"

The telegram, a lengthy one, arrived by messenger to the Boston Police Department. It detailed what had occurred in Santa Marinella. It came as no shock to Chief Christopher Belden. He'd known in his gut the woman, Mabel Vickers-Brighton, hadn't died. It would have been too easy. If there was one thing he'd learned working in this line of business, the good seldom came easily.

The chief had definitely decided to step down—retire. He was tired of the grizzly business, tired of dealing with the sordid side of life. The years had been good to him, but he was bone-weary of the evil man perpetrated upon man. He'd be turning the department slowly over to George Baxter. He was an excellent detective and would make a superb chief, and an important fact for Chris was that George was a Christian. He would deal fairly and keep the department section straight. Chris hadn't told anyone about his decision, but he would, and soon.

He walked to his window and stood with his hands clasped behind his back, staring out at the street. The tree just outside his window had lost its leaves and allowed a cold light, filtered only by bare branches, into the room.

It was still early morning, and snow lay like a thick, puffy duvet cover, blanketing the world in a virginal bed of white. Earlier, when he'd ridden to the office, the sky had been heavy with clouds, but the wind had blown them away. The glaring sun made his eyes water from the brightness reflected off the snow. Chris stood at the window and thought about Mabel May Vickers-Brighton and her son Charles, who'd told him he'd watched as his mother killed his father. *What a horror for that poor little boy. I pray, Father, that Brighton loves him and helps to ease the terrible memories. I pray for all three of those children. I lift them to Thee, that Thou wouldst bring healing to those children. May they grow up normal and leave the baggage behind. Thanks,*

Lord. Please be with Manning Brighton. It will be a horrible shock to find his wife is still alive. Comfort him, I pray. In Jesus name I ask these things. Amen.

Guess I'll go see what George makes of it all, if he's in yet.

George was nearly late getting to work. He'd overslept, which almost never happened. He and Adeline had been to a dinner party the night before and returned home quite late. The two had sat up even later talking about their evening as they held hands in front of the warm fire in the library.

"I was surprised to see the Bouviers there, weren't you?"

"Yes. He was sure trying to cozy up to Mrs. Honeywell, wasn't he?"

"Yes, but at the same time he kept preventing me from talking with his wife. I wonder if the poor woman has any friends at all. He's a bad one, George, a very bad one. I can't imagine why she ever married such a man in the first place. He's a lot older than she is."

"I know he is a bad one. We've had our eyes on both him and his business partner, who is Madam Bouvier's father. We've gone over and over all the information. We've contacted the businessmen, but so far, we can find nothing on either of them. They ruin the businessmen who trust in their loans."

"Who is Madam Bouvier's father?"

"Jacques Corlay."

"Oh my! That poor woman! I'll wager her father married her off to the scoundrel. Oh, I do feel sorry for poor Madam Bouvier. Why, if I had those two in my life, I'd probably hate all men, and I'd certainly never trust them."

"I'm thankful you don't have them in your life, my dear." George patted her hand, leaning over to give her a kiss. "Are you feeling all right? You look a bit tired."

"I'm fine, George, just fine." Adeline had not been feeling at all well lately, but she wasn't going to tell George until she'd seen a doctor. "It's been a busy week and I'm tired, is all. Let's go to bed. You need to get up early."

And so George, who was nearly always early, was not in his office when Christopher Belden walked down the hall.

Chris decided to get some coffee for the two of them and start George's fire. His office was cold. Stuffing the telegram into his suit pocket, he laid the fire and lit it. Running lightly down the stairs, he found Elsie already ensconced in her kitchen, and wonderful smells were wafting their way into the reception area of the department. With his mouth beginning to water, Chris hailed Elsie.

"Good morning, Elsie. Uhmm, it smells dee-licious in here! What is that you're making?"

"Good morning, sir. I'm trying ta get some meat on your ole bones, Mistuh Chris. Don't seem ta be working, but I still tries!" She smiled a wide smile with teeth startlingly white in her brown face. "Uh hmm, I be a makin' you some scones and you kin picks your fillin'. You want apricot or strawberry?"

"I'll have one of each, thank you." He watched as she pulled the baking sheet out of her woodstove. "In fact, I'll take two apricot, one for Baxter and one for me, plus the strawberry for me, too." He grinned at her. "If our cook ever leaves us, I want you to come cook at my house. You have an excellent way with food, Elsie. Yes, excellent."

"Thank you, kind sir." She laughed a full-bellied laugh, handing him a tray with the scones and coffee. "You jest take that now an' be satisfied. Go on now, you have work ta do."

"Thank you, Elsie." Clearly startling her beyond measure, he bussed her cheek before taking the tray. He headed on up the stairs and entered George's office. He was sitting at his desk going through his mail.

"Good morning, George. How are you today?" He asked the younger man cheerfully.

"In truth, I'm feeling a bit discombobulated. I'm not used to oversleeping, and I did this morning, sir."

"Well, you're not late, by any means."

"I skipped breakfast and by the looks of you, I'm going to be able to eat a bit after all. I had counted on Elsie to rustle something up for me, but I expected to have to wait a bit. Thank you, chief. Thank you very much. You laid a fire in here too, didn't you?"

"Yes, and you're very welcome, George. Sit down and have a cup of coffee and eat a couple of Elsie's scones. I'll run down and get myself another later. I got myself two, thinking you'd most likely have already eaten breakfast."

Chris sat down across the desk from George, the latter telling him about the evening before and how Armand Bouvier had tried to cozy up to Mrs. Honeywell all evening, but she seemed aloof to his attentions.

"I'm glad to hear that. Honeywell owns quite a nice company, and I'd hate to see him get caught up in Bouvier and Corlay's schemes. They'd take over his business in no time."

"Yes, that's true. Madam Bouvier had her eyes on Honeywell, and I saw a look pass between the two of them. I have no doubt that at some point she gave Honeywell a heads-up. We were at a function before Christmas, and Mrs. Honeywell was all smiles with Bouvier. Well, whatever the case, I'm glad she virtually ignored the man last night."

The two men spoke about dealings the department had. There was an ongoing investigation of a murder down in the salt flats, and both suspected the same man and were close to making a few arrests.

Daisy entered and said she was sent by Elsie to give the two inspectors a second cup of coffee and more scones, if they wished. After she left, Christopher broached the subject of the telegram. He'd wanted to give George time to settle in before talking about Mabel Vickers-Brighton. He knew George would be mightily upset.

"Well, George, I have some bad news...some exceedingly bad news."

George felt his stomach tighten. He watched as his chief pulled out a telegram. He dreaded what his chief might impart. *Whatever is coming must be mighty bad for my chief to lay a fire and feed me first. He's breaking the news gently. It must be bad.*

Chris handed the telegram across the desk to George, who perused it rapidly, his face turning a ghastly white.

"I knew it. I didn't want to believe it, but in my gut, I knew it. When the Vickers boy, Charles, said he knew his mother wasn't dead, I knew it to be true." He looked across the desk into Chief Belden's eyes. "She's coming after Brighton, you know. She's heading this way. Oh Lord, help us! She even poisoned a priest! The woman is evil, Chief, very, very evil."

"Yes, I know, but what shall we do? I hate to spoil Brighton's peace of mind, but we'll have to tell him. He's going to need protection. We'll have a couple of the younger men keep watch on 'em around the clock. We won't be able to control the docks. We have no idea if she'll arrive on a tramp steamer or a cruise line or something in between. At any rate, it's too easy to slip through and a waste of manpower. No, besides keeping watch on Brighton, I suspect a watch on the Brighton premises would be our best bet. There's two of her children to watch, but what if she decides to hurt Brighton by going after his daughter? We have no way of knowing who any of her contacts are here in Boston. Wonder where she'll stay when she comes? We've got our work cut out for us on this one, to be sure!"

The two men talked at length about the possible contingencies of what Mabel May Vickers-Brighton might do and how they could catch her.

The Contessa Viola Stella di Amalfi booked passage on a cruise liner headed for Boston. She'd been to the United States before, but only to New York and down the East Coast. Knowing her English was more than passable, the contessa looked forward to arriving in Boston.

Her first stop would be the police station. She'd sent a telegram ahead telling of Mabel Vickers' treachery. She also stated that she wished to speak to the man in charge. That accomplished, she'd find lodging, perhaps at Young's Hotel. She'd read of that establishment in a brochure and was sure it would be an amenable place to stay. Viola had enjoyed being honored at the captain's table for more than one night.

She was a beautiful woman and sought after by the single men as well as flirted with by married men who should know better. It was a cold crossing, and she could be found either in the lounge or in her stateroom. When she wasn't in the lounge, the contessa read, crocheted, or prayed, for the six days it took to cross the Atlantic.

She'd left Santa Marinella only after making sure that Lorenzo Stenali would be all right. He was a bit slow of speech and said his eyesight bothered him, but Luigi thought he would make a full recovery. How thankful to Sister Amalia she was for keeping her head and giving the priest the antidote as quickly as she had. She shuddered when she thought of the alternative.

CHAPTER XXVII

They will not frame their doings to turn unto their God:
for the spirit of whoredoms is in the midst of them,
and they have not known the Lord.

HOSEA 5:4

LIBERTY WALKED SMOOTHLY, picking up her skirts as she started down the stairs. She thought back to boarding school and how many times she'd been made to walk up and down a flight of stairs with books piled atop her head. She almost giggled at the memory of the countless times Madam Mosman had voiced disapproval of her dropping books off her head. Liberty descended graciously and turned toward the parlor, her back straight and her head well up.

As she entered, heads turned and some conversation stopped. Her eyes went straight to Armand's.

His lip curled sardonically at the showstopper who was his wife. His hand was on Edwina Peabody's arm, and he gave it a gentle squeeze and a pat as he left her to welcome his wife in front of all onlookers. He knew he was the envy of many men present, and it pleased him that his wife was so beautiful, but he never let Liberty know of his pleasure.

There was an elusive something about her that he'd never been able to penetrate. He'd tried to break her spirit, but it hadn't worked. He could see by the set of her head that she was self-contained and poised for whatever he chose to do. He surprised her by kissing her cheek in front of the guests and took her hand in his. He led her to Mr. Peabody. Taking his leave, he strolled back toward Mrs. Peabody. He had a fleeting thought that Liberty would never love him…he would never attain to the elusive something about her that held him captive.

There was a place in her, untouched by him, that would love only one man, and that man—forever.

Mr. Peabody, quite handsome but quite sexist, took his cue from Armand's amicable behavior. He turned to Madam Bouvier and spoke to her as an equal rather than speaking down at her.

"You're looking quite lovely tonight, madam."

"Thank you," she replied and then quoted, "'Beauty, like supreme dominion is but supported by opinion.'" She smiled up at him winningly, and he was suddenly at a loss for words, not only because of her charm but by the quote.

"Benjamin Franklin," he answered back. "I admire so many of his sayings."

"As do I… For example, another that has become my favorite is, 'He that is of the opinion money will do everything may well be suspected of doing everything for money.'"

Mr. Peabody looked down at her, puzzled. "That doesn't seem to be a quote a woman would care about. Why do you?" He was now quite interested in her answer. He'd thought her a showpiece, a woman with no thought in her head but to dress nicely and sit quietly, listening but unable to contribute. His own wife seemed to have no ideas of her own. She could barely read, but she came from a moneyed family, and that had been important to him. Now, he wasn't so sure. There was no companionship between the two of them. He leaned closer to hear Madam Bouvier's reply, as she spoke quite softly.

"Because, Mr. Peabody, Bouvier Enterprises does everything for money. Do you know, sir, that we've acquired upwards of eleven companies in the past seven years?" She nodded at his wife. "Looks as if my husband is now working on his twelfth." Her cheeks colored up at her daring conversation. She realized he could spurn her and tell all to Armand.

Mr. Peabody's discerning eyes swung from her to his wife, who was laughing, almost uncontrollably, up at Armand Bouvier. His lips tightened with enlightenment at the information he'd received. He turned back to Liberty and said quietly, "Thank you for your wise counsel, Madam Bouvier. I have no doubt I'd have been the twelfth without your warning. Please know I am discreet. Your notice to me will not go further. I've played quite the fool, but no more. Again, I appreciate your word of caution. Would you care to walk in to dinner with me?"

"I would be honored, sir, but I think, as Shakespeare said, discretion on my part is the better part of valor. I do thank you for your listening ear and the invitation. I simply wish to avoid the wrath to follow if my husband should, in any way, think I alerted you."

She smiled pleasantly and moved off to another group that contained the woman with whom she enjoyed conversation. She could feel her heart beating wildly in her throat from talking to Mr. Peabody, but she thanked the Lord in her heart that Peabody, too, had listened. She began to chalk up companies she'd helped save from her father and Armand's clutches.

Three days later, a woman dressed in deep mourning descended the gangplank of a huge cruise ship. The sky was pure pewter. Rain poured forth in huge drops mixed with snow. Slanting sideways, an umbrella was nearly useless. Everything was wet. It was cold.

Despite the miserable weather, a detective stood at a distance and watched the woman in black. He did not consider her twice after his initial perusal. He was thoroughly wet, cold, and miserable as he waited. The woman dressed in mourning went into the customs shed, and upon finishing, she exited out another door. She was met by a man dressed in elegant clothing. The detective's attention swung back to a beautiful woman descending the gangplank, but she was on a man's arm. Leaning back against the hard brick wall of the warehouse behind him, he figured this ship most likely didn't contain Mabel Vickers-Brighton either.

Armand met Mabel at the customs shed exit. He took her into his arms and publicly, to the disapproval of several passersby, kissed her long and hard.

The detective across the street watched impassively.

Armand took Mabel by the arm, and they strolled to the main street, where he hailed a hansom cab. Giving the cabby an address, the two climbed into the cabriolet.

"Everyone thinks you're dead, my dear, but it looks to me as if you are in deep mourning." Armand smiled at Mabel, patting her gloved hand.

"I would have been dead had it not been for a huge Italian who saved me when I was unconscious. At least to the best of my knowledge, that must be what happened."

"How did you get money to travel back to Boston?" Armand was fascinated by this wicked woman who had no more scruples than he. He knew she'd poisoned her husband and the banker, Burbank.

Mabel smiled, appreciating Armand's admiration of her, and told him everything that had transpired. She felt no shame for having poisoned the priest.

He admired her ingenuity and success. They traveled together, getting caught up on the happenings in their lives since they were last together. Neither thought to look behind them at another hansom that followed them through the busy streets of Boston.

Because of the Peabody's invitation, Liberty had no time to notify the police of the correct arrival time of Mabel Vickers-Brighton until midmorning. They'd arrived home from New York quite late the evening before. Armand, visibly upset all the way home, had never let her in on the reason for his irritation. She surmised that Mr. Peabody had told his wife to not talk to Armand. Breakfast had been a bit quieter without Armand's and Mrs. Peabody's heads together, laughing and carrying on the way they had the previous two mornings. Yes, Armand had been very upset.

Liberty sent a message to Inspector Belden, when Armand left the house that morning, to tell him of the ship's arrival time. She'd also hailed a hansom cab as soon as Armand left the house. Because of the telegram she'd inadvertently opened, she knew on which ship Mabel was arriving and had the cabby drive her to the docks. She sat in the deep shadows of the cab watching the scene unfold in front of her as if it were a play being enacted. She looked across the street to the customs shed where Armand was headed and saw the man watching the ship.

Liberty breathed a sigh of relief that her note had arrived early enough for something to be done. The young inspector carefully scrutinized every passenger who disembarked, but Liberty didn't pay any attention to the passengers. She kept her eyes on Armand. She knew he had several houses where he kept women, and she had decided to trail him and not worry about the ship. She could have taken her carriage but preferred the hansom cab. Their carriage had an ostentatious coat of arms on the doors. She'd not wanted to involve Jean-Paul in any venture that could ultimately get him dismissed from the Bouviers' employ.

George was visibly upset. Chris Belden had come into his office midmorning to tell him of the anonymous note that had just arrived. He hurriedly pulled his watch out of a fob pocket and checked the time.

"It's arriving right now," he said.

"I know, I know," Christopher Belden said. "This just arrived. I opened it and here's the information we've needed. I certainly hope Dufort keeps his eyes peeled. We have him watching the ships coming into port, and he's also keeping watch on the customs shed."

Traffic in the city picked up as people left their places of business to eat a bite of lunch in the fine restaurants and inns that afforded them a wonderful break from their offices.

Liberty rode in the cabriolet, craning her neck to see. She realized her cab driver had lost sight of Armand's hansom cab as it made a sharp right turn. She tapped her foot, impatient for the carriage in front of them to clear. As they turned the corner, she knew Armand had disappeared. The cabby, at her direction, drove slowly up the street, but the hansom cab had disappeared.

"I'm sorry, ma'am," he said. "I seem to have lost them in the busyness of the streets."

The rain beat loudly down on the roof of the hansom, and Liberty scooted forward to hear him.

Her heart sank at his words. "Thank you for trying. I'd like you to take me to police headquarters, please." She sat back and began to pray out loud. "Lord, oh my Father, please protect the Brightons. I pray You will give wisdom to the detectives and help them to be wise as serpents in ferreting out where Armand is hiding Mrs. Vickers-Brighton. I also pray for wisdom in talking to the detective. Give me favor, oh Lord. Thank You, my Father."

Liberty leaned her head back against the bolster. She thought about what she could relate to the inspectors, but was thankful they'd had a man watching. *It is to be hoped that everything is under control,* she thought.

The cab pulled up in front of the police station, and picking up a small bag she'd brought with her off the seat, she exited the hansom. Taking the cabby's outstretched hand with her gloved one, she smiled up at the man. His huge umbrella protected her head from the onslaught of rain pouring down, but her skirts were another matter as the rain slashed sideways. The cabby stayed with her as she ascended the steps. She pulled out her reticule and paid him, thanking him for his thoughtfulness.

He took her hand, closed her fingers around the greenbacks she held, and said, "Madam, I don't deserve to be paid. I didn't stay close enough and I lost that other cab."

Taking the money, she tucked it into his breast pocket and said, "Sir, you did your best, and I couldn't ask for more." Liberty smiled and the man smiled back, his cheeks reddening under her green-eyed gaze.

"Thank you," she said as she walked into the station. Libby was surprised by the smell of bread baking. Her stomach rumbled, as she'd not eaten before leaving the house. She'd wanted to keep her eye on Armand. With her back straight and her chin up, she approached the information desk. Anyone looking at her would never imagine she was anything but composed, but her heart beat a rapid cadence as the clerk walked up to the desk.

"Yes, how may I help you, madam?"

"I wish to speak to the chief inspector, please."

"May I tell him who's calling?"

Liberty fumbled about for a second before quietly answering, "Sir, I do not wish my name bandied about, so I will not give my name until I am speaking with him. I have something I am sure he would appreciate."

She hoped the clerk could ascertain by her speech and clothing that she was not a woman to be trifled with.

"Yes, madam, please follow me. I am sure Chief Belden will see you." He led her up the wide flight of stairs and down the hall to a door with an opaque glass window in it. A brass nameplate under the window read Boston Police Detective Branch. And under that was Chief Inspector Christopher Belden. The clerk rapped on the door and a voice said "Enter." The clerk opened the door and ushered Liberty inside.

"A woman to see you, sir."

"Thank you, Bobby."

Chris had been reading a missive from someone who said he had information about another case they were working on. He looked up as the door closed to see the most beautiful woman he'd ever set eyes on.

He rose and said, "Please, be seated." He waved to a chair across from his. Liberty sat down as he did, and the two of them looked at each other across the wide desk.

Liberty was nervous. She was well-aware that many men were in Armand's pocket. He paid public officials all the time, and she knew if this man was one of them, he could tell Armand about this visit. She handed him the small package.

"I found this reticule and wished to turn it in." She looked down at his desk and breathed a deep sigh of relief. A Bible lay open at Romans, the eighth chapter. She looked up to see his eyes looking kindly at her.

"My name is Madam Liberty Bouvier," she said.

At the name Bouvier, Inspector Belden sat up a little straighter. He was well-acquainted with Armand Bouvier's shenanigans. He had ruined many a good man, and yet the department could find no way to convict him of any specific crime.

"I'm Chief Inspector Christopher Belden," he replied. "Where did you get this?"

"I found it lying on a bench in the park when I was out riding, but it is not the main reason I am here. I needed some kind of an excuse to talk with you."

"How may I be of assistance?" Christopher Belden saw her nervousness and wondered at it.

CHAPTER XXVIII

But whoso hearkeneth unto me shall dwell safely,
and shall be quiet from fear of evil.

PROVERBS 1:33

LIBERTY, HER GREEN EYES SERIOUS, replied in a quiet voice to Inspector Belden.

"I wanted to tell you that Mrs. Vickers-Brighton arrived on time, and although I followed Armand, my cabby lost him in traffic. I know he has several houses where he keeps, ah, where he keeps..." Her face colored up as her voice trailed off.

"Are you saying you are the one who sent the note earlier today, and Mrs. Mabel Vickers-Brighton was met by Monsieur Bouvier?"

"Yes, that is what I am saying." She looked fully into his eyes, her eyes now full of misery.

This woman was beautiful inside and out, Chris surmised.

What she must endure at the hands of Bouvier doesn't bear thinking about, he thought. *It took much courage for her to come here like this.* Aloud, he said, "I cannot begin to thank you. We have a man watching the ship. Surely he will have followed and will know where the two of them have gone."

"N-no. I saw him. He never left the dock. After Armand met the woman, the two of them left the dock together, but your detective was still watching the ship."

"Please wait here." Chris Belden ran down the hall to George Baxter's office, but he wasn't there. Running lightly down the stairs to the information desk, he asked Bobby, "Have you seen Inspector Baxter?"

"Yes," Bobby said, "he told me he planned to go down to the docks and check on Dufort."

"Thank you." There was nothing more to be gained at that moment, so he headed back to get coffee and scones from Elsie.

"I'll fix up a tray, Inspector, and have Daisy bring it up shortly."

"Thank you, Elsie. You're a gem of the most precious kind." He left her grinning and ran lightly up the stairs. He reentered his office and closed the door behind him.

"Madam Bouvier, thank you for your help. I'm afraid with your husband's help, the Vickers-Brighton woman has slipped through our fingers. We have a detective watching the Brighton household around the clock."

Liberty pointed to his Bible. "I've been praying for the Brightons to be safe."

"You're a believer, then?"

"Oh yes! Quite frankly, I couldn't survive without Jesus. He's my strength, my shield and buckler, my protection against the world's woes, I suppose you could say." She smiled, a little shyly.

"Yes, He's that for me, also. He—"

"Good morning, sir!" Daisy entered with a tray of scones and coffee, much to Liberty's surprise. Her stomach rumbled as the smell of freshly baked scones wafted toward her.

"Good morning to you, Daisy, and thank you for this treat." Christopher Belden took the tray from her as Daisy looked curiously at Liberty. He opened the door and ushered Daisy back out. He knew of her curiosity and penchant for gossip. He closed the heavy door firmly behind him. "Thought I'd offer you a bite to eat before you leave, madam."

"I, in truth, am famished. I'm normally an early riser, but I also eat right after getting up and hadn't the time this morning." Libby took one of the scones and bit into it. It was filled with raspberry jam and tasted wonderful.

"How do you like your coffee?"

"Black would be fine," Liberty said once she swallowed the scone. "This is delicious. How ever did you find a cook for a police department?" She smiled at the inspector.

"It's a long story, but since you're here, may I ask, are you aware of your husband's dealings? Do you know anything at all about his business? I'm not trying to put you on the spot. I am simply wondering."

"Yes, I do know. He is a partner with my father, Monsieur Jacques Corlay, and the two of them loan money to unsuspecting businessmen and then, somehow, the businessman loses his company. I haven't figured out exactly how that happens. I've been trying to warn some of the men if I know about it, but too many times I have no idea with whom they are dealing."

"You must be very careful, Madam Bouvier. We too know that much, but the how is still a quandary."

"Yes, I am careful. I don't know what Armand would do if he found out I have warned some of his prospective victims. I am glad that this department is aware of it." She took a sip of the coffee appreciatively. It was hot and a Colombian roast.

The Brighton household enjoyed a bit of a holiday, as Manning and Olivia decided the children should stay home and not be cause for more work for the inspectors.

Manning was thankful Olivia fully agreed with his plan. He wanted the children to remain in the house, close to him and safe from Mabel's treacherous schemes. He wondered if she had any friends in Boston, anyone who would help her. It was curious to think he was married to her and knew nothing about her personal friends.

Olivia had arisen earlier than usual, but Cookie was already up and the coffee made. Gratefully, she took a cup back up to her room. She had some serious praying to do this day. Inspector Belden himself had come last evening to tell them that Mabel had slipped through their net and was on the loose somewhere in the city.

After praying, she dressed and went down to share with Manning what she believed to be a good idea. The door to the library was wide open, and she found him ensconced in one of the deep leather chairs with a cup of coffee. He stared into the fire. She entered and gently closed the door behind her.

Hearing the click of the latch, he turned, and his eyes warmed as they looked into hers. He stood and started to take her into his arms, but he dropped his hands to his sides as he realized he was still a married man.

"Good morning. You're up early," Manning said.

"Yes, there are a few things I wanted to discuss with you before the children are up."

Side by side in the deep leather chairs, they turned to face each other.

"The first thing is that I think we should tell the children about Mabel. Things like this shouldn't be kept secret from them. If something untoward should happen, I don't want them to be unprepared mentally. Do you agree?" Olivia asked.

"As much as I hate to upset them, especially Henry, I think it is only wise. Better a bit upset and prepared for the worst than to be kept in the dark. What else do you have on your mind?"

"I wondered if it would be all right for the contessa to stay here while she is in the United States. I know this is your house, but I believe it would be good for all of us to have her here. It's lonely for a woman traveling alone. I know that from experience, and I believe she'd enjoy staying with us while she is here."

"Of course it is fine with me. This will soon be your house too. You have every right to make decisions." He squeezed her hand and then brought it to his mouth and kissed it.

"Manning, I know I needn't remind you that you are still married."

His face darkened at her words, and he replied, "I do realize that, but whatever happens, remember...I love you." He slipped a hand into his pocket. "Oh...I nearly forgot." He smiled into her eyes, his warm with love. "Here." He took her hand again and slipped the garnet solitaire surrounded by diamonds onto her finger. "I don't know what is going to happen, but I do know if Mabel is caught, she will hang for her crimes. Olivia, my dear, I am sorry for the sordidness of all this. It has been such a nightmare, and I thought it was over. I had also asked Elijah to look into an annulment since the marriage was never consummated." He was a bit embarrassed by his words, and he began to pace around the room as he talked.

"Charles was right all along. Mabel was not dead, but it doesn't fill me with dread the way it would have. One thing I learned that very first day with Elijah is everything that comes my way, everything that happens to me, is filtered by the hand of the Almighty. When I am out of step, He may allow something to bring me to a place where I am dependent upon Him. Anything that furthers His kingdom, that draws people closer to Him, is good whether we view it that way or not. I have been meeting with Elijah Humphries and he is mentoring me. He said all of us, no matter where we are in our life's journey, need to mentor someone and have someone mentoring us."

"I've never thought of that before, but it is a good idea, isn't it? It would have to be someone totally trustworthy, but I can see the benefit of mentoring and having someone to pray with on a regular basis."

Olivia was fascinated with the idea of Manning's peace of mind. She knew of his distraught state of mind when he'd returned from Italy. *What a difference an encounter with Jesus Christ has made in his life!*

"So," he asked, "how shall we present the idea of a living. breathing Mabel to the children?"

"Right here. We'll tell them why they are not going to school and calmly explain why we have detectives watching the house. Let's pray Henry takes it all right. Charles is growing in his faith, and I believe he'll be all right with this."

They knelt right there and prayed together for God to be in control.

The next morning it was still pouring rain. The room, lit only by a few lamps, was opulent, the furniture beautiful but heavy and dark, looking almost Spanish. The walls, painted much like the Bouviers'

manse, looked as if the same man designed the interior of both. Heavy brocade curtains were drawn against prying eyes.

Mabel laughed across the table at Armand's jest about his Christian wife. "Why ever did you marry that little prude in the first place? I should have thought you could have found any woman you wanted. I know I've asked you this before, but you never answered me. So, I ask again, why did you?"

"Well, probably the most important reason is her name. It's opened doors into society for me that would have otherwise been closed. Her mother was a Browning, you understand, or perhaps you don't, since they've all died off except for Liberty herself. The second reason is, I don't believe in my entire life I've seen any woman more beautiful." He knew his comment would rankle Mabel deeply, and he laughed sardonically at her expression.

He continued. "There is something about my wife that holds my interest, which is amazing because no one else ever has. She is very self-contained, and there is a part of her that I don't know nor do I understand, but nonetheless, it piques my interest." To himself, he added, *And try though I may, I cannot break her spirit.*

"Well, let's change the subject, shall we? I've never cared for your wife. I believe she thinks she's better than anyone else."

"That's just it—she doesn't. She is unaware of her beauty, and I wish to keep it that way. She has no idea of the impact she makes on a room full of people." *Unlike you*, he thought, *her beauty will last into old age.*

"Well, I think she's full of pretension. A spoiled snob, that's what she is." Mabel had never shared the limelight with another woman and didn't plan to begin now. "So, dear Armand, will you help me plan a way to get rid of Mister Manning Brighton and get my son Henry back?"

"No! I don't like children and I don't care to have the police breathing down my neck any more than they already do. I've provided a place for you to stay and that is enough, my dear."

George Baxter was down to the docks to check on Dufort. An errand boy came running up with a missive for him. George reached into his pocket and gave a gratuity to the boy, who was drenched from the pouring rain.

"Thank ye, kind sir," the boy said. "Will I be waitin' fer an answer?"

"No, I plan to talk to the man who sent this note shortly, but thank you."

"Yer welcome, sir, ta be sure." The boy ran off, happy to have made a little money on both ends of the errand.

George opened the note and grimaced. "Dufort, did you see a woman come off this ship dressed in deep mourning?"

"Y-yes, sir, I did."

"Well, let's be going, then. We know who she's with, but I wonder where she went."

George didn't express it, but he was angry. Angry that a woman of Mabel Vickers-Brighton's ilk was on the loose. Angry that the department, for the past two years, had not found one shred of evidence that she was a murderess, and now that they had it, she was able to slip right through their fingers. She was dangerous, not only to the Brightons, but to anyone who got in her way. George hailed a hansom cab and the two men climbed on.

"I did see her after she came out of the customs shed, and it didn't even dawn on me to think about her being in black and kissing that man as if the two were lovers. That should have clued me in. Sorry, sir. I messed up for sure."

"Well, some days you win and some days you lose, but I would like you to report all you saw to Inspector Belden when we get back. We're going to have to put a hedge around the Brightons' premises until we can catch this woman, somehow." As the carriage pulled up to the station, George patted Dufort on the back. "See you later. I have an errand to run before I attack that pile of mail on my desk."

Contessa Viola Stella di Amalfi arrived into Boston looking rested and quite at peace with the world.

The Brightons and Olivia Anderson met the ship coming in from Italy with excitement.

George Baxter and Adeline were also there, as well as Franklin Dufort, who apologized to the Brightons for having let Mabel slip through his grasp.

Manning said, "It's difficult to catch a person when you don't know who they are or their physical characteristics." He could see Dufort's discomfiture and felt sympathy for the man, and yet wished he'd been a bit more careful. *Certainly there were not that many single women traveling alone. Ah well, I leave all of this in Thy capable hands, Father.*

He watched as a woman descended the ramp, several men surrounding her—all attentive to her every need—and surmised with an inward smile that she must be the contessa.

CHAPTER XXIX

A naughty person, a wicked man,
walketh with a froward mouth.

PROVERBS 6:12

TORY JUMPED UP AND DOWN. "That must be her. Look! I'll wager that's her! A real countess from Italy. Oh, Charlie, Henry, doesn't it make you want to swoon with excitement? Oh, I do hope she will stay with us! Don't you want her to stay with us?" Tory was excited. She'd been so upset to hear about Mabel still being alive and felt as if her emotions were on a bobsled going downhill with no way to put the brakes on. She'd been excited to hear that a real contessa might stay at her house. Now that she'd seen the beautifully dressed lady surrounded by men, her excitement rose even higher.

"Oh look, Aunt Ollie, Mrs. Baxter—see how lovely she looks. Do you think she can speak English?"

Adeline answered her. "I speak Italian, as does your father and Olivia. We shan't have a problem communicating. And yes, she looks lovely."

Olivia said, "I'm glad she's arrived safely and hope she will want to stay with us."

Although her papa and Olivia didn't say so, Tory had figured out on her own that when Mabel was caught, she would hang for murder. *Inspector*

George Baxter will see to that. She could tell her papa had fallen in love with Olivia and nothing could have made her happier.

Because of what they'd been told, Charles wasn't excited. Tory could tell his heart was heavy because of the conversation they'd had in the kitchen around the table. They'd met there so Frankie and Cookie could hear. And Ralph had been asked to come in from the stable. He was to keep a sharp lookout around the stable and back courtyard.

Now that Charles knew for sure his mother wasn't dead, he told Tory he needed to pray about his attitude because he wished she were dead and knew that was wrong. He told her he couldn't seem to help it. It wasn't that he wanted vengeance for his father's death; he simply didn't want to be afraid anymore. He wanted to protect Henry from her too. Both Tory and Charles knew Mabel would come for Henry, and they both agreed she probably wanted to wreak retribution on their papa for having left her to die, and not dying himself.

As they waited for the contessa, Henry was awash with emotions.

He'd been shocked when Papa and Aunt Ollie sat the children down around the kitchen table and explained to them about his mother having survived the ship going down in the Mediterranean. Henry had finally come to the conclusion that his mother was evil. He had adored his father, and although he'd known he was his mother's favorite, he never knew from one moment to the next exactly what she would do.

He looked over at Tory bouncing with excitement and wished he were as carefree. He turned to his brother and saw Charles' mouth. Henry could see Charles felt the way he did. He felt no remorse for not wanting to see her. His life was different now, and he liked it. He decided it would be better never to see her again. She would hang for murdering his papa. That much he knew.

The group remained at a distance, but George approached the woman still surrounded by men and said, "Excuse me, are you the Contessa di Amalfi?"

The woman nodded and smiled. "Yes," she answered. "I am Contessa Viola Stella di Amalfi." Her English held very little accent, which surprised George. The contessa held out her hand and George took it, briefly bowing over it.

"Welcome to Boston, Contessa di Amalfi. My name is George Baxter and I am with the Boston Police, detective branch."

As soon as George said he was with the police, Viola straightened her back, stared into his eyes, and asked, "Did you catch her? Do you have Mabel Vickers in custody? I...I'm sorry...please excuse my lack of good manners. It is nice to meet you, sir. I simply have been concentrating...is that the correct word? I have been brooding or preoccupied for the past six days. Well actually, ever since that woman poisoned my priest. I've thought of little else but to see her apprehended and held accountable for her crime."

"Yes, I can well understand. Please, let's go someplace where we can talk. I can accompany you through the customs shed since I am from the department. Also, there are some people who would like to meet you. It is to their house I think we should go first. Come with me."

George waved to Manning and the group to meet them on the other side of the customs shed. Taking the contessa's arm, he led her through customs. There was a bit of a wait, as one of the cranes used to unload the ship had broken, and men were bringing the luggage down the gangplank and into the customs shed to be sorted out by the passengers. Once everything was collected and checked, George led the contessa to the group awaiting her arrival.

"Well, you certainly can't bring anyone here!" Armand, his face red with anger, was nearly shouting at Mabel, whose eyes were a dark glittering blue. "I want no connection to your kidnapping anyone or murdering Brighton, for that matter. I gave you a place to stay, but you'd better be finding your own place to live if you decide to enact your plan. I want no part of it. I have my own interests to protect. The schemes you're concocting, well, you can just go elsewhere to accomplish them. I have helped you and will continue to do so for as long as you need it. Once you start crossing the law, you're out. Do you understand? I walk a thin enough line as it is with the Boston Police Department sniffing around me all the time. I certainly don't need to be accused as being an accomplice to whatever it is you decide to do!" Armand looked incensed that Mabel would even suggest bringing her brat to this hidey-hole of his. "So far, no one has ever found this place, and I intend to keep it that way. I have rented it under an assumed name."

"I will begin looking for a place to rent or perhaps just get a hotel room. My Henry will not be making much noise. He loves me and will do anything I say for him to do, so there are no worries there." Her eyes still glittered from the tone Armand had used on her. *Perhaps Armand is expendable.* She lowered her lashes so he couldn't tell what she thought. He seemed to read her fairly well. *I'm sick and tired of men telling me what to do. Ah, there it is. I know now what I can do. Yes, what a wonderful plan.*

George and Adeline had been invited to the Brightons' for dinner, as had the contessa.

She said she was delighted to stay on with them.

"You have a generous heart to allow me to abide here with you until…" Her voice trailed off as she realized the children were listening intently to her every word. She finished, saying smoothly, "Until my return trip to my beloved Santa Marinella."

Tory, her eyes wide with wonder that a real contessa would deign to stay with them, asked, "What's Italy like? Why do you love it so much?"

The contessa smiled across the table at this sweet, young girl and replied, "Italy, ah, yes…Italy, my dear girl, is a foretaste of heaven. It is a glorious country washed in sunlight, and the food…ah, the food…" She kissed her fingertips in an expression of appreciation. "The food is the nectar and ambrosia of the heavens. Yes, I think God, our Father, will have Italian food at the great feast for all the saints in heaven one glorious day." She laughed. "I love Italy, I love my people, and I love our customs and the beauty of it. It seems whenever I travel, I can't wait to get back to my beloved Italy!"

All three children were captivated by the powerful presence of the Contessa di Amalfi. She was beautiful, intelligent, and radiated contentment and peace, yet she sparkled with personality. She was a vivacious woman, and everyone at the table felt mesmerized by her. Even Charles, usually so quiet, was drawn into the conversation and enchanted by her charm.

Several times, Adeline spoke to her in rapid Italian and she replied in kind. The two had an instant rapport and Olivia, knowing a smattering of Italian, followed a bit of the conversation too.

George turned to Manning and told him, in an aside, that there were now four men guarding the house. They would be watching if any strange woman got even close to the edifice.

Manning nodded his head, but his heart was heavy, knowing Mabel would find a way. He could only pray that his newly found Savior would see fit to protect his household.

Liberty sat in her dark sitting room knitting sweaters for the children at the deaf school. Annie had come in with hot tea, and so laying her knitting aside, she sat sipping and thinking as she looked out the window. *What is Armand up to, Father? He's been away for three days now without a word. I know he's with the Vickers-Brighton woman. I wish I knew where. Lord, Maker of heaven and earth, You know, only You know our hearts' desires. I desire, my Father, that You would please protect Miss Anderson and the Brighton family. Lord, hedge them in with Your angels. Let no harm come to them, I pray in the name of Jesus. Lord, again I ask for Your Holy Spirit to woo Armand's heart to You. You have commanded women to respect their husbands, Lord. Please forgive me because I don't. I don't see anything in him to respect. If I'm to respect him, please, Father, help me to remember that my struggle is not against flesh and blood but against the spiritual forces of wickedness in the heavenly places. It's not Armand but the evil he does that I must contend against. Please change his heart. Grant him the desire to be good, I pray in Your precious, wondrous name. Amen.* Liberty prayed fervently for her husband but knew, too, that God had given Armand the freedom to make his own choices.

Armand entered the apartment. "Mabel, I've found a place for you. It's not far from here, and I think it's time you were on your own. If you need any help, you can contact either or both of these men." He shoved a piece of paper across the table where Mabel sat, looking bleary eyed. "They are both extremely discreet, and for the right amount of money, they will do anything. I've found them to be quite useful in my line of business."

"Thank you." Mabel had just gotten up from a nap and felt thick headed. She reached up to straighten her hair. Armand stood watching her as she pulled the remaining pins from her bun. It cascaded down in a ripple of blonde waves.

It was beautiful and he reached out a hand. Taking the length of hair, he wrapped it around his hand; she went willingly into his arms.

Olivia couldn't decide what to do about the children and their schooling. She'd spoken to Manning that morning about their school assignments, and he'd said they could get lessons from the teacher and work on them at home. He didn't want his children out where Mabel could easily grab them someplace.

He'd hugged her, planted a kiss on her cheek, and left for the bank. A detective was shadowing him at all times, and for that he was grateful.

Olivia had written out a list of necessities and wanted Lorna to get some things from the mercantile. She tapped her teeth with the end of her ivory pen. It had been a present from Manning and she loved using it. The nib was made of steel and was far superior to the quill pens she'd used all her life.

I don't believe it would be harmful to walk the half mile to the school and get the children's work. I don't want them to get too far behind. It's a boon the schoolmaster is so understanding and allows the children to miss so much schooling. It's been a full week now, and they're going to need to get caught up. That's what I'll do after lunch. I'm going to get their schoolwork. She smiled to herself as she descended the stairs. She could hear giggling behind her and turned to see Tory and Henry, both with eyes bright and full of laughter.

"What's so humorous this early in the morning?" she asked them, smiling.

"Tory stitched the cuffs of Charles' shirt together." Henry laughed a full-bellied laugh. "It was hanging on his chair, and she crept in there and took it. When she was finished, she put it back, and he's still sleeping. He's going to find it difficult to get his hands through unless he finds some scissors to clip the threads. She did a good job on it." Both children laughed again.

Charles strolled down the hall, the shirt in question buttoned up to his neck and looking none the worse for wear.

He looked at Tory and Henry and spoke pleasantly. "Good morning. Sure is raining hard, isn't it?" He brushed past an open-mouthed Tory, took Olivia's arm, and said, "Good morning, Aunt Ollie. It's starting to get lighter earlier every day, isn't it?"

They descended the stairs together. As Olivia looked into his face, his left eye winked imperceptibly. She smiled her beautiful wide smile at him and squeezed his arm to her side. *I do love this boy. What a lot of heartache he's had to overcome. I can't begin to imagine having a mother who was so cruel to him.* She reached over and ruffled his hair.

She whispered, "I do love you, Charles, very much, my good young man."

He looked at her with eyes that sparkled. "I love you too, Aunt Ollie."

CHAPTER XXX

LORD, how long shall the wicked,
how long shall the wicked triumph?
How long shall they utter and speak hard things?
and all the workers of iniquity boast themselves?

PSALM 94:3-4

EVERY DAY SINCE HER ARRIVAL in Boston, Mabel spied on the
Brighton manse and looked for a house to buy. She'd gone to a jewelers
and sold several of her gems so she'd have ready cash. After much
searching, she finally found a house in a perfect location down near the salt
flats, and she'd bought it outright. The house sat back, far from the road,
and was suitable for her needs. The property included a barn, small stable,
and a huge garden. Massive trees lined the long dirt road to the house. The
house seemed a bit run-down but was surprisingly clean and sufficient for
her. She figured it would be a much better place than an apartment or
hotel room like the one Armand had found for her.

Next, she'd gone to a tailor shop and purchased a few things off the
rack. She also stopped to buy a few necessary food items and stashed all of

it in her rented buggy. Lastly, she'd made a quick stop at an apothecary's shop for some chloroform, explaining to the man that the midwife delivering her neighbor's baby needed it for the pain. Chloroform was popularly being called *Anaesthesia a la Reine*, the anesthesia of the queen, because Queen Victoria had used it during childbirth. *Thanks goodness for that—the perfect excuse to buy some.* She took everything to the house and then went back to Armand's flat for the night.

He'd gone off first thing this morning. Mabel was finally ready and packed up her meager belongings and moved, leaving no trace of her whereabouts. *I believe I know enough about the man to understand if anything I do could reverberate back on him, he'd stab me in the back. What's that old saying? "There's no honor among thieves"? Or is it, "There's honor among thieves"? I can't remember. If he had even an inkling that anyone thought he might be connected to me, he'd spill his guts and tell the police about me.*

Now, she stood and regarded herself closely from the top of her head to her feet. Her reflection rippled in the old mirror, but she didn't care. *Perfect,* she thought, *absolutely perfect. No one will recognize me in this getup. No one here in Boston has any idea I'm alive, and I don't think anyone at the abbey in Italy is going to come looking for me.*

Mabel had done a good job watching the Brightons' house from the small buggy. She'd seen four detectives who guarded the house, and another walked with Manning to and from work every day. Now that she was ready, it was time to wreak a little havoc on this household. And she wanted her children back—Charles, because he was a good worker and did many of the chores; and Henry, because he adored her. *Perhaps I could get that Victoria girl too. She'd be fun to harass, and taking her would bring torment to Manning. Ah, Manning, you think life is good, but that shall soon come to an end, and so shall you, my dear man.* She laughed wickedly. *I'll not only end your comfort, but I'll put an end to you.*

She laughed again as she chewed on some bread and roast beef while she watched the Brighton manse from her seat inside the buggy. The little carriage was fashioned so that anyone sitting inside it could barely be seen, with the wide hood and the seat placed deeply within. It only seated two people, but with just one horse to worry about, it was perfect for Mabel's needs. As she sat eating, she saw the front door open, and she became agitated. *That woman is still here? The gall of that man! She's been with my boys all this time? I'll get them. I'll get them all. They will suffer.* She watched as Olivia Anderson smiled at the detective and spoke to him. She couldn't hear what was being said, but seeing that woman's winning smile, she clenched her teeth in anger.

It was late afternoon by the time Olivia closed the heavy front door behind her. She wanted to catch the teacher before he left the school. As she stood on the porch, she thought, *I don't know when I've been cooped up in a house for so long without poking my head outside! I'm glad to be out.*

She took a deep breath and inhaled the sweet, fresh air. Although it had poured down rain this morning, it had stopped in the early afternoon. She walked down the steps, and her high-topped boots splashed water with each step. The puddles, scattered everywhere, were impossible to avoid.

"Good afternoon, sir!" The detective started to talk, but Olivia quickly forestalled him. "It's all right, sir. Honestly, it is. I don't believe the Vickers woman even remembers me, and I simply must get some schoolwork for the children to do. They are getting too far behind." Olivia smiled winningly at the detective whose usually pleasant face was marred by a worried frown. She could tell he was in a quandary.

"It's all right, truly. You needn't come with me. You can stay right here and guard the house, and I'll be back in two shakes of a lamb's tail." Olivia smiled widely, her eyes alight with good humor.

He acquiesced with an admonition. "You keep a sharp watch out for that woman, and don't let anyone get anywhere close to you unless you know them. Do you understand?"

"Yes, sir, but I don't think I have to worry. No one in their right mind would be out in this unless they need to be. It's nearly a sea of mud." She laughed, and with a wave of her hand, began to walk to the school, her skirts already beginning to hang heavy as they soaked up water from the deluge earlier in the day.

Charles sat in his room reading a book. His room faced east, which he'd found perfect. When his father had been alive, all three children had shared a bedroom and there had never been any privacy. Now, he had lots of privacy and he loved it. Occasionally, Henry would come in during the night and crawl into bed with him. He knew Henry was plagued with bad dreams and sought solace from him. He tried his best to be a comfort to his younger brother.

Charles was an early riser, and when the sun came up, it would stream into his window, making his room a pleasant place to be. This day it had rained so hard they couldn't go out riding. Mozart lay at his feet. The dog seemed to be wherever Charles was, and the boy adored the dog. Moe slept at the foot of his bed on a special blanket just for him. Charles spent time feeding, grooming, playing, and training him.

This morning Charles had enjoyed playing games and hide-and-go-seek with Tory and Henry. Moe seemed to know not to give him away and would sit patiently at the head of the stairs unless Charles was the one seeking, and then he was a great help. The other two children had not yet caught on that it was Moe that led Charles to them. Sitting quietly, Charles could hear Henry practicing on his violin. *He's getting quite good. I'm sure glad all the squawking-type music is over.*

He let the book slide to his lap and as he did so, he glanced out the window. *Aunt Ollie! What is Aunt Ollie doing? She's not supposed to go out of the house. Where's the detective?* As he watched from his window, he saw a small carriage wend its way down the street, stopping next to Olivia, who left the path and moved closer to the carriage. A man jumped out and quickly wrapped his arms around her, holding a cloth against her mouth and nose. As Charles watched, dumbfounded, Aunt Olivia struggled against the man but then crumpled to the street. The man began to drag her toward the buggy.

Charles dropped his book and ran out of his room, yelling at the top of his lungs down the hall. Swinging his leg over the bannister, he slid down and was out the front door, still yelling. Moe was at his heels, barking. He stopped yelling and dodged the detective, who reached out hands to grab him as he quickly slipped past. Now silent, he ran as fast as his legs could carry him down the street, but he was too late. The carriage pulled away and started off at a fast clip. Charles stood helpless in the middle of the street. Moe smelled the area.

The detective finally caught up to Charles, all out of breath and with an angry stance. He stared down at the boy and started a blistering harangue, but seeing his stricken face, the anger drained away and he caught at Charles' shoulder.

"What is it, boy? What's the matter?" But even as he asked, his heart sank. He was quite sure of the answer.

"She took her. My mother took Aunt Ollie."

"I saw that buggy pass by, son. There was no woman in it..." His voice trailed off as he stared into the honest blue eyes of the boy, and he knew in his gut what the boy said was true.

"She was dressed as a man, sir, but believe me, it was my mother."

Charles' shoulders sagged as he turned back toward the house. He felt misery in every ounce of his body. He knew how cruel his mother could be. He turned his face up to the detective and asked, "What will you do now, sir?"

"Report to headquarters. We'll make a search for her...a thorough search."

The detective, Andre Dufort, was more than desolate. He wondered if he should find another profession. He certainly hadn't proved himself adept on this case. This was the second big mistake he'd made. His shoulders also sagged with the weight of the wet wool coat, but even more with the knowledge he needed to report, immediately, his failure.

Turning, he ran back to the house and told the other detectives to report back to headquarters, except for one man to keep watch on the house. Charles was right behind him, and he hurriedly told Charles to let the occupants of the house know what had happened. He headed his horse at a gallop toward the police station.

Charles stood looking forlornly after him. When he turned toward the house, he saw everyone standing on the front porch, waiting for him. The contessa nodded her head as if she was not surprised. The boy looked in wonder at all of them for a second before he remembered he'd gone screaming through the house before running out the front door. He ran to Frankie and buried his head in her waiting arms, sobbing, with Tory, Henry, Cookie, and the contessa looking on.

"She got her...m-my m-mother got Aunt Ollie!"

Henry, his face blanched in shock, clenched his fists. "She'll not dare to hurt her...she'll not dare!"

"We must wait for Mr. Brighton. He will know what to do." The contessa spoke with an assurance she did not feel.

Frankie hugged Charles for a long moment and led the group back inside and to the kitchen. Cookie began to make tea for everyone, and Frankie spoke to Tory.

"I want you to go get Ralph. Don't elaborate—just get him. We need him to go as soon as possible to the bank and get your father."

Charles, still shaken, said, "The detective went to see his boss to report what happened, but it won't do any good. My mother will hurt Aunt Ollie, maybe even kill her the way she killed my father!" He tried to hold back his tears, his lips quivering, and he shuddered from cold, wet feet.

Frankie said, "Wait here while I go up to help Charles into some dry socks and shoes."

Moe bounded up the stairs ahead of them.

She spoke quietly to the boy. "Charles, I think you and I should pray for Olivia. Don't you think that would be a good idea?" She wrapped her arms around him and they sat together on his bed. She held this boy who had so won her heart close to her side.

Armand dropped by his manse to pick up some papers. He was in a foul mood, as his last two attempts for business takeovers had failed.

Jacques Corlay, his father-in-law, had been livid when Armand told him of his failure to gain the mercantile from Mr. Peabody. It had been bad enough when he failed with Honeywell.

Liberty heard him come in, yelling at Sigmund to fetch his mail, which lay on the salver in the front entry.

She tiptoed over to Armand's library door after it slammed shut behind him and pressed her ear to the door.

"I will be going out and need the carriage hitched up. I don't care to ride my horse. See to it Jean-Paul has the carriage ready and my horse stabled. Where's Madam Bouvier? I wish to see her immediately."

Liberty hurried across the hall and entered her sitting room, quietly closing the door. Silently she prayed, *Lord, please help me. I need Your guidance for whatever it is Armand is angry about and how to respond to him when Sigmund comes for me. Please be with me.*

In the meantime, Sigmund bowed to Armand and said, "All will be accomplished as you wish. I will inform madam to see you posthaste." He turned to exit the library and heard a book being thrown against the wall. With measured steps, he gained the door as he heard glass crash to the floor. He closed the door behind him. Taking the stairs two and three at a time, he knocked on madam's boudoir door.

Annie answered. "Yes, Sigmund, what is it? What's the matter?"

"Monsieur wishes to see madam, forthwith." He turned to leave and said over his shoulder in a whisper, "He's in a foul temper, Annie."

She spoke quickly. "She's in her sitting room." Sigmund ran lightly down the stairs and tapped on the sitting room door.

"Please enter."

Opening the door, Sigmund said, "Monsieur's in the library, madam. He wishes you to join him—immediately."

Liberty stood as she replied. "Thank you, Sigmund." He bowed slightly and left the hall. He ran out to the stables but Jean-Paul was not there. Turning, he breathed a sigh of relief when he saw the groom coming around the house with the white stallion Bouvier was currently riding. The man switched horses constantly and had quite a selection in his stable.

"Hello, Jean-Paul. Monsieur wishes a carriage posthaste, and of course he wants his horse stabled."

"I'll get right to it," the groom replied.

Back at the house, Liberty straightened her skirts, took a deep breath to settle her breathing, and entered the library. She wondered exactly what was causing Armand's show of temper. Swallowing, she closed the door behind her.

Armand picked up a paperweight and threw it at the wall of books, tearing the back of a beautifully bound tome and scarring the oak shelf.

Liberty stood straight, her shoulders back and her chin raised. She waited rather than say anything, but a telltale pulse beat rapidly in her throat.

In the dim lighting, Armand could not see it.

He only saw a self-contained woman who seemed to have no fear of him nor any adulation, which he craved from her above all things.

His voice seethed with anger and he hissed at her. "Did you perchance drop by the police station yesterday? Are you reporting on me, my dear?" His rage emanated from every fiber of his being.

Chapter XXXI

For the enemy hath persecuted my soul;
he hath smitten my life down to the ground

PSALM 143:3a

LIBERTY LOOKED HIM STRAIGHT IN THE EYE. "Yes, Armand, I did go to the police station yesterday. I found a lady's reticule on a park bench the day before and thought I should turn it into the police. Perchance someone will check with them and be able to retrieve it." *How grateful I am, Lord, that you gave me that excuse.*

The rage in Armand's face seemed to fade away. He knew she never lied.

"You may go. Tell cook I won't be in for dinner."

Armand watched as she turned and left the room. Something vital seemed to leave with her; the room seemed empty without her presence. His shoulders sagged as he sat, collecting his thoughts. He began to sort through his mail.

Mabel drove the cabriolet right up to the steps of her house and went inside. Grabbing a throw rug, she went back to her vehicle and placed it on the ground. She eyed it and was satisfied it would be big enough for her purpose. She noticed Miss Anderson's woolen scarf. It had caught on the wheel when she'd dragged the woman into the cabriolet. Now, wrapped around the hub, it was in shreds. *I'll have to remember to bury that when I bury her*, she thought. Olivia was still unconscious. Mabel perused the woman closely. *I didn't think much about her looks before, but she is quite pretty. She won't be when I finish with her.* Mabel hauled her out of the carriage, and with a dull thud, she let her drop to the rug. Pulling on it, she was satisfied that it would aid her in getting the woman up the steps of the porch. She dragged her, thumping up each step and over the threshold. When Olivia started to slide off, Mabel dropped the rug and planted her feet on both sides of it to haul Olivia back onto it. It was work, but finally Mabel maneuvered her to a small room off the side of the kitchen where she'd placed a mattress. *She'll be one sore woman when she wakes up. Serves her right, trying to take my children's affections away from me.* Mabel had the key ready on a string around her neck and locked the door.

Both Christopher Belden and George Baxter showed up at the Brighton manse before Manning got there. George paced back and forth in the front foyer. He needed to settle his thoughts, as he was incredibly angry. Mabel had again slipped through the department's fingers. Knowing of her fiendish, malevolent behavior, he prayed as he paced. He was extremely worried about what the woman would do to Olivia Anderson.

Manning rode into the back courtyard at a fast pace, hooves skidding slightly on the cobbles as he drew to a halt. Ralph grabbed the reins as his employer dismounted.

Manning nodded at his groom and then yelled as he took the back stairs. "Don't unsaddle him!" As he entered the kitchen, he saw Charles, pale and shivering, before the open flame of the kitchen fireplace. He immediately went to the boy and hugged him. He spoke to all who were gathered there.

"We'll find Mabel before she causes any more harm. We'll get Olivia back." He prayed that what he said was true. Releasing the boy, he squeezed Tory's shoulder as he strode past. "I mean it. We'll find her!"

"In the front foyer, sir," Frankie said succinctly.

Without another word, he hurried to the front entry, where George paced.

Christopher Belden was in the library trying to calm the contessa, who was in a rage.

"You are telling me, sir, that there is no way to find where that horrible woman has taken Olivia? *Certamente* there must be a-someone, a-someone who know her." Her speech was becoming heavily accented in her anger.

"We will do the best we can, but we have no way of knowing where Mabel Vickers has taken Miss Anderson."

Chris Belden decided right then to pay a visit to the Bouviers' manse to see if Monsieur Bouvier had any idea where the woman might be. He stared at the contessa as she paced back and forth, kicking at her skirts as if she could kick away her problems.

"We will do our best. Believe me, we will try to catch the Vickers woman before she wreaks any more havoc on Olivia Anderson, or on anyone else for that matter. Now if you'll please excuse me, I have work to do." He strode to the front foyer to find Manning talking in a low voice with George.

They shook hands and Belden said, "I'm going to ride over to the Bouviers' and see if he knows anything."

Manning nodded and said, "I'm going to see if my lawyer can get access to any records of housing purchases. Mabel wouldn't dare try to haul an unconscious woman into a hotel or apartment complex. She must have bought or rented a house."

"Good thinking," George said. "Let's have a quick word of prayer before we go. Can we gather in the kitchen where the family is?"

"Yes," Chris Belden agreed. "I'll get the contessa from the library."

The family, the contessa, the staff, and the detectives held hands in a circle and Christopher Belden led the prayer.

"Our Father, Almighty God, we come before You humbly. We know that Thou knowest all things. Our prayer is that Thou wouldst keep Thy servant Mistress Olivia Anderson safe. We pray for guidance and for Thy provision to find her. We, each one of us here, beseech Thee on her behalf. We thank Thee that Thou are a compassionate God, abounding in loving-kindness. We give Thee praise for what Thou wilt do in advance. Thank Thee. We praise Thy holy name. Amen."

Amens echoed around the circle.

George said, "Let's be on our way. I'll go back to headquarters and get every available man out searching the streets, carriage rentals, and simply to ask questions. Someone must have seen something."

Manning turned to the group standing in the kitchen. "I'm going to try to find out where Mabel has taken Olivia. First, I'm going to my lawyer, and Chief Inspector Belden is going to the Bouviers' home because he's seen Mabel with Monsieur Bouvier."

"He's evil too." Henry stated the obvious, but everyone listened because they were interested in the young boy's reaction to Mabel's behavior. "I think he's just as bad as my mother."

Henry had grown to love Olivia and the stability and love she'd given him. He looked over at Charles. "I just know they're going to find her. I'm worried too, but Jesus will take care of her."

Charles looked over at Henry, dumbfounded. "Did you ask Jesus into your heart too?"

"Yes," said Henry simply. "I did. I saw the change in you, and I want to be just like you." He turned and hugged Manning's waist. "Please find her, Papa. Please find her!"

"I'll do my best, son." To Cookie and Franke he said, "Don't wait dinner." The door banged shut behind him in his haste.

Mabel shook Olivia to awaken her, a bit worried that she'd given her too much of the chloroform. She wanted to torment the woman awhile before getting rid of her.

"Wake up," she said to Olivia. "Wake up!" She yelled at her again.

Someone was screaming at Olivia.

Olivia awoke to see Mabel standing over her but couldn't maintain a coherent thought. She felt sick and wondered if she were dreaming. Rolling onto her side, she threw up into a bucket that sat next to the mattress. Her conscious mind seemed to be asleep. "Oh, I feel so sick." Her voice sounded thick and slurred. She stayed on her side, curling up in a fetal position.

Mabel slapped Olivia's face and screamed. "I said, wake up!" The slap was ignored.

Feeling as if she were seasick, Olivia spoke in French. "*Je suis le mal de mer.*" Saying she was seasick in another language was Olivia's last thought for quite some time.

After the men went their separate ways, the children and the contessa tried to eat, but no one was hungry.

Charles said, "I think I'll turn in early. Good-night to you all."

Frankie looked at him closely. "Good-night, Charles. You've had quite a day. I don't blame you for going to bed early."

Charles turned away because he felt uncomfortable under Frankie's careful perusal. A plan had been percolating in the back of his brain ever since the men left.

"Before I do," he said, "I'll go up and take Snuggles out. The poor thing is probably wondering where Aunt Ollie is."

"Put him in my room when you bring him back in, please. He's not used to sleeping alone and he'll be lonely." Tory spoke over her shoulder to the departing boy.

"Sure, I'll do that. I'll put his blanket bed in there too. Good-night, everybody." He left the group with Mozart at his heels.

Henry was tired but didn't want to go to bed too early. He knew he'd wake up while it was still dark and not be able to go back to sleep.

Charles stopped at the bottom of the stairs, picked up the dog, and whispered into his ear. "We're going to find Aunt Ollie soon as I let Snuggles out and put him in Tory's room. I'm trusting you, Moe, to find her scent and show me where she is." He put Moe back down and ran lightly up the stairs, grabbed his coat, and went down to Olivia's room. He opened the door and Snuggles was right there, ready to go out. The two dogs wagged and sniffed and wagged some more.

Frankie wasn't the only one who watched Charles closely.

The contessa had been watching him with eyes veiled by her lashes. She sensed the boy was up to something, and she wanted in on it.

She stood, reached out a hand to ruffle Henry's hair, and said, "*Buona notte.* I too shall turn in early." She smiled around at those remaining in the kitchen. "I think we must continue to pray for Olivia's safety most of all. Again, I say good-night."

Charles led the dogs down the hall, and as he descended the stairs, the contessa was on her way up. They said good-night to each other again, and Charles followed the dogs out into the night.

The sky had cleared and it was cold, but the moon shone brightly. A breeze made it feel even colder as Charles waited on the porch for the dogs to finish their business. He pulled on his woolen hat as he stood. Snuggles made straight for a bush and took care of business. It'd been too long since he was let out. He began to sniff and sniffed around in circles. All the sudden, he took off like a shot down the street, his nose to the ground.

Charles called after him, but he didn't stop. Calling the dog again, he ran down the steps, buttoning his coat as he went. He'd thought he would try to get Moe to smell Aunt Ollie's scent, but the little dog's behavior decided him. Snuggles was a smart dog. He stopped right where Olivia had been dragged into the carriage. With his little tail wagging, Snuggles, followed by Moe, headed straight down the street after Olivia's scent. Charles, right behind, was wishing he'd put the dog on a leash. As he ran, he slipped his cold hands into his pockets and found his gloves. He was grateful and pulled them on.

At the house, the Contessa di Amalfi had run up the rest of the stairs as Charles had come down with the dogs. The contessa slipped into her room and hurriedly untied her petticoat, letting it fall to the floor. It was an encumbrance she could do without. She grabbed her coat, jammed a hat on her head, and picked up her gloves from the chiffonier, slipping them on as she ran down the stairs.

She could hear voices in the kitchen and quietly let herself out the front door. She heard Charles yelling at Olivia's dog as he ran down the street. The contessa hurried after him.

Christopher Belden, usually a calm, level-headed man, wanted to slug the smirk off Monsieur Bouvier's face.

"We know you harbored that woman. Where is she?"

"And I'm telling you, I don't know. Tis true she telegrammed me and asked if I would meet her and if I had a place to stay, which I did. I took her there, and late this afternoon I found she was gone. Left without a by-your-leave or a thank you. Such seems to be my lot in life. I help someone and don't even get a thank you, just the police breathing down my neck. What has the woman done, anyway?" His lip curled disdainfully as he spoke to the chief detective.

"Is this really the best you can do? You're telling me you have no idea where Mabel Vickers has gone?"

"Mabel Vickers? Mabel Vickers? I thought her name was now Brighton. It's Mabel Brighton you are talking about, is it not?"

Chris Belden replied heavily, "Yes, yes, it is Mabel Brighton of whom we speak."

Armand rang a bellpull and Sigmund appeared at the library door.

"Please tell madam I wish her in the library."

Armand decided he would see if she had been telling the truth about the purse. He had an informant at headquarters and wondered if, with the two of them together, one would make a mistake about their knowing each other. Armand trusted no one.

Liberty came into the library and seeing Detective Belden, she proffered her hand, saying smoothly. "Detective Belden, how nice to see you again. Did you find the owner of the reticule I turned in to you?"

Christopher Belden took his cue from her and said, "Yes, in truth, I did. It belonged to a nanny over on fifth who left it on the park bench when her charge fell down and bloodied his knee. She ran directly over to him and forgot all about her reticule in her haste to get him home and cleaned up. I'm glad you found it instead of some shady character who would have taken the poor woman's money. Again, I thank you."

Liberty inclined her head.

"May I ask why you are here today, sir?"

"Certainly. I was simply inquiring of your husband if he knows the whereabouts of one Mabel Vickers-Brighton. Sadly, he seems to have no idea where the woman is, so regretfully, I must be on my way. Good day, madam." He bowed slightly to her and Armand. "Monsieur."

"Good-bye, sir," Liberty said.

Belden turned, and Sigmund, who hovered by the door, showed him out.

Manning used the knocker of the Humphries' private residence. He hoped he wasn't overstepping the bounds of their relationship by showing up at the Humphries' door. It was opened by a servant.

"Yes?"

"Good evening. My name is Manning Brighton and I wish to speak to Mr. Humphries, if he is available."

"Come in. Come in out of the cold, suh. I understand yore a new brother in Christ!" His dark brown eyes were warm as he spoke. "Let me take yore coat and I'll tell the master yore heah."

Manning was surprised at the man's comment. "Yes, yes, Elijah introduced me to Christ not long ago. What's your name?"

"I'm Thomas Fuerst, suh. Please take a seat there in the parlor and he'll be with you di-rectly." He left hurriedly.

After he departed, Manning suddenly realized the futility of his visit. All the city offices would be closed for the day. Elijah couldn't get to any records of transactions any more than he could. His shoulders drooped in frustration and the beginnings of embarrassment that he would be bothering Elijah for no sound reason.

Olivia was very sick but Mabel wasn't too worried about it. *If she dies, she dies. I've got a big backyard where I can bury her.* Mabel put away some victuals she'd purchased from a small shop on a side street and looked forward to a good meal.

CHAPTER XXXII

"That thou doest, do quickly."

JOHN 13:27B

CHARLES, STILL FOLLOWING SNUGGLES and Moe, was able to catch up because every so often, it seemed Snuggles lost the scent and would circle a bit, nose to the ground, and then take off again.

The contessa, not used to running, had a stitch in her side. She hoped she was not on a wild-goose chase. Moe seemed to have picked up Olivia's scent as well. It was already dark, but the lamplighter had lit the streetlamps and a soft orb of light lit the way, but the streets were dim. Charles had not yet noticed her following him.

Suddenly, Moe made a right turn. Snuggles circled a bit and followed Moe. The road they were now on was an unlit dirt one that led down to the salt flats and the bay.

Both dogs, with Charles right behind, ran down the road toward the source of the tangy night air, which turned into wisps of fog as they neared the salt flats. Houses here were few and far between. Snuggles started to yelp and whine as he ran to the porch of a house set far back from the dirt road. The windows were dark, and it didn't look like anyone was home.

Charles hadn't thought about Snuggles making any noise and tried to shush the dog as it barked sharp, yapping sounds. The front door opened, and his mother stood there in the dark, looking like an apparition, with a dull lantern in her hand. Still dressed in a man's breeches and frock coat, a breeze blew her loosened hair across her face.

Charles was crouched behind a bush by the porch. Moe was at his heels, not making a sound. Snuggles yapped and barked at Mabel.

"Oh, oh yes, I know who you are. You're my prisoner's dog, aren't you, you little rat of a dog. How did you get here?" She held up her lantern, which cast an eerie glow on her face. Charles drew even further back behind the bushes on the side of the front porch. Moe didn't move nor make a sound.

From the path, the contessa could see Mabel outlined in the doorway. She stopped, knowing Mabel couldn't possibly see her. But she didn't want to snap a twig or kick a stone to draw attention to herself. She was breathless, her heart pounding. It was difficult to hear what Mabel said since Snuggles was still yapping.

"Come here, little dog. Come on. Ole Mabel won't hurt you. Come on." Snuggles continued to yap at Mabel, and as she stepped down from the porch, Snuggles made a dash for the doorway. He slipped easily past Mabel and into the house. "Aha, now I have you." She ran up the steps and slammed the door behind her.

Charles decided the best thing to do was to run back to the city and get Detective George Baxter to come to this house. He figured Mabel wouldn't be going anywhere else tonight. Starting at a run for the dirt road, he was brought up short when he saw the contessa.

"Yes," she said in a low voice, "I followed you and I am too old to do so! I will stay here and watch the house. You go tell your papa, yes? I run after you an-a I have no more energy to follow you. I stay here. Run now, quick! Get-a help!" She shooed Charles with her hands, talking urgently all the while.

Charles ran as fast as he could. He wondered what his mother would do to the dog. She didn't like them. His breathing was labored and his lungs were seared by the cold air, but he felt sweaty with his clothing sticking to him. He hadn't paid much attention to the route they'd taken, so he trusted Moe, who ran ahead of him.

When he reached the cobbles, it surprised him how much traffic was moving about. He'd paid no attention on his way to Mabel's house. He wasn't ever out at this time of night and didn't know about the bustle of Boston. Moe kept just a few yards ahead and seemed to know when to stop for street vehicles. *He's an awfully smart dog. Must be 'cause he was out on his own so long.* He began to pray as he ran. *Lord, right now I pray not only for Aunt Olivia's safety, but for her dog, Snuggles. He's such a sweet little guy. Please, Lord, protect them both. Thank you. Amen.* He felt much better for having prayed.

They were on their own street now. Looking ahead toward his house, he saw Detective Baxter running up the front steps. Charles tried to yell, but his voice came out in a gasp and made no sound.

Moe ran up the steps past the detective, who turned around, obviously surprised. Charles made it up the steps as Frankie opened the door to the detective. She stood there welcoming Mr. Baxter, clearly startled to see Charles right behind him.

"Charles! Where have you been? We've been looking everywhere for you!"

He looked up at Frankie, and his eyes filled with tears. "She got Snuggles too! My mother has Aunt Olivia and Snuggles." Charles gasped for breath. "I took the dogs out to wee and Snuggles took off like a shot, smelling the ground. He smelled in circles where my mother put that handkerchief over Aunt Ollie's nose." Charles paused to grab some air to his tortured lungs. "I think Snuggles followed her scent, because I followed him all the way to the salt flats. The contessa was right behind me and said she would watch the house and make sure my mother doesn't go anywhere."

George Baxter took the boy and hugged him to his side. "Good work, young man. You have the makings of a great detective."

Manning was right behind Frankie when she opened the door, and after listening to Charles, he grabbed his heavy coat off the coat tree. "Let's go!"

"My carriage is out front," George said. "Let's take it. We'll need something big enough to carry all of us." He said to Frankie, "Make some good, strong coffee, won't you? If Olivia's been chloroformed, she'll need it." The two men and Charles, along with Moe, ran down the front walk to the carriage.

George had a driver and spoke to him, saying, "Head for the salt flats. The boy here will show you the way, and hurry!"

Charles climbed up the carriage but felt chilled as the sweat began to cool off his body. Even more chilling was the thought of his mother's treachery.

Mabel had opened the door to Olivia's little prison, but she was still asleep or unconscious. Mabel didn't care which. The room was cold and smelled of vomit. Snuggles scooted in and ran to his mistress. He licked her face as Mabel pulled the door shut and locked it.

Mabel tripped over an ottoman. She cursed and lit several lamps. *Oil. I'm going to need more lamp oil.* She threw a few logs onto the fire and rubbed her shinbone, which was scraped. Going to the kitchen, she lit two lamps, one over the table and one beside the stove. She fed some more wood into the wood stove. Hungry, she began to make something to eat. As she sliced a piece of ham and peeled a potato, she thought about the last two days and how busy she'd been. Mabel realized the evening before, she'd neither counted her money nor looked at her jewels. The bag was made of black velvet, and in the lamplight the stones glittered beautifully on it. Excitement filled her. She loved letting the jewels slip through her fingers and sparkle in the lamplight. It had become a ritual, and the anticipation filled her with a consuming longing to touch the gemstones again.

Quickly, she put some ham into the skillet, and once the fat melted, she sliced the potato into it. Her stomach began to rumble. She went out the back door and filled a bucket with water from the pump. *Once I take care of Manning, I'm going to live on the continent and in style. I'll never lift a finger again. I have enough money to last me a long time. I won't have to marry for money. I have enough of my own. Too bad I didn't realize I could steal money instead of marry for it. Ah, well, I'll make Manning pay before I go. Tomorrow, first thing, I'll take care of that woman and her dog.*

She dished up her ham and potatoes on a plain white plate that had come with the house. She walked to the drawer in which she'd hurriedly placed the bag of jewels and returned to the kitchen table. She sat the bag on the smooth pine top of the table and ate a few bites, nearly gulping her food. She poured herself a glass of water, and then placing a towel under the bag, she sat back down and pulled the drawstrings open. She poured the gems and money out onto the towel and gasped in surprise. At least half the jewels were gone, but the weight of the bag was nearly the same as before because rocks had been used as filler. Anger infused her and she gasped again.

Armand! Why, that thief saw my jewels and helped himself! She stood and shoved the bag and towel of gems to the center of the table. She was so angry she could scarcely think. She ran to the front door and opened it, but when the cold air hit her, she turned back to the bedroom for her coat. *I'll kill him. That's what I'll do. I hate him for this. I hate all men. I'll get him. Yes, I'll get him.* She slammed out the door and pulled a hat on. Still dressed in men's clothing, she buttoned her coat as she headed for town. Once she got to the end of the dirt road, it was a mere few blocks to the apartment Armand owned. She didn't wish to waste time hooking the horse to the carriage. She moved fast, as the cold penetrated her clothing. It seemed to clear her head, and her thoughts became less jumbled. *I'd better make a plan. He could be at his own house.*

The Contessa Viola Stella di Amalfi had been standing, stomping her feet in the cold. *No wonder I live in my beloved Italy. It is so cold here. Why anyone would live here in this cold clime is beyond me. Brrr!*

As she stood there, clapping her arms and stomping her feet, she saw lights come on in what she guessed was the living room. She could smell wood smoke in the cold air and knew Mabel had stoked her fire. Another light lit in another room. *Oh, I do wish Charles would come back with help! I have a bad feeling about this. I don't know, but I have that stomach-churning bad feeling like Sister Amalia gets.*

Time seemed to drag. All the sudden, the front door crashed open, screaming on rusty hinges. Mabel appeared in the doorway, disappeared, and returned as she slammed out of the house. The contessa pulled back behind a tree and watched as Mabel hurried past her, so close she could have reached out and touched her.

The contessa did some fast thinking. *The woman is crazy, and I do not believe I could overcome her. I will follow her and see where she goes. Yes, that is a good plan.*

Baxter's driver had no idea what Mabel looked like, and because of the dark, Charles missed seeing her as she walked hurriedly past them. The contessa saw the carriage and flagged it down.

She spoke through the window. "There—that's her right there!" The traffic was still busy as horses and carriages made their way home at the end of a workday, but George Baxter could see her by the light of a streetlamp, nearly running. Without a word, he jumped out of the carriage and started after Mabel.

Manning spoke. "Get in, Contessa. Please get in. He leaned out and took her hand, nearly pulling her into the carriage. He leaned out again and spoke to Baxter's driver. "Turn us around and please hurry!"

Meanwhile, George began to jog and shortened the distance to Mabel. It wasn't the first time he'd followed this woman. For the past two years he'd followed her often, hoping against hope that something would give her away, that somehow he would be able to catch her in the act of committing a crime. Horses and carriages passed by, and the noise was a loud din in his ears.

Mabel suspected nothing until she turned toward the building where Armand's apartment was located.

She turned to look both ways for carriages and caught George's face in the lamplight not five feet from her. *It's him! It's that face I see following me, watching me, knowing what I've done.* Everything seemed to stop.

George paused as he saw her look at him.

Their eyes caught and hers looked suddenly like a trapped animal. She turned and ran straight into the path of a heavy wagon that rode on down the street, the driver having no idea his wagon bounced the woman off its wheels as if she were a rag doll. George ran to her and knelt in the mud and slush. Mabel Vickers-Brighton looked at him quite lucidly and said clearly, "I'm not sorry—not for Horace or his brothers. Not for Bradley, nor the priest." Her voice lowered to a whisper, and George bent closer to hear.

"I'll never"—she coughed, choking on blood—"I'll never get Manning, will I?" Her eyes glazed over and her head fell sideways. Mabel Vickers-Brighton was dead.

Baxter's carriage pulled up and Manning jumped out.

He forestalled Charles from getting out, but Charles jumped down after Manning turned his back to the carriage. Charles headed over to George Baxter. The contessa followed the boy out of the carriage.

George saw Charles approach and said, "She's gone, son. She's gone."

Charles walked slowly over to the detective, who stood over his mother. He took one look at her and turned back to the carriage. The contessa did the same.

George said to Manning, "Go home. I'll take care of this. It's part of my job. Go home and tell your family they are safe." He turned wearily to his driver. "Please take them home and then get Dufort. He needs to know everything is all right. Manning, we still have a detective at your house. Tell him to report to headquarters."

George thought quickly and walked over to the carriage. "Charles, thank you. I pray you find no guilt for your part in this." Suddenly, he smacked his forehead, knowing that all of them must be in a state of shock. "Manning, you must get Olivia."

He spoke again to his driver. "I'll get a hansom and take her," he said and nodded at Mabel, "to the morgue. You help the Brightons and then go home."

As Manning climbed into the carriage, Charles spoke. "I needed to see, Papa. I needed to see with my own eyes. I'm sorry for the whole thing. If I'd spoken to you before you married my mother, you wouldn't have gone through all this."

Manning pulled the boy onto his lap. "If all this hadn't happened, you wouldn't be my beloved son, I wouldn't be a believer in Jesus Christ, and most likely, you and Henry wouldn't be either. The ways of the Lord are unsearchable. We all make choices, but what may be meant for evil, the Lord can take and turn for good. His Word says so. Don't be sorry for what has gone before. Look forward to the good we will have as a family. I love you, Charles. I love you as if your were not adopted, but my own son." He hugged the boy to his heart, tears of relief, shock, sorrow, and joy mingling as they rolled down his cheeks.

"You are a good man, Mr. Brighton. Now, we must get Olivia," the contessa said.

"And Snuggles," Charles added as he cuddled closer into Manning's arms, which tightened around him.

EPILOGUE

O give thanks unto the God of heaven:
for his mercy endureth for ever.

PSALM 136:26

ARMAND BOUVIER SAT AT HIS DESK with several companies'
records copied onto sheets of thin vellum. He'd found that money opened
doors, and greasing a palm here and there definitely paid off. Drumming
his fingers, he compared the assets and expenditures of four different
companies. He planned a takeover of the one that made the most money.

He'd already met the men owning each of the companies and curried
their favor. He planned to establish a cordial relationship with each of
them. He thought about his father-in-law, who was greedier than he was.
Jacques Corlay had gathered the information on the companies.

He thought back on his dealings since meeting Jacques Bertrand
Corlay. Armand had married Liberty for her name and place in society,
and he had taught Jacques Corlay, her father, various schemes as a means
to make money. He knew a few things about Liberty that Jacques would

not like her to know. Perhaps he could make a little money off his father-in-law.

He sat thinking about his wife. *She's definitely an asset. Because of her mother's place in Boston society and long memories, doors are open to me that never would have been had I married any other woman in this city. I am fortunate I had the foresight to marry for the name rather than for money. Jacques was penniless, deeply in debt when I first met him. He should be grateful for what I've done for him.*

Too bad about Mabel. Let's see—she's been dead about six weeks. I have half her jewels, and when she signed for the house, she made me the beneficiary. Yes, Mabel, you did me a good turn by dying.

It was Sunday morning, and Liberty was at the little chapel on Rice Street. She bowed her head and prayed again for Armand. He'd been extremely unpleasant the last few weeks, more so than normal. *I don't know how he can sleep at night, the way he treats people. I struggle, Father, to find anything to respect in him. I suppose each of Your children struggle in some way. We'd probably become too independent of You if we didn't. I simply am at a loss as to what is good in him other than that he is Your creation.*

I am thankful that Manning Brighton is free to marry Mistress Anderson. I know they will be happy together. Lord, please bless them. Help them as they raise Mabel's children. I praise You. I praise You with my whole heart.

She continued to pray and praise the Lord. *Father, I thank you for the privilege of praying for people. Many times, they don't even know they are being lifted up to You. You know, and You are a God of compassion and mercy. Thank You. I thank You.*

The Brighton family had taken to eating in the kitchen around the huge oak table. It was relaxed and cheerful, and Frankie and Cookie could join in the conversation. The contessa had left two weeks after a quiet burial for Mabel. She telegrammed to let the Brightons know that her priest seemed to have lost his memory of only that horrible day and had made a full recovery. She'd given money to add to the remaining jewels and money found in Mabel's house, and the orphanage would be renovated as planned. The contessa also invited them to come stay, anytime, in her beloved Santa Marinella. The Brightons were more than welcome.

Madeline had arrived home after her mother's burial and planned to extend her stay. The boarding school had winter break, and she could make up any classes she missed. She hadn't wanted to come for the funeral, but now that she'd been adopted, she wanted to get to know Manning.

She looked at her brothers in amazement. The change in Henry's behavior, and even Charles, who'd always been such a quiet mouse, was a shock to her. Charles was now happy and seemed to have a confidence about himself she'd never witnessed before. Her youngest brother was the most changed. She could scarcely credit it and was astounded at his ability to play the violin.

Olivia was grateful that she could remember little after leaving the front porch of the Brightons' house on her way to get the children's schoolwork. She looked over at Manning, and their eyes caught and held. "I love you," she mouthed to him.

He said out loud, "I love you too, Olivia."

All eyes swiveled to focus on the two of them, and color rose to Olivia's cheeks.

Tory said, "Why do you have to wait a year to get married, anyway? I think you should get married right away. It's not as if anyone is mourning. Do you see any of us dressed in black?" She stated the obvious and grinned around the table, receiving nods of approval and affirmation from the other children.

Manning felt he'd never been happier. He looked at his family with eyes that glowed with thanksgiving and love. He lifted up a silent prayer as his heart filled to overflowing. *God, dear God Almighty, thank You. I thank You.*

EDEN'S PORTION PREVIEW & PROLOGUE

In the secret places doth he murder the innocent:
his eyes are privily set against the poor.

PSALM 10:8b

MR. AND MRS. CHANDLER TOOK their coats from Francis Harding and laughed at Theo's jest as they descended the steps of their friends' house. The couple hosting the party, the Hardings, were close friends, and their stableman was bringing around the Chandlers' carriage.

"Eldon Chandler, you drive carefully now, do you hear?" Francis Harding admonished as she waggled her finger at him.

"I will. I will," he replied. "Camilla will be sure to make me." He chuckled, and his wife laughed along with him.

"It was a lovely evening, and we had a delightful time," Camilla said as she donned her wrap. "And I do make him drive carefully. He'd always rather be on a horse than in a carriage. When we do take the carriage, he wants to go as fast as he would on his horse." She smiled at her hostess. "But I won't let him."

"At least there's a full moon, and you'll be guided by it," said their host, Theodore Harding. "Thank you for coming. We always enjoy your company, and we certainly couldn't do without your jests, Eldon."

"Well, again, we thank you," Camilla said. "We had a lovely time. Good-bye now," she called out as they started off down the long drive to the main road.

The night was beautiful with nearly a full moon. Stars twinkled in the inky blackness. The air had cooled, although the day had been unseasonably hot.

Camilla pulled her wrap closer around her neck as she turned to listen to her husband.

"Eden was out again with that young whippersnapper last night, wasn't she?" Eldon asked. "I know we haven't talked about it much, dear, but do you like the Kerrigan's son? I simply can't see what Eden sees in him."

"Oh, I can see what she *sees* in him," Camilla replied. "He's quite a handsome, strapping young man. The problem arises when he opens his mouth. He seems to be quite open minded and perhaps because of that, everything else has fallen out of it." She laughed at her jest, but her husband's eyebrows creased to a frown.

"That's the rub, isn't it?" Eldon sighed. "He seems as brainless as his father."

"What do you think about Caleb?" Camilla asked. "He seems to be personable enough. He's a hard worker, and Eden enjoys his friendship."

"He's nice enough, but I don't care for his mother. She seems almost syrupy, doesn't she?" He turned to look at his wife with a rueful smile.

"Eldon, watch out!" Camilla yelled. She saw a body lying in the road.

Eldon pulled hard on the reins, and the carriage came to a halt.

He drew out his gun once he descended the carriage. They'd had no robberies in the area as far as he knew, but a man couldn't be too careful. All the sudden a shot rang out, and he clutched at his shoulder as Camilla screamed his name. Another shot, and he knew no more.

Sobbing, Camilla grabbed for the rifle. Another shot sounded.

The funeral was over. Everyone had left the graveside to attend the reception except Eden Rose Chandler. She stood at her parents' graves, tears running down her cheeks. *How could this have happened? Who in the world would want them dead? Why...why...why?* Questions with no answers bubbled up within her. She'd had no sleep for the past two nights, as she'd kept vigil with both bodies lying in the parlor. Questions and remorse haunted her, not allowing her to rest.

The sky was seamless. No cloud marred its surface. The rainy season was over, and warm weather was here to stay. The early June sun beat down on Eden's honey blonde hair, pulled back into a severe chignon and held in place by a diamond-studded onyx comb.

She wiped at her tears with an impatient hand as soft gusts of wind pulled at her hair, whipping a few strands around her face. She'd talked with Buck, but he had no answers.

Sheriff Buck Rawlins of Napa could find no suspects, no evidence except the two dead bodies. He'd told her again today that he couldn't find the shooter or shooters, no shell casings, no hoofprints. He was at his wit's end to find the perpetrators of this heinous crime. Eldon and Camilla Chandler had been a couple of the sheriff's closest friends, and he mourned them.

Caleb McHaney and Taylor Kerrigan had both wanted to stay and console Eden, but she'd sent the young men packing with a few curt words.

Her neighbor, Liberty Bannister, wanted to talk with her, but the press of people at the funeral had come between them. Many had driven miles and miles to attend the funeral of Eldon and Camilla Chandler. The couple had been stanchions in Napa society and well-known in San Francisco and beyond.

Eden stood now, a lone figure, heartsick and grief stricken. "Oh, how I wish I hadn't yelled at you before you went to the Harding's party. How shall I ever forgive myself?" Eden spoke to the two dirt mounds as if they could still hear. She fell to her knees and bowed over in grief as she cried tears of remorse and sorrow.

"Father, Mother, please forgive me. Oh, how I wish I could do so many things over. I knew you didn't want me seeing Taylor, and I reckon you worried about my relationship with Caleb. It was mean of me not to tell you Caleb and I were just friends. It was horrid of me to go on seeing Taylor simply to cause you worry." Grief and remorse cut deep into the young woman's soul.

Her parents were dead, and the bitter truth was…she had no one.

Learn more about *Eden's Portion* at:
www.maryannkerr.com

My books can be purchased on Amazon
My website: www.maryannkerr.com (signed copy)
Inklings Bookshop, Yakima, WA
Songs of Praise in Yakima, WA
Or by writing me at:
Mary Ann Kerr
10502 Estes Road
Yakima, WA (I charge no tax, sign the book, and the cost of shipping is $5.65)

My public e-mail is: hello@maryannkerr.com
You may message me on Facebook on my author page:
Mary Ann Kerr—comments are welcome!
When readers take the time to write or e-mail me their experience reading my stories, I sometimes put their comments on my blog if they don't mind.

Liberty's Inheritance	(sale price. . . . . $14.99)
Liberty's Land	(sale price. . . . . $14.99)
Liberty's Heritage	(sale price. . . . .$14.99)
Caitlin's Fire	(sale price. . . . . $14.99)
Tory's Father	(full price. . . . . $14.99)

Books by Peter A. Kerr (my author son)

Adam Meets Eve (nonfiction)—$10.00 + 5.65 shipping and handling
The Ark of Time (science fiction)—$12.00 + $5.65 shipping and handling

Book by Andrew Kerr (my author son and my cover and design guy)

Ants on Pirate Pond (children's black-and-white chapter book with darling illustrations)—12.95 + $5.65 shipping and handling

Made in the USA
San Bernardino, CA
23 April 2018